BLOOD FINALE

GOD WARS SERIES, BOOK FIVE

CONNIE SUTTLE

Print Second Edition (2018)
Print ISBN: 1-63478-048-5
Print ISBN-13: 978-1-63478-048-3
eBook ISBN: 1-93975-925-0
eBook ISBN-13: 978-1-93975-925-2

Published by:
SubtleDemon Publishing, LLC
PO Box 95696
Oklahoma City, OK 73143

Cover art by Renée Barratt @ The Cover Counts

To Walter, Joe, Larry, Lee, Dianne, Sarah and Mark.
Thank you.

And for Chloe B. Welcome to the family.

ACKNOWLEDGMENTS

As always, this book is the result of collaboration. If it weren't for the support of my editor, my cover artist and my beta readers, it would be less than it is. All mistakes, as usual, are mine and no other's.

About the Author:
Connie Suttle lives in Oklahoma with her husband and a conglomerate of cats. They have finally banded together to make their demands, which has proven disconcerting to all humans involved.

You may find Connie in the following ways:
Facebook: Connie Suttle Author
Twitter: @subtledemon
Website and Blog: subtledemon.com

Blood Destiny Series:

Blood Wager

Blood Passage

Blood Sense

Blood Domination

Blood Royal

Blood Queen

Blood Rebellion

Blood War

Blood Redemption

Blood Reunion

Blood Destiny Series Boxed Set (Books 1-10)

Blood Recall

Blood Alliance*

Legend of the Ir'Indicti Series:

Bumble

Shadowed

Target

Vendetta

Destroyer

Legend of the Ir'Inditi Boxed Set

High Demon Series:
Demon Lost
Demon Revealed
Demon's King
Demon's Quest
Demon's Revenge
Demon's Dream

God Wars Series:
Blood Double
Blood Trouble
Blood Revolution
Blood Love
Blood Finale

Saa Thalarr Series:
Hope and Vengeance
Wyvern and Company
Observe and Protect*

First Ordinance Series:
Finder
Keeper
BlackWing
SpellBreaker
WhiteWing

∾

R-D Series:

Cloud Dust

Cloud Invasion

Cloud Rebel

∾

Latter Day Demons Series:

Hot Demon in the City

A Demon's Work is Never Done

A Demon's Due

∾

Seattle Elementals Series:

Your Money's Worth

Worth Your While*

∾

BlackWing Pirates Series

MindSighted

MindMage

MindRogue

MindMaster*

∾

Black Rose Sorceress Series

The Rose Mark

CHAPTER 1

*E*arth—*past*
  Adam's Journal

"Martin?" I stepped carefully through piles of fallen pine needles and broken twigs to get to Martin Walters. I knew he was werewolf. He had no idea what I was—a former vampire, turned Saa Thalarr.

"I didn't know you were in the area," Martin turned to me. I'd startled him, but at least I'd found him human and not werewolf.

"I came looking for you. No, Mack's fine. Justin's fine. Anna has a broken leg. There was an accident outside the school this afternoon; a child was hit by a speeding car. Three are dead; I just wanted you to know in case you heard anything. Mack's safe at the house with Justin —Joey's babysitting. Anna's staying overnight at the hospital, just as a precaution."

"Three children?" Martin Walters stared at me in alarm.

"No, two adults in the car and one child on the school grounds. I didn't want you to panic in case someone called you with the news."

"All right. Thanks for letting me know. That's horrible about the child. Do we know who?" Martin asked.

"So far, they've been unable to identify the child. No parents are missing a child and there was no identification."

"Not good," Martin shook his head. "Adam, what do you make of this?"

"What is it?" I walked forward to see what Martin meant—it looked to be a pile of rags.

"I think it's a towel, but there are strange—scales, I think—on it."

"Scales?" I squatted to examine the towel—it seemed to be an expensive one—lying on the ground. Martin was correct; the black, thumb-sized spots were indeed scales and much too large to belong to any serpent native to California. I was used to Ra'Ak scales, but those were much larger than this and copper in color.

"Strange scent, too," I glanced up at Martin. I knew he'd smelled the scent—his wolf's nose would certainly notice that.

"I didn't know whether you'd get that or not," Martin shrugged. "Think we ought to take it with us or leave it here?"

I had the head off the creature that leapt toward us from a nearby pile of brush and pine needles before Martin could blink and then stood there, grinning sheepishly as Martin stared at my vampire claws in shock.

~

Kent, England—present

Conner's Journal

"I've been called to a meeting, that's what," I shook a finger at Shane, who'd demanded I tell him what was going on and why I was dressed to go out.

"What kind of meeting? With whom?"

"None of your beeswax, that's with whom," I said.

"Are you taking anyone with you?"

"I asked Kee to come with me," I huffed in righteous indignation, lifting my nose in the air.

"Is Kiarra safe to go traipsing about with you?" Shane narrowed his gaze and gave me a frown only he might produce. "I thought the bad guys were after her."

"They were. Are. She'll be with me," I said. "Don't you think that's safe enough?"

"Nope."

"How about if I," I began.

"Nope."

"You didn't even let me finish," I complained. "How about if I take Dragon and Gracie with me?"

"Still nope." Arms crossed tightly over Shane's chest; that meant stubborn had moved in—with baggage—and planned to stay awhile.

"Plus Adam, Merrill, Pheligar and Devin?"

"Nope."

"How about all the Saa Thalarr, including healers and Spawn Hunters?"

"Seriously? You want to take the whole bunch to a meeting?" His arms uncrossed. I was softening him up, looked like.

"If I have to, Mr. Grumpy Drawers."

"I do not have grumpy drawers. They have hearts and ice-cream cones on them."

"They do not."

"Hummingbirds and flamingoes?"

"Nope."

"Saguaro cactus and coyotes?"

"Really? Where did you get them? I want some," I said, waggling a finger in his face.

"I bought extras. They're in your armoire," Shane grinned.

"You're kidding? I'll wear those tonight."

"You're not spending the night with Martin, are you?"

"Yeah. Why?"

"Because it's coyotes with neckerchiefs," Shane pointed out. "Not wolves. He'll get all huffy."

"And he'll rip 'em right off," I said.

"TMI," Shane muttered and opened the refrigerator door. I can't say how many discussions and/or arguments he and I'd had in front of the fridge, but it was a lot. "Do I get to go—as a healer?" he muffled, scooting things around on the lower shelf. "Are we out of orange-pineapple again? I want a French martini."

"You can go," I sighed. "And you probably should wait until after the meeting to have a martini—or three."

"What?" Shane's head poked around the refrigerator door so he could stare at me.

"Just what I said. Be ready to go in half an hour. I have mindspeech to send." I flounced out of the kitchen, considering what was about to happen and the shock—of all involved—when we arrived at the meeting in question.

∾

Le-Ath Veronis—present

Lissa's Journal

"Here's your mail." Grant placed a small stack of envelopes on my desk. Yes, in the days of comp-vids and electronic messages (and gadgets) dropping out of everybody's ass, I still got paper mail.

Six months had passed since Breanne, Ashe and Wisdom disappeared. Kalenegar had given Belen the information—Charles had been under everybody's nose for centuries and nobody guessed. He'd disappeared off everybody's radar for a while, too, and nobody noticed.

I had theories about that, and they included the fact that a lot of people (mostly vampires) had forgotten about me for a long time. It was probably a good thing Charles wasn't in front of me. God or not, we had some things to discuss.

"Not possible," I sighed and lifted the first envelope. It contained an invitation to a gathering on Karathia—Bel's birthday, actually. Of course I'd go, provided we were still alive. I was waiting for the shoe to drop—for the General to command his troops and start wiping out populations. We were all sitting ducks and he probably knew it.

I couldn't imagine that he'd be immobilized with Acrimus' destruction—I'd read Kalenegar's report, after all. He'd allowed those who had ties to the Larentii to read it, so most of us knew what happened on that terrible day. Kiarra was lucky to come out of it with only a broken leg in the past.

I set the invitation aside after sending mindspeech to Ry—to tell him I wouldn't miss Bel's birthday—and lifted the next envelope. Made of expensive cream linen, the envelope was something I hadn't seen in a long time. I recalled that Gavin had once sent a message to me using the same stationery. Where had this come from?

"Grant?" I called out, examining the envelope—it was thick and felt heavy.

"Lissa?" Grant poked his head through my study door, a puzzled expression on his face.

"Where did this come from?" I lifted the envelope to my nose and sniffed—there was no detectable scent.

"It came with the rest of the stuff and went through the detectors, just like the others. Why?"

"No reason. It just jogged a memory, that's all." I motioned with a hand, telling him it was okay to go. His head disappeared. Forming a short claw on my right index finger, I carefully slit the envelope open. The note—and something else—dropped out. I stared—the bracelet— the one Gavin had given me eons ago and I'd handed to Merrill's housekeeper because I was angry, lay on my desk. It looked new—as if it had never been worn.

I'd be lying if I said the hair on my arms and the back of my neck didn't rise, because it did. With shaking fingers, I opened the note.

What we lose, we find again, the note read. The words were handwritten, with beautiful penmanship. There was no signature.

Gavin, Merrill? I sent. *I need to see both of you. Now.*

"I forgot about that," Merrill raked long, well-shaped fingers through black hair in confusion. "I remember dropping it in a desk drawer after getting it back from Lena and offering money in exchange."

"You bought it back from her?" I stared at Merrill in disbelief.

"I worried that you might have second thoughts and merely

considered holding it until you were sure about Gavin's courtship. Obviously, as I said, I forgot about it."

"Gavin, where did you get the stationery to send that note to me back then?" I turned to him. He was just as surprised as I was and held the bracelet in his hands, examining it. It was made of eighteen karat gold, I knew that, now, with tiny diamonds winking at the center of each flower.

"From Charles," Gavin sighed, handing the bracelet back to me.

"No, put it on my wrist," I handed it back to him.

He did, his hands steady as he opened the clasp and placed the strand of tiny, gold hibiscus flowers about my wrist, the cool metal settling against my skin. "I bought this because I loved you," he murmured. "I still do. More than anything."

"I'll go." Merrill disappeared swiftly. Gavin pulled me from my seat and wrapped his arms around me. I kissed him. *Thank you*, I sent. *I love it*, I added.

~

Earth—past

Adam's Journal

"Thanks for calling the Grand Master." Director Bill Jennings studied the beheaded body on the ground. Martin and I had talked briefly before he pulled out his cell phone and dialed Weldon Harper, Grand Master of the Werewolves.

That call had generated other calls, until the Director of the Joint NSA and Homeland Security Department was deposited nearby by a Larentii. Before that moment, I'd seen few Larentii and blinked in astonishment that this one was transporting and assisting humans.

"What is this thing?" Martin asked, pointing to the beheaded body.

"A Sirenali," Director Jennings explained. "I have agents coming to collect the body. Have you found anything else?" Bill lifted his eyes from the creature and glanced from me to Martin.

"Nothing, Director," I shook my head.

"I'm surprised they left this one behind," Bill murmured. Martin and I heard the softly spoken words clearly.

"A Sirenali?" I said aloud while sending mindspeech to Pheligar, linking him to me so he could see and hear those around me.

Extinct, Pheligar's voice huffed in my mind. *Wait,* he added. *This is not good. I am still with Kiarra,* he added. *Do you need me?*

No, just asking what a Sirenali is and why the Director of the Joint NSA and Homeland Security Department might know that when I didn't.

I will investigate and return with an answer. Pheligar's mindspeech cut off.

"I know they're supposed to be extinct," Bill Jennings nodded toward me as the Larentii stepped up beside him. "Connegar," Bill said, "do you have anything to offer Mr. Chessman?"

"What?" He'd just used my real last name, when nobody should know that name.

"Don't worry," Jennings held out a hand. "I've gotten a real education in the past few weeks. You won't believe what I've seen and heard in that time."

~

Avendor—present

Kay's Journal

I was thankful that Trajan—the one in the future—came to get me in the past. I'd been transported to SouthStar in the present, where things were still unsettled. Trajan, Kathleen, Trace and several others attempted to make me understand what had happened to Breanne and Ashe, but it defied reason. I'd asked on numerous occasions for reassurance that they were still alive. Trajan suffered just as I did with their loss, but he did his best to explain that they were together and inseparable now.

Too many questions remained and I was afraid nobody had the answers. I wanted to talk to a Larentii, too, but they were curiously absent and I was too timid to ask Trajan or Trace how to contact them.

"Kay?" Kathleen broke into my thoughts as I sat on the wide deck outside my suite. Avendor was beautiful in the early evening glow and a light, cool mist lay over gishi trees far down the valley.

"Kathleen?" I studied her—she looked so young. Far younger than her sixty-plus years. Casimir stood behind her—I often saw them together. He'd comforted her when she learned months ago that her estranged husband was dead. It was only a matter of time before Casimir declared his feelings, I think.

"Dinner," Kathleen smiled and held out a hand to me.

"I'm really not hungry," I began.

"Kay, you have to eat. You know that. What if they come back and find out we've been starving ourselves with worry? They're somewhere, at least. We know that much, don't we?"

"Yeah." I'd found Ashe and Breanne; those two meant more to me than anything, and I'd lost them again. At least I'd lost what I'd known of them—that precious contact that had become so important to me.

Ashe might never know it, but I cried every night for him. And for Breanne. I wanted to curse the one responsible for this, too. Trajan explained that it was a powerful rogue god who'd made the mistake of killing a Larentii.

At least the rogue god had been destroyed. I heard Trajan and Trace talking about other rogues, though. That frightened me. "I'll eat," I said and followed Kathleen and Casimir into the house.

Earth—past

Adam's Journal

"Sweetheart, I don't know what is going on." I carried Kiarra into the house while Joey watched. Pheligar had already healed the break in her leg, but the hospital stay was mandatory as we were doing our best to fit into the local population.

"How did the Director know your name?" Kiarra's blue eyes were worried as I seated her on a chair at the kitchen island.

"No idea, and he had a Larentii with him. Called him Connegar.

Do we know why the Larentii might be working with the Director of the Joint NSA and Homeland Security Department?"

"Adam," Pheligar appeared beside Joey, dwarfing our healer, "It involves events in the future, which are now having an impact on the past. At the time you are now, Connegar hasn't been born. Actually, I am Pheligar from the future, and not the one with whom you are familiar. I cannot give more information without confusing everything, so you will have to trust me—us."

I'd never seen Pheligar with something resembling confusion on his face. "Kiarra, how are you feeling?" he turned to her, now.

"Better, now that I'm out of that ridiculous hospital. Thanks for healing the leg."

"You are most welcome." He actually smiled at her, and I wasn't sure I'd seen that much warmth from him, even when he was standing in full sun on a hot July day.

"You can't tell us anything?" I asked.

"Only that Kiarra was in danger, yesterday, and the child who died was no child. It would be prudent for you to travel to Kiarra's home offworld; Justin can be tutored there and time can be bent when it is safe to return."

"What the fuck?" Joey joined the conversation, then.

"I did not want to be forced to do this," Pheligar sighed impatiently. "Saxom has been resurrected and has renewed his obsession with you." Pheligar shook his head at Kiarra. "This time, he has more powerful allies than the Ra'Ak to help him."

"Yeah. We'll go. Right now." My wife turned green and looked ready to vomit.

"I will move your belongings," Pheligar said. "Go. Now."

⌇

Avendor—present

Reah's Journal

"Lara'Kayan, I think we should hold off on our search for these criminals," Nefrigar said.

"Honey blue, you look sad." I went to him and stroked his face with my fingers. He sat on a glider outside my suite while we talked. I understood his sadness—the Larentii race was still in mourning for Ferrigar, although his son, Kalenegar, had taken his father's position as Head of the Larentii Council and according to accounts, was doing very well.

"We are all saddened by recent events, and my sons and I must place records in the archives, detailing the God Wars and Ferrigar's death."

Nefrigar didn't add that he'd be forced to record that the Mighty had been taken out of the fight early, because of Ferrigar's death at the hands of Acrimus. Few of us understood Acrimus' role in the God Wars, other than he seemed to be the General's right hand in all things related to wrongdoing and death. Nefrigar also didn't add that many Larentii felt the God Wars were lost and that their race would be the last standing, as it was the first to be created.

"Honey blue," I placed both hands on his face, then. "Even though things look their dimmest now, there are children who need to be rescued. The time for the mortal may be over, but they deserve an easier life—and death—in the meantime. Besides, Breanne asked this of me. How can I refuse that last request?"

"You were uncomfortable around her," Nefrigar pointed out gently.

"I know," I agreed and hunched my shoulders before turning away. "I'd heard that she could read anyone—that's why Teeg wanted her help. I didn't want her to see everything about me if she looked. Some of it makes me ashamed for anyone to know."

"My love, those things are not your fault. Do you think she wouldn't see that as well? Don't you think she might have given you what she gave to others—*Love*?"

"I hear that it's a comfort and a joy," I muttered. I felt as if I'd missed a chance at something wonderful, because my insecurities stood in the way.

"That is what I hear as well, and it is a shame that Kalenegar cannot receive it, as he grieves in private—for her and for his parent."

"I think I'll go hunting in two days," I said and turned back to Nefrigar. "I know you worry about me," I held up a hand. "I'll take Farzi and Nenzi with me, plus anyone else who wants to help. I'm planning to fold to Campiaa tomorrow, to talk with Tybus."

"Yes. Talk with Tybus. He is wise," Nefrigar conceded. "Ask him what he thinks of this errand."

"You know, I'll do that." I nodded stubbornly at Nefrigar. I had no idea what Tybus might say about the hunt for Hordace Cayetes and his crowd, but my mind was already made up. Edward had offered to come with me, so I hoped a High Demon and the Elemaiyan War Eagle, plus two deadly lion snake shapeshifters might be enough for this mission.

"Please do not place yourself in danger. I hear that some of the remaining rogues outrank you."

"I know. Lissa and I had this discussion already."

"There is something else," Nefrigar said.

"What's that?"

"I have been instructed to bring you to a meeting. In the Archives. Edward, Tybus and your reptanoids must come as well."

"When?"

"Now."

~

Avendor—present

Adam's Journal

"We're on Kiarra's planet in the past," I handed a glass of wine to Merrill. He preferred wine—I was having a Jameson's on the rocks.

"We have a meeting with Conner, and then we can go into the past if you want," Merrill held up his wineglass in a silent toast. "Pheligar says Belen has given all of us carte-blanche on tracking and destroying the enemy."

"I'm interested in this meeting with Conner," I muttered. "She came for Kiarra earlier, and I'd be worried except that Pheligar, Renegar, Graegar and Barrigar went with them. Pheligar said that Connegar and Reemagar went to collect Lissa, who didn't know about the meeting."

"Nefrigar and his sons have been sent to collect Reah, Edward and several others," Kalenegar appeared inside my study. "Are you ready? It is time to go."

"You're escorting us?" Merrill asked.

"I am. Bring your drinks. You may need them."

Lissa's Journal

"What's this about?" I studied my surroundings—we were in the Larentii Archives. I'd never been there. Reah, who was mated to Nefrigar, had been several times, but she always said she'd only seen parts of it.

All the ceilings were clear and the building—if you could call it that—stood far in the north on the Larentii homeworld. Calling it huge would belittle what it was. Calling it huge to the hundredth power might come close.

Everything inside was in stasis, and some might consider it a museum as it held books, recordings, drawings, valuable sculptures and works of art. I stared at a Caspar David Friedrich painting that was supposedly destroyed in World War II. The piece was beautiful, haunting, and I'd only seen black and white photographs of it in the past. Here was the stunning reality.

"That is the original, *Pulled* away before the building housing it was bombed," Nefrigar and his sons appeared, accompanied by Reah, Edward, all eight reptanoids and Tybus.

"Lissa, how nice to see you again," Tybus came forward, took my hand and leaned in to kiss my cheek.

"Hey," I put my arms around him and hugged him tightly.

"Daughter, it is wonderful to hold you again," he whispered against my ear. I felt like sniffling against his crisp, white shirt. I had a father, but he and I were estranged. This man was offering something I'd never experienced—a father's unconditional love.

"Come," Nefrigar smiled as Tybus and I drew apart. "It is time."

"Time for what?" Reah whispered to me as we followed Nefrigar farther into the Archives, past storage systems I didn't recognize and shelves of items that defied explanation.

"No idea," I muttered as we walked. Reah and I gasped as we passed through a wide, marble entrance into what appeared to be a grand hall, where tables were lined up in neat rows.

I imagined so many Larentii young had studied at those tables at one time or another; every Larentii had a parent and a surrogate, along with others as they matured, who taught them what they should know and how to use their power properly.

"Choose your seats—all are open," Nefrigar smiled as he held out a hand, inviting us to sit. "Others will arrive quickly."

They did. The Saa Thalarr, Spawn Hunters and all their healers began arriving in groups. All were accompanied by Larentii.

Others I didn't expect appeared, including Erland, Gavin, Winkler, Rigo, Drake, Drew, Roff, Toff, Nissa, Ry and Trik. Ildevar Wyyld appeared, accompanied by two Larentii. The Starr brothers—all four of them, came with Garegar and his Protector, Lanigar.

Trevor appeared, accompanied by Lenigar. I blinked—Lanigar and Lenigar were brothers, with Lanigar being the eldest. He'd been a Protector for the previous Wise One, who'd separated his particles after a very long life. Garegar had taken his place and convinced Lanigar to remain as his Protector.

Merrill, Adam and Kiarra came to join Tybus and me at the long table I'd chosen. Ry, Nissa, Toff and Trik came next, followed by Karzac, Grace, Devin, Dragon and Crane.

Trajan and Trace appeared last of all, with Bill Jennings, Kevis Halivar, Bear Wright, Amos and Flossie Thompson, Kay, Opal Tadewi and Jayson Rome. Yes, I was shocked when Jayson appeared—in the past he'd given up that identity and assumed that of Matt Michaels, who'd eventually take Bill's place as Director of the Joint NSA and Homeland Security Department. Here he was, however—no longer in disguise, and that defied logic.

Everyone talked quietly—this was a library and an Archive, after all, which lent itself to quiet study and contemplation. "May I have your attention?" Conner spoke. Silence fell on the crowd.

"I have several announcements to make, but first, the others of my kind will join us."

The others of her kind? Gavin, who'd moved others aside so he could sit beside me, sent mindspeech.

No idea, I returned. I knew she could transfer the dead to the other side, or call back some to deliver messages to those left behind, but it was the first time I'd heard her make an announcement like this.

Conner, Kiarra's half-sister, was just as beautiful as Kiarra, but her hair was a honey-blonde instead of platinum, and she had a lovely Southern accent.

"We are here."

I stared—two more had come. There was no mistaking The Ear— I'd seen him once before. The Eye—I wasn't sure anyone in the crowd had seen him. "I am The Mouth," Conner announced to dead silence. These were the Shining Ones—those who spoke and acted on behalf of the One. I think my breath caught—I can't recall.

CHAPTER 2

issa's Journal

"Before Wisdom, Strength and Love were reunited, a task was assigned to us," Conner went on. She was the only one of the Shining ones who maintained her appearance—the other two glowed softly in the Archives. Larentii dotted the large space, as if they were guarding those present.

"That task," Conner said, "was simple—we were instructed to form an army. For the One—who is also the Three."

"As you know," The Ear began, "many rogue gods were eliminated by Love—whom you know as the Mighty Heart. She has chosen one-third of those present."

"I was instructed by Strength to approach another third of those present—to replace what was lost with those better, stronger and more resolved," The Eye added.

"And I was directed by Wisdom to choose the final third," Conner —The Mouth, said. "That is why you are here. If you choose to decline the invitation you are about to receive, there will be understanding and no recrimination. The choice is yours to accept or not. Should you choose to accept, then you agree to hunt the enemy in all its forms and destroy what you hold the strength to destroy."

"You are held to the normal requirements—no killing of the innocent," The Eye said. "No unnecessary interference. No intentional tampering with timelines."

"Here are the invitations." The Ear held out a glowing hand. Envelopes appeared and plopped onto tables before all of us. They were cream linen—exactly like the one I'd gotten recently that held the bracelet and the note.

With shaking fingers, I lifted my envelope. It wasn't sealed—perhaps there was no need. I pulled out the enclosed card.

Should you choose to accept,
the title—and honor—of being a member of the Al'Riyu is yours.

My breath caught again.

~

Reah's Journal

All around me, envelopes were opened. Farzi and Nenzi showed me their invitations—they'd been selected as Nameless Ones. I hugged both of them. Their brothers, with the exception of Chazi, received the same. Chazi turned his invitation around so I might read it, his eyes huge in surprise—he'd been selected as Pan'Warha, a level above the Nameless Ones.

In most instances, the one singled out as a superior might have been outcast because of jealousy. Not this time, or with these—Chazi—perhaps the quietest of all of them, had been given an honor and they were all happy.

"Sweetheart, open it," Ry pointed to my envelope. I saw that he hadn't opened his, either.

"Open yours at the same time—I'm afraid," I muttered.

"Yeah. I get that," he nodded in agreement. Both of us lifted the flaps at the same moment.

Should you choose to accept,

the title—and honor—of being a member of the Al'Riyu is yours.

I turned the card to show Ry, who did the same for me. His said En'Nurifi, a level below mine. Edward's was the same—En'Nurifi.

~

Lissa's Journal

Gavin was a Nameless One. Rigo and Aurelius had been given invitations to join the Mil'Karha. Drake and Drew—Ba'Mirha. Their father, Dragon, was chosen as Al'Riyu, joining Reah, Adam, Merrill and me.

"Look." Winkler handed his card to me—he joined my Falchani twins in the Ba'Mirha.

"What should I do?" Corent approached me with a heavy sigh, a card in his hand. Until then, I hadn't known he'd come. Fes, shockingly enough, was right behind Corent.

"Honey, I don't believe you would have gotten that if they didn't think you might be able to do something," I said, lifting the card from his fingers. En'Nurifi was printed on it. Fes' said Pan'Warha. A master cook was going to war. Well, it wouldn't be the first time.

"Will we know what to do?" Fes sounded worried.

"Fes, I've always gotten the message, one way or another," I nodded to him.

"Then I will accept," Corent seemed determined, suddenly. "I will find a way," he added.

"Maybe a little peace is what some of them need," I suggested.

"I hope so," he replied.

"Lissa, I have received a promotion," Belen sounded nearly breathless as he joined the growing crowd around me.

"Belen?" I blinked at him.

"I am Ghi'Yisi—with Kiarra," he said. "She was offered a place with the Nameless Ones long ago—and kept refusing to take it in order to stay with the Saa Thalarr. Her long wait has been rewarded."

~

Trajan's Journal

Yeah, I used to be a sportswriter—before Winkler made me his Second. Then Ashe came along, changing the game called my life. I became his Second. I stared at the card in my hand. Only one other had received the same offer on his card, and he was just as surprised as I was. So many others I imagined would be in line for this, rather than me.

My card—and Karzac's, offered a position with the Ko'Ahmari.

"What shall we do first?" Karzac dropped his card on the table where I sat, stunned and immobile.

"I think we ought to track down Hank, I guess. Maybe he has some ideas."

"Sounds as good as any other suggestion," Karzac pulled out a chair and sat beside me. He'd been a physician and healer for the Saa Thalarr for nearly sixteen thousand years. He and I were about to join one of the highest echelons of gods. Would I refuse this offer? *No.*

Too many things needed doing, and I'd watched Hank carefully, ever since he'd wiped the dojo floor with my body. He didn't hurt me —he only showed me what he was capable of doing. That impressed me greatly.

"Mine isn't nearly that impressive," Winkler dropped his card on the table on my other side. His card said Ba'Mirha. Still very impressive and not as shocking as my elevation.

"There must be a reason," Karzac said.

"Healer?" Winkler turned a puzzled gaze to Karzac, who handed his card over. "Well, it makes sense, I think," Winkler began. "We have humanoid bodies, and we're going to war. Who's gonna fix us if we're injured? Face it—if we lose this," he tapped his chest, "we're energy after that, unless we form or find a new body. I hear that's next to impossible, unless you're Al'Riyu or above. Somebody on the other side was finding bodies for their rogues. Whether it was Acrimus or someone else, who knows?" Winkler shrugged.

"I may be in the business of reforming bodies?" Karzac studied his card with renewed interest. "That is more than fascinating."

"I think it's your calling," Winkler agreed. "You can do alone what it took most of the Larentii race to accomplish for Breanne."

"I miss her," Karzac sighed. "Kevis misses her more. I cannot sufficiently convey my sorrow, werewolf, for your loss." He turned green-gold eyes filled with sympathy toward me.

"Yeah." I nodded. "Nothing may heal that."

In truth, my heart felt empty at the best of times, and there was no concrete entity to blame or hold accountable. Ashe's absence also created a void within me—we'd worked together for centuries. Kay cried herself to sleep most nights, and I had little comfort to give her; I was so desperately in need of it myself. The only good thing, perhaps, to come of Ashe's disappearance was that Aedan and Adele had begun to lean on one another in their grief.

"May I have your attention, please?" Conner spoke again. The room went quiet and our attention turned to her and the other two once more.

~

Lissa's Journal

"Is there anyone here who does not accept?" Conner asked. "There is no stigma attached to a refusal, and your honesty will be appreciated."

Nobody spoke.

"Good. By dawn tomorrow on your respective worlds, the transformation will be complete. Now, Nefrigar has something to show all of us." We watched as Conner, The Ear and The Eye stepped aside. Nefrigar came forward and lifted his hand. A wide, rectangular section of the floor beside him opened and a platform rose. Yes, I gasped, right along with everyone else.

"They are in stasis," Nefrigar sighed. "But this is only their corporeal forms." The bodies of Ashe, Charles and Breanne lay on individual blocks of marble, dressed just as they were when their energy combined to reform the One.

"How?" Kiarra spoke first.

"They appeared here immediately after," Nefrigar replied. "This is the Archive. Dead races, books, languages and many other things are here. It is fitting, is it not, that these are also here?"

"I guess." I watched as Bill Jennings rose from his seat and walked toward the bodies.

"Do not touch," Nefrigar warned. That's when Bill wept.

"Meanwhile, back at the ranch," I muttered to myself. I sat in the arboretum at the top of my palace, staring at the pinpoints of light marking homes and businesses throughout Lissia.

"Cara?" Gavin sat beside me with a sigh. The glider swing was comfortable and rocked both of us gently as we contemplated the city beyond the palace.

"Gavin, I don't know what to say," I began. One of my sons—Rylend—would become En'Nurifi. Nissa, Toff and Trik would be Pan'Warha. Travis and Trent were still too young for consideration. My remaining son had been left out completely. Yes, he deserved some punishment, but there were many at the meeting who'd done the same or worse than my High Demon child. I'd said those things aloud without really meaning to.

"Perhaps you should consult Kifirin—or Li'Neruh Rath. Neither were at the Archives," Gavin pointed out.

"Do you think Li'Neruh Rath will just drop everything and come if I call?" I blinked at Gavin in disbelief.

"I will if it is important enough," Li'Neruh, whom my sister always called Hank, appeared before us, arms thick with muscle crossed tightly over his chest. "You ask why Torevik was not included in the meeting," he nodded to me, his eyes darkening while curls of smoke escaped his nostrils. "I have plans for the High Demon race, and I asked that no High Demon be allowed at the meeting."

"You did this?"

"Yes. The High Demons must prove their worth—since they failed so miserably in the past. Had they been vigilant as instructed, many things could have been prevented. You know better than anyone how that turned out."

"Yeah," I sighed. "I know how that turned out." Races had been exterminated, while others were allowed to run amok. The shield between the Light and Dark halves of the universes had come down. Gavin reached for my hand and stroked it as I hunched my shoulders.

"The Larentii were asked to lower the shield," Li'Neruh said. Somehow, he'd read my thoughts easily.

"By whom?" I stared—I was hearing this for the first time. Until now, I didn't know that the Larentii held the shield between Light and Dark.

"Wisdom. You may as well know, since you will join the Al'Riyu in a few of your hours—as you currently measure time."

"You knew who he was all along."

"He made himself known to me, yes. I cannot say that it was all along."

"How long did he know who he was? When he was born as human?" I demanded. It probably wasn't wise to demand answers from a superior, but if Charles stood in front of me I'd do exactly the same, even knowing he was Wisdom.

"The Ear was instructed to carry a message to him when he reached his sixteenth year," Li'Neruh dropped gracefully to the floor, his legs crossed elegantly. I had no idea what training he'd endured, but the Falchani warriors did the same—to perfection. Drake and Drew often did it when we had tea inside my suite. I usually joined them, although my sitting wasn't nearly as graceful.

"So he knew—when the others didn't."

"Ashe became aware when he was sixteen, as should have been. Breanne," he shook his head. "So many things went wrong with Breanne."

"Thorsten and Griffin," I muttered angrily. "I have a question, though. Who placed the mind cloud on Gavin, Cheedas and my son?"

"I have a theory," Li'Neruh said. "And it will bear investigation. If my suspicions are correct, many of our troubles did not die with Acrimus."

"That doesn't sound good," I stared at Li'Neruh in alarm.

"It is not good, sister," Li'Neruh agreed. "It is my desire to get to the bottom of this, as humans often say."

"What are we going to do? Without Bree?" The tears began to fall, then.

"I do not know." Li'Neruh rose just as gracefully as he'd sat. "My heart is empty," he said and disappeared.

Reah's Journal

"It was a request from the Mighty Heart," I said.

"Then we will wait until our power manifests and hunt this filth," Tybus said, his voice firm, his decision final.

"I agree," Edward nodded.

"We go," Farzi and Nenzi declared.

"You're going with us?" I blinked at Tybus in surprise.

"My dear," Tybus approached me carefully and touched my face with a gentle hand, "I have been given a great gift. Do you suggest I sit behind a desk and ignore it when there is a need for my talents elsewhere? I adore children. It burns my soul to know so many suffer."

One of Lissa's words almost pushed past my lips—*wow*. I stared at Tybus with respect and awe—he planned to utilize what he had immediately.

"Dormas—Dee—can handle things in my absence," Tybus continued. "He knows as much as I about the difficulties our Alliance faces. If there is need, he will contact me and I will make myself available."

"Where should we start?" Aurelius asked. We'd gathered at EastStar, before returning Tybus to Campiaa.

"I say we start with Kay—and Kalia's memories," Astralan

suggested. "We know, now, who you are," he nodded toward Tybus. "Pheligar informed us."

"A wise decision," Tybus agreed. "I hold within me what Gavril was, as well as what I am."

"Pheligar said so," Stellan nodded. "We are relieved."

"How do we approach Kay? She is fragile, no matter what," I pointed out.

"I can help, I think," Kevis offered. "It would be better if Bree, well, that won't happen." Kevis shook his head.

I knew Kevis loved Breanne—he'd discussed it with me before her disappearance. I didn't mind at all—I felt Kevis often received only the bits and pieces of my time that weren't demanded by the rest of my mates. He never complained, either, and I'd hoped that a relationship with Breanne would help him as much as it might her. That wouldn't happen, now.

"I'll contact Trajan," Aurelius offered. "He or Trace will come for us."

~

Avendor—present

Adam's Journal

"I think we should go back to Fresno in the past and wait for the bastard to show up again. You know he will," Kiarra paced inside the solarium. Merrill, Pheligar and I watched her agitated march, first this way and then that, as she attempted to discharge restless energy. All of us knew she spoke of Saxom.

"My darling, Moxas is with him. What might occur, should they realize we are from the future and not that particular time?" Merrill asked.

"I don't give a damn," Kiarra muttered. "I just want him to come for me, so we can kill him again. And as many times as it takes to make him dead forever."

"Lissa killed Moxas the last time, and this appears to be one of his clones," Pheligar observed.

"You think we ought to take Lissa with us?" I asked.

"Perhaps, although I can't say that she'll be able to come alone. I believe many of her mates will insist on coming with her."

"Perhaps I should make arrangements for additional housing," Pheligar said. "It may be needed."

"Can we put up another compound—like we did in the past? Is there land available?" I asked.

"I will do research," Pheligar nodded and disappeared.

Avendor—present

Reah's Journal

"Kay, we just want to track these women and take them out," Kevis said gently. "We'll make sure no children are harmed."

"Then you need to be careful," Kay brushed tears away. "They're awful. They'll kill all of them rather than turn them over," she added.

They'd treated her cruelly, I could tell. At that moment, I wished for Breanne's talent of reading someone, so I would know how much damage these women had caused. Not just to Kay, but to untold others.

"We want Hordace Cayetes and his crew as well," Kevis said softly. "Can you give us anything to go on?"

"Song and Serenade have contact information on them." Kay's voice was thick with her tears.

"We can hand that over to Kooper and Lendill," Edward muttered. "I believe that is in their domain."

"What will you do with the children?" The question bore pain and I wanted to weep with Kay as she asked it.

"Amara and her new mate will care for them." Aurelius had remained quiet until now. I turned to him in surprise. Yes, I knew who Amara's new mate was. Edan Desh. My reincarnated father—thanks to Kifirin. He'd become a healer for the Saa Thalarr and was now immortal, just as Amara was. My shoulders sagged at the thought.

"Yes. Amara and Edan will take care of them," I agreed.

My love, you are pale, Aurelius' words brushed softly across my mind. *He is not the same as the one you knew. He merely wears that face.*

I know, I replied. The Edan I knew had never had a kind word for me. This one—he would welcome me if I went to visit. Too much pain stood between us and I wondered if that would ever subside.

"Kay, I'll find them," I found myself making a promise to her. "They'll never harm children again."

"Thank you." She surprised me by wrapping her arms about me and hugging me tightly.

"You're welcome." My arms went around her shoulders and I hugged back.

~

Kifirin—present

Hank's Journal

"My Lord?" Nedevik Weth approached me cautiously as I stood atop the high dome of the palace. He was in his smaller Thifilathi, just as I was. Surprisingly, he could speak quite well in that form—most High Demons couldn't.

"Lord Nedevik?" I turned and nodded to him, taking my eyes away from the city of Veshtul below us.

"May I speak with you?" Nedevik asked politely.

"Of course. Do you wish to speak here or elsewhere?" I asked.

"I would invite you to my home, if you are willing to come. I offer food and drink as well, should you choose to accept."

"I accept." I nodded to the Patriarch of the House of Weth. Before he could skip away, I folded both of us to his home near the eastern mountains.

~

"I have watched through the years," Nedevik sighed over a glass of wine later. We'd eaten—he'd seen to that first.

"What have you noticed?" I asked. Nedevik was the eldest of the High Demons, slightly older than Gardevik, who was quite old.

"I have studied genealogy lately," Nedevik said, pulling a comp-vid from a nearby table drawer. We sat in his private study, finishing drinks after a fine meal. Nedevik waited until now to talk of anything important. I felt it was to spare the members of his household, especially his wife, who appeared quite worried.

"Genealogy?" His remark intrigued me.

"Yes. All High Demons except Reahrok are from Kifirin. You see where our race has fallen," he said bluntly. He'd given the honorific to Reah, too, and Jaydevik Rath had failed—or refused—to do it in the past.

"I understand that," I agreed.

"In fact, all the Dark Realm races have fallen—in one way or another."

"I know that as well," I nodded. All of them—either dead, dying or in disgrace. Only a few had escaped that fate, and they were constantly threatened. Except the High Demons, of course, and they were, in my opinion, at the top of the disgraced list. "What does this have to do with anything?" I asked.

"I believe it is connected with our creation," Nedevik breathed. "May I give you the rest of my observation in mindspeech? Might you shield us against intrusion of any kind?"

"Of course," I nodded to him and placed a shield. Nedevik was deeply concerned about something and I was now determined to find out what it was. If my suspicions were correct, then he and I might have traveled similar paths to reach our conclusions.

In our archives, Nedevik began, *the tale of our beginning is recorded. Kifirin placed it there himself, if the legend is true.*

It is true, I nodded.

Good. I have been concerned on that point. That supports my theory, he sent.

What theory is that?

As you know, Kifirin did not hold sufficient power to create the Dark Realm. That power was lent to him by his parent.

Yes, it was. I was surprised that Nedevik had searched through the archives to read these records—most never bothered, including Jaydevik Rath, King of the High Demons.

You see that everything touched by that power is now dead or deteriorating. I fail to believe that it was only because Kifirin slept. It has also troubled me greatly that he did sleep. Why was that? Did he not realize that he was tiring? How did that come about? Any parent who cared for his child would point out that flaw. Perhaps even step in when his child was exhausted. Nedevik blinked at me, waiting for me to confirm or deny his statement. I breathed a curl of smoke, instead.

Then, Nedevik continued uncertainly, *we see that parent briefly—but only when Kifirin is about to fall into disgrace for struggling to keep a promise. Now, all find Kifirin abhorrent, even his mate, because he erred. Where was his parent when he began his journey down that path, or was his absence merely to allow the disgrace of his child and leave him without allies?*

How many, Nedevik's sending was a trembling question, *of the rogue gods were more powerful than the one assigned to oversee the Dark Realm? Before you accepted that assignment?*

He worried that I'd be offended. I wasn't. His concerns mirrored my own. I couldn't recall seeing Kifirin's parent. Only Lissa and a few others had seen him in the past century, and then he'd disappeared. Nedevik was correct—as Kifirin's parent, he should have stepped in to help a struggling child. He didn't. He only observed the mistakes and forced an apology afterward.

I had no godling children. I'd chosen not to make any. All below the Ghi'Yisi were parented by others, however—until now. Many had been promoted in the past few hours. The Ear had informed me of this. How many of the rogue gods had parents still within our ranks? A chill raced down my spine, more smoke curled from my nostrils and my Thifilathi threatened to manifest.

"Lord Nedevik, thank you for this conversation," I rose unsteadily and nodded to him. "Gather your household. I will transport you to Avendor, where you will be safe."

～

Avendor—present

Trajan's Journal

"We have room," I said. "Marco, will you and Cori make sure they're comfortable and have everything they need?"

"Sure thing," Marco nodded. "Is there anything we ought to tell the others? They're not used to High Demons."

I understood what he wasn't saying—that he wasn't used to them, either.

"They're just like us, until they turn Thifilathi," I pointed out. "Hank tells me that Nedevik and his household won't be a bother. In fact, Nedevik may want to go through Ashe's library. Tell him he can read anything he likes and that he's welcome at the big house anytime."

"Okay," Marco said. I realized then that he was a bit depressed—his younger brother, Sali, had gone to a meeting and he'd been left behind. Sali would join the ranks of the gods in a few hours, while Marco would remain Marco.

"Marco, everybody is important in this war," I said. "A meeting will mean nothing if everything falls anyway."

"You think it will?" Cori blinked at me.

"Cori, I don't know what to think anymore," I reached out to tuck a blonde curl behind her ear. "I always thought Ashe would be with us, here and now. He isn't." I didn't add that I thought Breanne would be with us, too. Charles? I couldn't muster enough emotion to miss him as well. I was too depressed over the loss of Breanne and Ashe.

"Look, man, I didn't mean," Marco sighed.

"I know. Things are different now. We all have to adjust." I folded space to a quiet spot on Harifa Edus before I broke down.

Le-Ath Veronis—present

Lissa's Journal

Yeah, I stared. Li'Neruh Rath was inside my bedroom, pacing. Drake, Drew and Karzac had arrived earlier; we'd been discussing what might happen in the morning when Li'Neruh appeared. So far, he hadn't said anything.

"Healer?" Li'Neruh finally stopped pacing, coming to a stop at the foot of my bed. Karzac sat with me, leaning against the headboard. At least all of us were fully clothed.

"Li'Neruh?" Karzac said.

"Call me Hank. It's simpler," Li'Neruh sighed. "I know what you will be in a few hours. I need your help—and Trajan's. Care to join me as I travel to Avendor?"

"I'll come." Karzac was off the bed immediately. They disappeared in front of me without saying good-bye.

Avendor—present

Hank's Journal

"I need generals. For an army of High Demons," I said.

Trajan blinked at me in surprise. Karzac studied the problem for a moment without speaking. When he did speak, his words were weighted with wisdom. "Ask Dragon and his children," he said. "They all have experience in leading armies, and Dragons may be able to command High Demons when no other might rise to the challenge. You may also consider Dragon's brother, Crane. He was Dragon's General for a very long time."

"Why not all the Falchani?" Trajan turned to me and asked. "Plus Sali. He has war experience, too. Let me tell you, Caylon Black is a badass. Nobody messes with him. Not even Dragon."

"I like that idea," I said. "I will make contact, beginning tomorrow."

The General didn't want to admit that he was weak in any area. He also hated admitting—even to himself—that Acrimus had carried much of the weight. All he'd had to do was wave a hand and Acrimus would see any task done.

"Calhoun, gather the Hidden," the General commanded.

"I cannot command them—I hold insufficient power, my Lord," Calhoun bowed warily.

"Then who might command them?" The General's anger rose. Calhoun took a step back—he felt the General's wrath.

"Only you, my Lord," Calhoun quavered.

"Do you still command V'ili and his subjects?"

"Yes. And the chimeras and all others less than I."

"Then humanity is ours. You know what to do. I will command the Hidden."

∾

Le-Ath Veronis—present

Lissa's Journal

"Where do you think they'll strike first?" Drake asked. We couldn't sleep, although we were in bed—Drake on one side, Drew on the other.

"I don't know, but consider this," I said. "How many of the Three were from Earth?"

"Three," Drew answered immediately.

"How many of the Saa Thalarr are from Earth?" I asked.

"A lot," Drake blinked dark eyes at me. Was he handsome? He and Drew were so handsome it dripped off them. "Kiarra, Adam, Merrill, Grace, Mom, Fox, Justin, Martin, Mack, Daniel, Joey, Conner, Norton, Brock, Stephan, Russell, Will, Wlodek, Weldon, Steve, Jeff, Kyle, Franklin, Radomir, Dalroy, Rhett and Christi." He'd ticked off all the Saa Thalarr and associated healers from Earth. There were other Saa Thalarr, but they were from scattered worlds and none in such numbers. The second largest contingent was from Falchan, actually.

"You think they'll strike Earth first? To wound us and make us bleed?" Drake asked.

"It makes sense. So many of us are invested in that world, one way or another. Dragon is married to your mother, who is from Earth," I pointed out. "Most of the others have a mate from Earth. I figure since they've already had a victory there, they'll push to take it first."

"They have a decent start already," Drew said. "All they had to do in a few instances was play on the hate or prejudice already in existence."

"True," I agreed. "In the past, anyway."

"Then that's where they'll strike again, most likely. If that world succumbs in the past, they'll have allies in the future."

"Makes sense," I agreed.

Lissa? Mindspeech came from Merrill.

What, hon? I returned.

May I visit? If you're awake, that is.

Yeah. We're all awake.

I wasn't expecting Kiarra and Adam to come, too, and I may have blushed at being caught in bed with both my Falchani. At least I was wearing pajamas.

"Lissa, we were wondering if you'd like to go with us when we return to Earth in the past. We think they'll strike there again," Kiarra began. She didn't seem concerned at all that I was flanked by two bare-chested Falchani.

"We were just discussing that," I said, misting out of bed. Merrill placed his arms around me when I shivered at the change in temperature. Drake and Drew had kept me warm.

"You'll consider it?" Adam asked.

"I think it's a foregone conclusion," I said. "Where, though?"

"We're going back to Fresno. I think Saxom won't be able to stop himself from trying again," Kiarra muttered.

"There's a nasty thought," I said. "And probably true. Plus, wherever Saxom is, Moxas will be, too. If we get them, maybe the others will come hunting. I hope we're ready for the challenge when it comes."

"As do we," Merrill kissed my forehead. "As do we."

CHAPTER 3

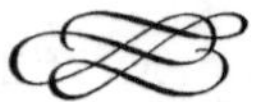

I knew the power was there the moment I woke. Sleep hadn't come for a very long time, but when it did, it descended heavily. Now, there was work to be done and I considered where to start.

Jayson and Opal had returned to Avendor with Trajan and me—at least the Jayson Rome and Opal Tadewi from old Earth had. Jayson, posing as Matt Michaels, had disappeared from the past, as had Opal. Somehow, Belen achieved that minor miracle and I didn't want to examine it too closely for flaws. I was afraid of what I might find.

Folding out of bed and into the kitchen, I found Jayson, Opal and Trajan there ahead of me. All three had cups of coffee in their hands, as if waking up as gods was an everyday occurrence.

"I have an idea," Trajan said, pouring another cup of coffee and handing it to me. I nodded my thanks and drank.

"What's that?" Jayson asked, settling on a barstool at the island.

"I hear that Adam and Kiarra have been taken to a safe place in the past so their more powerful selves can move in and deal with the enemy there. I think we ought to do the same."

"You mean remove the beta versions of Trajan and Bill, so we can go back and kick ass?" Jayson asked.

"Yeah," Trajan shrugged.

"Works for me." Jayson sipped his coffee.

"I'm for that. We all have our memories from back then. At least I do," I said. "I think we can handle this."

"I really want to kick ass," Opal chimed in. Not surprisingly, she had her Ranos pistol tucked in the waistband of her jeans.

"Then I'll contact Adam, asking if we can send two guests from the past to Kiarra's private planet," Trajan said. "I just don't know how to explain things to my former self."

"Let's not explain it," I suggested. "Let's get Lissa to explain it." Trajan laughed for the first time in months.

$\sim$

Earth—past

"Something has happened, brother, and I find it difficult to unravel. Images are blocked, which shouldn't be." Moxas studied the lawn outside his window—Calhoun had moved them to a vacant home in Sausalito. Calhoun wasn't present at the moment, therefore Moxas was comfortable making his confession to Saxom.

"What might have happened? We have won, brother. The Three are no more and those who remain have clearly reached a stalemate in combatting the General and his army. All that is left for us to do is take everything and let chaos rule. I only wait for Calhoun to return so we might continue our search for Kiarra. A promise was made to us and I will see it fulfilled."

"I have suggestions for how we might take everything," Moxas' mood lightened.

"Good. We can offer that as an incentive to continue the search for Kiarra."

$\sim$

Avendor—present

Kay's Journal

I can't say why I felt as I did, but things had certainly changed. Power waited for my command; all I had to do was use it. I also felt just as I had after receiving an infusion of *Love* from Breanne—and I couldn't explain that, either.

Reah, I sent mindspeech for the first time in my life. *I want to hunt with you. It's time my torturers became victims.*

Are you sure? I would appreciate the help as you are more familiar with these than I, but I don't want to upset you in any way, she returned.

I'm sure, I replied. *It's time I stood up to them. It's time for them to realize they no longer have power over me. I've spent too many years being afraid of them as it is.*

I understand that, Reah said. *More than you know.*

It was then, I think, that the realization hit me. Kalia and I—our souls had been forged into a single entity. Our memories were my memories, and seemingly, I'd been left in charge. What was left of Kalia didn't seem to mind at all that our separate selves were now combined. In fact, there was no *we*. There was only *I*, now, and I was determined to see justice done.

We should contact Jett Riffler, I sent. *One of Hordace's strongholds is located on Du'Ferias. Jett has extensive knowledge of survival in that sort of environment.*

The jungle planet? Reah asked.

Yes. I was there several times with Hordace, whenever the ASD came too close and he wanted to hide for a while. I didn't know where I was then, but I know it now.

Sounds like a good place to start. Do you think Song and Serenade are there with him? Reah asked.

No, but he'll know where they are and how to contact them. We need him alive—at least for a little while. If not him, then his lapdog, Q'Ind Ribalo. Q'Ind is Hordace's procurer—he looks over each new crop of children and makes selections for Hordace. Those get special training. Yes, my voice was bitter when I transmitted that bit of information.

And his brother, Q'And, is a prick who fed vital information on the ASD and its agents to Cayetes for years while posing as a sympathetic psychologist.

I could tell from Reah's bitterness that she disliked Q'Ind's brother greatly.

I'm coming with you, Kevis' mindspeech broke in on our conversation.

Kevis? Reah sounded puzzled.

You may need a healer—in more ways than one. I'm Mil'Karha, remember? We're mates, too, remember?

Then you'll come with us, Reah said. *At least we can shield ourselves well enough. I hope they never see us coming.*

Oh, I want them to see me, I said. *Right at the last, I want them to see me.*

That gives me an idea, Kevis said. *Where can we meet to discuss this?*

~

EastStar—present

Reah's Journal

Kevis spent a few moments explaining Kay/Kalia's past to everyone before she arrived at EastStar with Trace. Trace nodded to all of us before returning to SouthStar. He and his brother had their own mission to discuss—with Lissa.

"I don't want Kay to do this alone," Edward said.

"I agree with Edward," Tybus said immediately.

"I was hoping at least one person would go with me." Kay seemed shaky but determined to see this through. "All we have to do is find Rezil. He'll take things from there. I and whoever is with me will have to convince him to take me back to Hordace instead of shooting me on sight."

"I can see to that," Aurelius offered.

"As can I," Tybus nodded. "Actually, as Rezil will recognize me as Teeg, he may want to kill me instead and then take Kay back to Hordace, just to discover what she may have told me, the CSD and ASD."

"We can fake your death at Rezil's hands," Aurelius nodded at the logic in Tybus' plan. "And then travel with Kay, keeping ourselves shielded. We will be with her all along, but the enemy won't know it."

"My dear," Tybus touched Kay's hand gently, "how would you feel about posing with me as a couple? I can make arrangements to have our images shown in the media. That should draw Master Rezil to us quickly, don't you think?"

"Y-yes," Kay agreed unsteadily.

"Kay, you have more power now than Rezil can ever dream of," Kevis reminded her. "Tybus will lay compulsion to make Rezil believe that he's killed the Founder of the Campiaan Alliance, and he'll also tell him not to harm you. I'm confident that will work."

"Then I should pose with both of you, to let everyone know the arrangement has my blessing," I said. "We don't need a scandal. We need to show the Alliance a legitimate courtship of another mate."

"That would be wonderful," Tybus smiled at me. I could tell he hadn't wanted to make the suggestion, for fear of making me uncomfortable. I wanted to sigh but held it back—this man was quickly winning my heart and I had no idea how to tell him.

"We think this good idea," Farzi spoke for all the reptanoids. "We have talents for jungles, too. These grz-gitch not escape."

I wanted to laugh at Farzi's words. We understood—finally—the reptanoids' personal language. Grz-gitch meant illegitimate in every way. Farzi was calling Hordace Cayetes and his cohorts bastards.

"All we need to do is set a date to invite the media in," Tybus said. "Then we sit back and wait for Rezil Foculis to fall into our trap."

～

Le-Ath Veronis—present

Lissa's Journal

"Look, they know Kiarra is in Fresno. With me," Adam pointed out. "Bill, Trajan, Jayson and Opal want to go back with us. It would be easiest if you convince the past versions of Bill and Trajan to stay on Kiarra's private planet until it's safe for them to return."

"I have a house there," I reminded Adam. "I just never use it. They can stay there."

"If we send Fes and Corent to stay with them, they won't starve and those two can provide extra shielding or run errands," Merrill suggested.

"That's a good idea," I said. "Is there anybody else we need to send there to keep them safe?"

"That's something to consider," Adam agreed. "So you'll go and explain to Bill and Trajan that we need to keep them safe while other forces do the dirty work? You know they won't want to leave. We have to tell them that Jayson and Opal are safe where they are, too," he added.

"I know that, but I'll have to convince them that they need to stay alive then to be alive in the future. Maybe that will work."

"I sure as hell hope so," Kiarra sighed.

Earth—past

"Where the hell do you suppose Rome went?" Bill shook his head. "Opal's gone, too." He and Trajan found Opal and Jayson's rooms empty at the compound in Fresno. Bill had extra agents there, and he imagined the place was still shielded, only he had no way to prove it. Both disappearances puzzled him and Trajan greatly.

"No idea. We sure could use Hank right about now," Trajan said.

"Hank's busy," Lissa appeared beside them.

Lissa's Journal

Bill gaped for a few moments before closing his mouth. Trajan, however, didn't waste any time. "What the hell?" he snapped.

"I said Hank's busy," I repeated. "I need you two to come with me. Jayson and Opal are safe, by the way. You need to be safe, too. That's why I'm here—to take you to safety so we can sort this mess out. When we're done, you'll be brought back."

"I have things to do," Bill found his voice.

"And those things will get done. Just not by you. Don't worry, nobody will realize you're not here. Trust me."

"What about the President?"

"What about Winkler?"

"Neither of them will ever know you were gone," I said.

"Isn't this building shielded?" Bill asked.

"Yeah," I said. "But I have permission to get through the shields."

"What if we don't want to go?" Trajan asked.

"Trajan, you have to come with me—this is to save your life. You're needed in the future, and you won't be there if you're killed here and now. I hope that makes sense," I said.

"Why does everybody think you're dead?" Bill asked the big question.

"Bill, every time you see me, memories have to be modified. It's to save me, just as I'm here to save you. If I die here and now, I won't be alive in the future, either, to do what I need to do. If you must know, I almost died—twice. Ashe and Breanne put me back together."

"So that's how it happened." Bill took a seat at the kitchen island with a sigh. "Will we forget you're alive again?"

"At least you remember me. The vampires don't," I pointed out dryly.

"Yeah. That's true." Trajan took a seat across from Bill. "Where will you take us? So we'll be safe? And I'm still not convinced I'll be safer there than here."

"Trajan, you'll just have to trust me on this, and it's nowhere on Earth."

"Do we need to pack?" Bill sounded resigned. "I know Bree isn't here to protect us anymore. Or Hank or Ashe."

"Bill, don't worry about packing." I put an arm around his shoulders. "Bree was my sister. I miss her, too. Your things will be transported with us, and if you need anything, all you have to do is tell Fes or Corent."

"Who are they?" Trajan's dark eyes were puzzled.

"Fes is one of the best cooks anywhere. Corent, well, Corent should explain himself, I think. Don't worry, the hair is natural."

Kent, England—present

Conner's Journal

"I think it's for the best, don't you?" I nodded to Wlodek, Weldon, Winkler, Russell, Will, Radomir and several others. "I can gather all of you in the past and place you with the others on Kiarra's planet with Bill and Trajan. That'll allow your present selves to step in and work toward taking down the enemy."

"This plan coincides with my own," Wlodek said. "Only I was unsure how to replace myself."

"It won't be a problem," I shrugged. "And there will be no disagreements," I pointed a finger at him and then at Weldon.

"Fox is coming with me," Weldon began.

"I beg your pardon?" Wlodek turned dark eyes on the former Grand Master of the Werewolves.

"You think the sudden appearance of a woman in your bed will reassure the Vampire Council?" Weldon growled.

Wlodek cursed in Greek before agreeing. I wanted to laugh. I didn't.

"I'll be back in an hour. Be ready to go." I bent time, heading toward Earth of the past.

"The agreement was that I and the others like me would stay hidden until such a time as the opposition was destroyed or contained. You also agreed that Acrimus would act as your liaison. As unfortunate as it is, Acrimus is no more. We have held to our bargain, yet now you wish to alter it."

"You are Acrimus' child, are you not?" The General studied Quislus intently.

"You know that well enough," Quislus snapped. "I'm sure Acrimus described our relationship in detail. I sacrificed my own child in deference to my parent's desires. I will do my duty as I have made a promise, but I refuse to revise our original agreement."

"You will revise it or I will see you destroyed. I brought down one of the Three, never forget that."

"I have no corporeal body, do not forget that," Quislus pointed out, his voice cold and harsh.

"Shall I make my first attempt at doing to you what the One did to your parent? Shall I hold you up as an example to the other Hidden? Be assured, should I not be able to destroy you, I will contain you. I certainly have enough power for that."

Quislus studied the General. He knew, as did the others, what Calhoun and the General's subordinates were plotting. He saw the beginning of it in the General's shrouded gaze. At that moment, he wished he'd never created the Sirenali or the Dark Elemaiya. The Ra'Ak had been useful tools for millennia, but these—he'd made them too clever. Too grasping. The General had come to depend upon them to assist in his war. For a moment, Quislus wished for time to reverse and to begin again.

"I will do as you say," Quislus said, defeat evident in his words. "I will contact the others. All will be revealed soon as the traitors they are."

"Good. When that happens, I will command a body and you will join me. Calhoun is effective but not powerful enough. You and the others who come to me are the foundation of my new army. All will bow or fall before us."

"As you will it, General."

"As I say, so it is," the General replied.

~

Campiaa—present

Tybus' Journal

"Dee, you will bear my likeness," I said. "If anything happens to me, I know you can run this Alliance with no difficulty."

"I prefer to be what I am," he replied, his voice rough. He hated the spotlight and wanted to be exactly what he was—a powerful voice without the trappings of the media or the requirements or personal appearances to keep others happy. He hated official functions and refused to appear longer than a few moments at any of them.

"Please do this for me. Please," I pleaded. "You know everything there is to know already. We think alike. We act alike much of the time. Use that to protect us and the Alliance. I will pose with Reah and Kalia. When the assassin arrives, compulsion will be placed, he will believe me dead and take Kalia with him to Cayetes. It is up to you to remain here in my stead. I realize that Hordace may attempt to spread the rumor of my death, but that will be difficult to prove, as you will appear to be me in every way."

"Am I to understand that this may be used to further confuse Cayetes?"

"If necessary, yes. It may make him more than willing to question Kalia on her knowledge of me, and that will get us to him."

"Then make this expedition a swift one. I hate the media, I despise small talk, but most of all, I detest politicians."

"I feel the same, brother," I laughed. "I feel exactly the same."

~

Kiarra's private planet—present

Fes' Journal

"What the hell?" Trajan from the past looked about him as he and several others appeared inside the spacious beach house. If I hadn't been elevated to Pan'Warha, I'd never have understood the language of old Earth.

"Welcome." Corent's hair became a blue-green, reflecting the waters of the ocean below the massive house. "We have accommodations for the vampires among you," Corent added. "For the moment, I am shielding you so you will not be damaged by the light."

Wlodek, still the vampire he was in the past, gazed uncertainly at the waters beyond and the sun shining far to the west.

"I'll be damned." Russell, also a vampire, whistled as he stared at daylight for the first time in two centuries.

"We have rooms prepared for everyone, if you will follow me," Corent explained. "Each enclosed vampire suite holds a refrigeration unit with bagged blood or blood substitute available. For the others, Fes will provide meals. For any of you with cooking experience, I'm sure he will welcome any assistance while you are here."

"I will welcome assistance," I agreed, studying those who'd arrived. The Mouth had offered a mental description of likes and dislikes where food was concerned, and I was prepared to offer a variety of dishes they would appreciate during their stay.

"Where the hell are we?" Weldon Harper, the one who still held the position of Grand Master for the Werewolves, demanded.

"I can answer that," I said, waving a hand. Power is an amazing thing. A three-dimensional image of the universe appeared before me. I smiled as I began explaining the distance (and time) between where we currently were and where our guests used to be.

~

Campiaa—present
  Tybus' Journal
"Jett, you're in charge of these," I nodded toward Keith and Philip. "Philip is a shapeshifter who becomes a large mountain lion. Keith has experience in jungle conditions. He has worked the southern reaches of SouthStar, which borders the jungles there."

"We are to track Cayetes from the opposite side—through the worst of the jungles on Du'Ferias?" Jett asked.

"Yes," I said. "Cayetes may have shapeshifters, Sirenali or any number of nefarious creatures sprinkled throughout. Three others may accompany you, just in case."

"What about Macy, Luanne and Lizzy?" Keith asked.

"They will work with others," I said. "The rogue gates are still a problem, and Trevor, Kooper and Lendill may need their help."

"Who may be coming with us?" Philip said.

"Chazi, Roff and Bear Wright," I smiled. A lion snake shapeshifter, a winged vampire and a grizzly bear shapeshifter, all with power, might prove quite useful.

"When are you inviting the media to San Gerxon Palace?" Jett asked.

"Tomorrow afternoon. Be prepared to go anytime after that."

Kifirin—present

Hank's Journal

I wanted to laugh. I didn't. Dragon had just taken down his third High Demon swordsman. The High Demon army hadn't seen real action in nearly a century—not since Lissa had come to help dispatch a load of rogue Copper Ra'Ak. Dragon and his sons, all in dragon form, had taken down their share of Ra'Ak and a few rogue High Demons in Full Thifilathi during that battle.

Jayd and Garde stood nearby, blowing smoke as the former Falchani Warlord made a laughingstock of their best. For too long, High Demons had depended on their size and fierce looks to defeat what came against them. That time had passed.

"They have fallen, haven't they?" Kifirin appeared at my side.

"Long ago," I nodded.

"I failed to see it. I cannot say why."

"I think I may have an explanation, but it may not be easy for you to hear," I turned to him. For the first time, perhaps, I felt sympathy for him.

"I would prefer to hear it elsewhere," Kifirin sighed.

"I'd prefer that, too. I have taken Lord Nedevik and several of his household to Avendor. He and I agree on this, therefore, his safety is a concern."

"You think it might present a danger?"

"I have no idea how much danger, but yes, I believe that."

"When do you want to meet there?" Kifirin asked.

"Tomorrow morning. I'll be waiting outside the northern boundary."

"I'll be there," Kifirin agreed and disappeared.

Turning back to Dragon and his fourth opponent, I watched as Dragon blocked a blow with one blade and held the tip of the other at the High Demon captain's throat. "I had no idea we were so poorly prepared," Jayd muttered.

"I feel that undue influence has been present for a very long while," I said and folded away.

~

"What did he mean by that?" Garde asked.

"No idea," Jayd shook his head. "How did we get to this point? Not one of ours has made Dragon break a sweat, brother."

"We have a long way to go," Garde replied.

~

Earth—past

Lissa's Journal

As it turned out, we didn't need to put up a new compound—Bill Jennings—the current Bill Jennings, offered the building Ashe had put together in the past.

He, Trajan, Jayson Rome and Opal Tadewi accompanied Adam, Kiarra, Merrill and me to Fresno of the past. Adam, Merrill and Kiarra would be staying at their old home in Fresno, to bait the trap. Saxom would come—he wanted Kiarra too badly.

"There's plenty of room," Bill set two comp-vids on the kitchen island. "I can cook if necessary."

"I'll help," I offered. "I haven't had much time in the kitchen lately."

"We'll be at the house if you need anything," Kiarra nodded to me. "And you can come over anytime. We're only four miles away."

"I will be staying with Kiarra," Pheligar announced almost before he appeared.

"And we'll be with Lissa," Connegar and Reemagar coalesced right behind Pheligar.

"You're guarding us, aren't you?" Kiarra looked up at Pheligar, who offered a lovely smile before lifting her in his arms and giving her a kiss.

"I love you," he said in answer, before disappearing with her, Adam and Merrill.

"Are you sure?" I turned to my Larentii.

"Very sure," Connegar replied.

∾

Campiaa—present

Tybus' Journal

"Just stand here, with your arms around both," the journalist's assistant posed me with Reah and Kay.

"When will the marriage take place?" the journalist tapped notes on a comp-vid.

"Six moon-turns," I replied. "My assistant is working out the details now."

"Yes, just like that," the assistant said as I pulled Reah and Kay closer. The cam-recorder dutifully reproduced our image, which would be broadcast across both Alliances before the day was over. Our part of the attack had been initiated.

∾

Breanne's Journal

"This is always the most difficult part," Charles sighed. "Separating." It was. I did and didn't recall that memory. He was the Mind; of course he'd remember.

"How many times?" Ashe lay naked on the tiled floor nearby, where his corporeal body had been left. The bodies in the Larentii Archives? Decoys.

"Four."

"Will we get it right this time around?" Ashe heaved himself into a sitting position. As he was strength, obviously he'd rise first.

"I sure as hell hope so," Charles muttered. "Bree?" He turned his head in my direction. I drew a weary breath as I blinked into his gray eyes. He was himself instead of the Charles everyone else would recognize. It took power to assume a disguise. None of us had that at the moment—handing power to a new crop of godlings and coming back to a corporeal body exhausted all of us. I was the only one still too tired to speak, however.

"Where?" I croaked eventually.

"We're at your house. The one you asked for," Charles managed a grin. "It's huge, just as you wanted. Nobody knows where this is—I hid it on purpose. Are you cold, Love?" All of us were naked—it wasn't just Ashe. Likely, Charles had arranged for the clothing we'd worn before to be transferred to the decoys.

"I'm cold. Too tired to do anything about it."

"Hey, now," Charles scooted toward me. "None of that. We'll get warm together."

"What will people think?" I asked.

"Someday, maybe we'll tell them that we were Three in the beginning, instead of the One," he smiled before kissing me. "Maybe we'll tell them that we joined our energy to defeat other versions of the General in the past."

"Someday, maybe I won't care what they think." Raising a shaking hand, I rubbed my forehead. I'd forgotten what it was like to have a headache. I had one now, and it throbbed against my skull.

Bones. Something I'd been without for six Earth months. I felt every one of them, now. "Do you ache, too?" I asked Charles.

"I do," Ashe volunteered. "Corporeality sucks, sometimes."

"You weren't complaining after energy sex on Avendor," Charles pointed out. "Give me a hand, I need to get up."

"Was that a pun?"

"Take it any way you want."

"How long will we be like this?" I asked as Ashe rose unsteadily to his feet and held out a hand for Charles to take.

"A while," Charles grunted when Ashe pulled him upright. "All we can do now is watch and wait."

CHAPTER 4

Earth—past
Trajan's Journal

I listened while Jayson's cell phone rang in the media room next door. "Hey bro," he said. James Rome Jr. was calling. Likely, the call concerned their father's estate. With everything that had happened in the last six months, I'd forgotten about Rome Sr.'s death.

I'd suggested reactivating Jayson's old cell number, in case someone from the enemy camp started looking for him again. Bill had seconded that suggestion—we could work from this end of things to start tracking them. This call came almost immediately.

"Yeah, I can come," I heard Jayson say after several seconds had passed. "When? All right, I'll be there." I folded into the media room as Jayson ended the call with a sigh. "Are we allowed to have bank accounts now?" he asked.

"Bree did."

"Yeah, I guess she did. Dad divided the estate three ways in his will. I'll have to bring Mom, I guess. We're supposed to meet at the lawyer's office in L.A. next week."

"Don't go alone," I said. "Take Bill and Lissa with you."

"Sounds like a plan." Jayson shook his head. "Never thought the old man would go like this. Can't help but think I'm partly responsible."

"Don't even start," Lissa walked in and held up a hand. "I'll go with you, for sure. Bill will come and I'll bring Merrill, too, just in case. Trajan can stay here with Kiarra, Adam and Opal. That ought to be enough, and we'll be mindspeech away if they need us."

"Somebody say my name?" Opal folded into the room. "Connegar taught me how to use nexus echo. Cool, huh?" Opal grinned at me.

"Very," I agreed. "Ashe taught me, long ago. I didn't use it much. We probably should all do it, now."

"You know what I like best, though?" Opal said.

"What?" Bill joined us by folding in next.

"Only using the bathroom to take a shower."

"A definite advantage," Lissa laughed. "That's the first thing I appreciated about being vampire."

"I have a question," Bill said.

"What's that?"

"Who else knows about the reading of your father's will, Jayson?"

"The lawyer, his staff, Jamie, his wife Laurel and probably half of L.A. if Laurel's been talking," Jayson sighed.

"Are you thinking we could be ambushed?" I asked.

"Yes. Your brother, his wife and your mother are vulnerable, Rome. If the enemy knows anything, they know that," Bill pointed out. "What they won't know is who might be coming with you, or that you're more than mortal, now."

Our conversation was interrupted by Jayson's phone ringing a second time. "Hello," he answered after checking caller ID. Everyone else listened in as Bob Sullivan, Ross Gideon and Rome Sr.'s private investigator, told us he had a line on someone who had information about their deaths.

"Why are you contacting me instead of Jamie?" Jayson asked.

"Because I called him first," Bob Sullivan snorted. "He said your old man was dead and that was the end of it. That the police were doing their job and for me to stay out of it."

"So he isn't paying you?" Jayson asked.

"Nobody is paying me for this. I got pissed when I kept getting the runaround from the police, so I started looking into it myself."

"Where can we meet?" Jayson asked, cutting his eyes toward me. I nodded. We'd check this out, in case Sullivan was now obsessed or coerced. I wasn't the one who could tell whether there was an obsession, though.

"Yeah, I can be there in an hour," Jayson agreed before ending the call. Well, we were about to meet with a private investigator. *Hank?* I sent. *We need your help.*

An hour later, Hank, Jayson and I sat in a booth at a coffee shop just outside Hollywood, waiting for Bob Sullivan to arrive. He was likely having difficulty parking—the lot was nearly full when we folded in.

"Jayson," Bob Sullivan nodded to him before taking the open seat. "Here's what I have on Marc Cummings." He handed a file folder to Jayson.

"You tracked down Marc Cummings? I'm impressed," Jayson said after flipping the folder open. "Look," Jayson handed a photograph to Hank, who in turn handed it to me. It showed Marc Cummings talking to a waitress at the all-night café in Tyrone, New Mexico.

"Did you approach him?" Hank's eyes were darker than usual as he studied Bob Sullivan.

"Hell, no. I heard what happened to Ross and Jayson's dad. We had no idea we were in over our heads on this one. Cummings never knew I was there."

"Does anybody else have this information?" I asked.

"No. I would have given it to Jamie, but he wouldn't talk to me."

"What else do you have?" Hank asked.

"This," Jayson handed over a second photograph. Hank held it up to cover the smoke flying from his nostrils. "Calhoun," he growled and handed the photograph to me.

"And Obediah Tanner," I nodded. I recognized the rogue werewolf, who stood in the late afternoon light in New Mexico, discussing something with the rogue god Hank identified as Calhoun.

"When was this taken, and how close were you?" Hank asked.

"I tailed Cummings for a little while. Turned off on a dirt road while he went on up that hill. Had to take that photograph with a high-powered telephoto lens. I already had a picture of Cummings—he was going to meet those two. Something made the hair on the back of my neck rise, so I got the hell out of there after I took that shot."

"Probably a good thing," Jayson muttered. "Bob, don't approach any one of these. They'll kill you. I'll pay for your time and take this information to Director Jennings. He'll help with this."

"Heard you were with him—at least for a while," Bob shook his head. "If he needs my help with any of this, you have my number."

"I'll send a check," Jayson said. "Thanks, Bob."

"Anytime, kid." Bob rose, nodded to Hank and me, then walked out of the diner before the waitress made it to our table.

"No compulsion," Hank breathed a clear breath as he drummed his fingers on the Formica tabletop. "This is real."

Avendor—present

Hank's Journal

I had to bend time to meet Kifirin outside the grove boundary, but I was there when he arrived. The information gleaned from the private investigator on Earth confirmed a few of my suspicions, too.

Jayson and Trajan had taken the photographs to Bill while I left to attend to this errand. "Are you ready?" I asked Kifirin. He gave a slight nod. I folded us to SouthStar, where Trace and Lord Nedevik Weth waited for us.

"Lord Rath, Lord Kifirin," Nedevik bowed respectfully to us and invited us to sit. Trace lounged against a nearby doorway at the villa given to Nedevik and his family on the southern edge of SouthStar.

"Tell him what you told me," I said, inclining my head toward Nedevik.

"I have been reading in the archives and watching for a very long time," Nedevik began. "I became especially watchful while you slept, Lord Kifirin."

~

"It is, in our opinion, best to prove their beliefs to them," Moxas declared.

"What beliefs?" Calhoun was immediately interested.

"Oh, many, but let's start with this one." Moxas turned the reference book around for Calhoun to see.

"I knew Acrimus was wise to bring you to us," Calhoun breathed. "This is indeed genius."

"Might we consider taking Saxom's love? We were promised this," Moxas reminded Calhoun.

"Let us begin with this, and depending upon its success, this may motivate the General to provide even more help. I hear help is coming," Calhoun studied the image closely as he held up a hand. "Never fear, the woman will come to you. I swear it."

~

Earth—past

Lissa's Journal

"It's too bad Sullivan didn't hear what they were discussing," Bill dumped the photographs on the kitchen island. "They could be plotting a takeover or their next meal, for all we know."

"I heard from Weldon, Wlodek and Winkler," I said, rubbing Bill's back. "They're all here and in place," I added. "If we need help with this, all we have to do is ask."

"It's daylight in England, right now," Trajan pointed out. "Wlodek could come if we called a meeting."

"Then let's do that," Bill said. "Lissa, call Kiarra and the others. Maybe they'll have some ideas about this." He tapped the two photographs.

"It's a cinch that Zeke Tanner is involved, if Obediah is," Trajan observed. "That means drug money may be backing whatever schemes they come up with."

"Yeah." This Trajan would know everything there was to know about Zeke and Obediah Tanner, whereas the one who'd been taken off-world wouldn't. Not yet, anyway.

"You call Wlodek," Trajan nodded to me. "I'll get Weldon and Winkler here."

～

Winkler sat with his arms around me while we talked in the media room. If he'd been wolf, his tail would be thumping and he'd be panting, I knew. "I think we might be able to put a tracer on the money," Bill suggested.

"It would be easier if Ashe were here to hack their system, but I think I can handle it," Winkler's attention turned back to the reason for his visit.

"Joey can do it," Wlodek pointed out. "He's Mil'Karha now. That ought to help."

"Is he?" Weldon turned to Adam and Kiarra.

"He's at the house now; he followed us," Adam grinned before sending mindspeech. Joey, MIT graduate and former vampire genius, joined us in seven seconds.

"Joseph, we need a computer system hacked," Wlodek began.

"Just say where and when," Joey grinned. "I'm ready whenever you are."

"We know where Obediah is, we just have to get past his guards," Weldon said. "We'll have to scope out the area beforehand—we need to know if any of the powerful are with him, guarding that wildlife refuge."

"I can mist in," I volunteered. "They won't know I'm there."

"Take me with you," Winkler said, nuzzling my neck.

"Then I should ride along as well," Joey pointed out. "Why waste the opportunity if it's there?"

"Sounds like a plan," Bill slapped his knee. "Let's go to New Mexico tonight. I believe there's a compound outside Albuquerque we can borrow," he said. "The rest of us will wait there, in case Lissa needs help."

~

"I really want to kick Obediah's ass," Winkler muttered as we waited for midnight to arrive. The compound outside Albuquerque was the same one Bill and the others used before, and Winkler and I ended up in Hank and Breanne's bedroom. Shaking off the feeling of melancholy that came with that thought, I turned to Winkler. "No deliberate manipulation of the timeline," I pointed a finger at him. "If we could do that, I'd join you in kicking his ass."

"Lots of ass needs kicking," Winkler grinned at me. "Wanna fuck first?"

"How long will that take?"

"I think we can bend time if it takes too long."

"Then what are you waiting for, furball?"

"Did you call me furball?" Winkler growled and began stalking me with slow, deliberate movements.

"Oooh, the wolfman cometh," I pretended to be afraid.

"Not yet. Hopefully soon," Winkler leaned in to kiss me. "Very, very soon."

~

This place is a maze, Joey whispered mindspeech as we traversed Obediah Tanner's compound shortly after midnight. Connegar and Reemagar insisted on folding us to the compound in New Mexico, and the others stayed behind while I pulled Winkler and Joey into my mist and carried us to the wildlife refuge outside Albuquerque.

Joey was right—Obediah was obviously paranoid—there were warrens of rooms and hallways inside the massive residence he kept near the center of the refuge, and he kept dozens of werewolf guards around his centrally located private suite.

Bastard wants to save his own skin by putting everybody else in harm's way first, Winkler growled silently. *His computer will be in his private study, you can bet on that.*

I wanted to gasp as we misted inside Obediah's private study—his bedroom was nearby and all of us heard his snore—he was asleep. Several werewolves patrolled the outside of the compound, but we'd slipped past them easily. My worry was Wildrif; he slept in a bedroom down the hall from Obediah's.

As long as we're shielding while Joey works, there shouldn't be a problem, Winkler pointed out when I mentioned Wildrif.

Is that? Joey asked as we misted past the stuffed white buffalo taking up much of the floor space in Obediah's study.

Alex Thompson, Amos Thompson's brother, Winkler growled again. *Obediah is the worst kind of bastard, but his brother Zeke may be worse. If they hadn't found Wildrif or vice versa, we'd have had them long before we did.*

We shouldn't mess with the timeline, I pointed out judiciously as I released Joey from my mist. I knew what Winkler was thinking— destroy Wildrif while he slept and let Obediah try to hide from the Grand Master afterward.

While Winkler and I held our mental standoff, Joey settled into the chair behind Obediah's massive, walnut desk and powered up his desktop. It didn't take long for Joey to slip into Obediah's records.

"Rezil." Hordace handed a comp-vid to his best assassin.

"I saw it," Rezil muttered angrily, tossing the comp-vid on Hordace's desk with contempt. "Who knew she'd have so little intelligence? She knows this is a death sentence." Hordace's comp-vid held the images plastered across both Alliances—of Kalia, Teeg San Gerxon and Teeg's first mate, Reah Silver.

"My concern is what she may have told him," Hordace snapped.

"Find her and kill him. I want her alive so I can torture what she knows out of her. Take one of the Sirenali with you. I don't care what you have to do to accomplish this—just get it done." Hordace smashed his fist against the comp-vid, cracking the fragile screen and sending a few splinters of shatter-resistant glass tinkling across his desk.

Rezil didn't reply; he stalked angrily out of Hordace's study instead.

~

Lissa's Journal

What is he doing? I asked Joey silently as I peered over his shoulder at the records he'd uncovered. Reservation after reservation appeared —for arenas and convention centers across the United States. Obediah was using drug money to rent large spaces? What the hell for?

This defies logic, Winkler observed.

~

Quislus stood on the edge of Baetrah, waiting for Kifirin to arrive. His child had called out to him, when he'd instructed Kifirin never to do that. He was concerned—there was no doubt. Should Kifirin learn the truth, he'd be forced to destroy or contain him.

Acrimus had advised Quislus long ago, as he contemplated the creation of Kifirin, to make him in such a way that he might be destroyed easily should the need arise. Kifirin had existed with that shadow, completely unaware.

Acrimus no longer survived; therefore, that avenue of advice had disappeared, leaving Quislus to make decisions for himself—at least where Kifirin was concerned. The thought of the General and what he might demand was a constant concern to the rogue god, who'd helped Acrimus recruit and maintain the Hidden—an army prepared to wait until it was safe for them to be revealed.

Quislus quashed the thought that the General was risking

everything by bringing the Hidden forward now. Many, however, believed as the General did—that with the elimination of the Three, everything was now theirs anyway. All that remained was to assert their dominance over the created races.

We are the masters, Quislus repeated Acrimus' oft-spoken mantra. *We are the masters.*

～

Lissa's Journal

I have it, Joey crowed, holding up the flash drive with a grin. *I'm ready to get out of here, now.*

～

"Father, I hear terrible things about you," Kifirin began as he settled—in Full Thifilathi—on the steep edge of Baetrah's caldera.

"From whom?" Quislus demanded.

"That does not matter. What matters is whether those things are true." A cloud of smoke escaped Kifirin's nostrils as he rustled massive, leathery wings.

"You dare to insult me this way?" Quislus snapped. "Keep your breath clear and your wings still before me."

"I am done bowing to you, Father." Kifirin turned his back to Quislus, exposing his wings to the one who'd created him. Quislus raised his hand in reply, destroying Kifirin's essence with a thought.

～

Lissa's Journal

Perhaps he imagined I wouldn't feel Kifirin's death. He was wrong. Screaming out my grief, I folded to the world Kifirin had created long ago.

Quislus still stood there—blinking at his handiwork. Kifirin's

Thifilathi lay on the edge of the caldera, his body lifeless—his spirit destroyed.

"You," Kifirin's parent lifted his eyes as I appeared before him, tears blurring my vision and anger controlling my breaths.

"I," I answered.

"And I." Li'Neruh Rath appeared at my side, Kiarra, Dragon, Adam and Merrill not far behind him.

"You created him thus, did you not?" Li'Neruh became Thifilathi and breathed smoke. Kifirin's parent took a step backward. "How long did you and Acrimus plot his death? Did you allow him to live so long as he served your purposes?" He stepped forward, following Quislus. "Did you love him, or merely pretend to do so? I recall lofty words concerning love, Quislus."

"I loved him," Quislus' corporeal body quaked. "I swear it."

"Yet you killed him." Li'Neruh tossed out a hand, indicating Kifirin's still form.

"The General would never have allowed him to live," Quislus quavered. "He would have treated him more harshly than I."

"So his death at your hands was a mercy?" Li'Neruh wasn't buying it as he took another step forward. "I name you coward, Quislus. Hiding within the ranks, waiting for others to defeat what you see as the opposition, so you might take an easier place among the warriors, is that it?"

"What—are you going to do?" Quislus cowered before Li'Neruh Rath.

"Confine you to Baetrah," Li'Neruh's voice rumbled like thunder. "I will wait patiently for the General to come for you."

"He will not come," Quislus bowed his head.

"And yet you offered your allegiance to him."

"Through my parent, Acrimus."

"Ah. Acrimus. Where do you suppose he is, now?" Li'Neruh asked.

"Wh-where my child is," Quislus sobbed. "Gone forever."

The word forever echoed across the caldera, and I wept harder. I'd always thought Kifirin would return to me. That could never happen, now.

"You placed the mind clouds, didn't you?"

"On two," Quislus claimed. "The third transferred onto a weakened mind." He knew about Gavril. Knew my son's spirit was being sapped away. Had likely had a hand in it.

"So, two murders are on your hands," Li'Neruh declared. "What does that make you besides a coward, Quislus?"

"A traitor," Quislus muttered. "A killer."

"Did Acrimus create you to kill?"

"Yes." Quislus hung his head.

Get ready, a voice filtered into my mind. Recognition of the voice danced on the edges of my mind, but I couldn't grasp it.

It's a trap, I whispered to my allies.

As expected, Hank whispered mentally back. *Get ready*, he echoed the previous instruction into my mind and to those around me.

We are here, Connegar and Reemagar arrived.

"Why are there Larentii here?" Quislus suddenly seemed terrified.

"Why should we not be here?" Kalenegar also appeared and stood beside Connegar and Reemagar, his arms crossed over his chest—he was angry, that was easy enough to see.

"No reason," Quislus cowered.

"Quislus, what have you done?" The ground trembled beneath our feet as the voice thundered over our heads. I was forced to slap a shield over my ears, the words were so loud.

Jayd's Journal

"Jaydevik!" Glinda's cry brought me to her side immediately when the planet trembled beneath the palace.

"What the," Gardevik skipped to our suite as the palace shook about us.

Baetrah is exploding, came the message.

CHAPTER 5

Le-Ath Veronis—present
Lissa's Journal

"Hank and the Larentii are the only ones I didn't have to reconstruct," Karzac informed me when I woke four days later. "If the Larentii hadn't surrounded him there at the last, I might have had to repair his body as well."

The General had made his presence known, and after snatching Quislus away from us, he'd proceeded to show us what he was capable of doing. At least the General knew to leave the Larentii alone—he'd seen what happened to Acrimus, I was sure.

"I feel weak," I attempted to sit up in bed.

"You are not alone," Karzac brushed hair away from my face gently. "I have heard from those left on Earth in the past at least four times a day, asking how you and the others are."

"What did you tell them? I imagine Winkler is going crazy."

"As is Gavin and all your mates," Karzac smiled. "I told them that you would be fine. As you are."

"Thank you," I sighed. "Is there anything to eat? I'm starved."

"I believe we might find a place at the table for you," he said, his smile turning into a grin. "Tomorrow, I'll allow you to walk about your palace."

"How much work was this—to put me back together?"

"That is none of your concern. Come, let me help you up. I will accompany you to the dining hall."

"Kifirin's gone."

"I know. Nefrigar holds his Thifilathi in the Archives. With the Three."

Fresno—past

Trajan's journal

Hank told me to stay put. I'd stayed put while Lissa, Kiarra, Adam and Merrill were almost destroyed. I now saw the complete wisdom in selecting Karzac as Ko'Ahmari. He'd reconstructed what had nearly been obliterated by the General. A lot of power had been collected on the edge of Baetrah, but the General had swept it away with little effort. That terrified me.

How could we combat something that powerful? What the hell was the General, anyway? I had a feeling Breanne had seen what he was; she'd just never explained it. Perhaps it was too frightening for any of us to know.

Hank? I called out.

Trajan?

When you feel up to it, I'd like to talk.

I'll be there in a few days, he promised.

Good enough, I replied.

"Traje?" Bill set a sheet of paper in front of me. I'd chosen to do my ruminations during a coffee break on a warm Fresno morning at the compound.

"What's this?" I lifted the paper to study it while I sipped coffee. Keeping it hot was child's play, nowadays. All I had to do was think it hot.

"The list of dates for the arena and convention center rentals," Bill replied. "They're hitting twenty out of the fifty states, and Joey is wondering if maybe this isn't the end of it—that they might go global with this before it's over."

"You think they've abandoned the church idea in favor of larger venues?" I asked, handing the sheet back to Bill. I'd already committed the information to memory. I didn't need a physical reminder, now.

"I don't know. What if this is just a ruse? Maybe they want us to find this, so we'll be in the wrong place at the wrong time," Bill shook his head and crumpled the paper in his fist. "Face it, money means nothing to those in charge, but that's our first gut reaction—to follow the money. Speaking of money, we're supposed to meet with the Romes' lawyer tomorrow. Do you think Lissa will make it back?"

"She'll be here, even if she has to bend time," I said. "The others, too. Karzac says they're just weak—their bodies are fine."

I didn't say what I was thinking, though. That the General had shown up once already. What if he decided to visit a lawyer's office in Los Angeles, too?

~

Campiaa—present
  Tybus' Journal
"Reah, please don't make yourself ill with worry." I took the lounge chair beside hers on the patio behind San Gerxon Palace. The pool was a transparent blue before us, and I heard clearly as a stray leaf dropped with a tiny plip onto the water's surface.

"Have you ever noticed how we ignore the breeze most of the time —as it blows through the trees or ruffles the grass?" Reah turned lovely, green eyes to me and blinked.

"True," I agreed. "Generally we are focused on other things, so the winds are of no consequence."

"Until they become strong enough to destroy buildings," she said. "How strong do you think the General is?"

That question concerned me—just as it did all the others who'd received power recently. None of us knew. I imagined that Li'Neruh Rath, whom Breanne referred to as Hank, didn't know either.

"I cannot answer that, as I cannot make even an educated estimate," I replied as evenly as I could. "We cannot focus our worries there—we must focus on what we can accomplish instead. I feel Rezil Foculis has been sent already, and if my guess is correct, he may be accompanied by at least one Sirenali."

"I think that as well, since we can't *Look* to find him anywhere," Reah nodded. "It only takes a day to get here from Du'Ferias, by traditional means. They may not bother to travel that way."

"Yes, I have considered that," I agreed. "They may already be here, although I have all my forces on alert. With a Sirenali, they may have been seen and obsessions may have been placed to ignore that, or to assist them, even."

"I worry about that, too."

Reah and I had shields around the palace; nothing came or went without our knowing. Kay often stayed in her suite on the second floor—she worked constantly to fight off her fear of Rezil Foculis, Hordace Cayetes, Q'Ind Ribalo and the sadistic women who'd stolen her childhood and abused her during her training as a sex slave.

"It's almost too painful to comprehend—what Kalia went through. Isn't it?" Reah asked.

"It is." I reached out to pat her hand, but she surprised me by linking her fingers with mine.

"Reah?" I said. Just the one word, but a mountain of questions lay behind her name.

"I can't help myself," she squeezed my fingers, then attempted to let them go. I didn't allow it. Instead, I pulled her hand to my lips and kissed it gently.

"Neither can I," I acknowledged.

~

Kifirin—present

"I remember the comesuli making their trek to Baetrah to ask Kifirin to take them home," Glinda sighed.

Baetrah lay wasted before her as she stood on the edge of the volcano with Jayd and Garde. Lava rock crumbled beneath their feet; the caldera, cold and empty, waited below.

"The heart of Kifirin is no more," Garde shook his head. "What will become of us, brother?" He turned to Jayd.

"I can't answer that," Jayd replied.

"I fear for our future," Glinda said. Jaydevik Rath, King of the High Demons, pulled her close as he gazed upon the ruin of Baetrah.

Earth—past

Lissa's Journal

"He refused to stay behind," I sighed, dropping a small bag of toiletries on the kitchen island. Gavin rumbled a growl behind me as he thumped his leather suitcase on the tiled floor.

"All help appreciated," Trajan shrugged. "Ready to travel to L.A.?"

"I'm ready. I heard from Reah this morning before we left—she and Tybus are waiting for Rezil Foculis to show up on Campiaa. Merrill will be here in a minute—he, Adam and Kiarra are at the other house, right now."

"What about the Gavin here and now?" Trajan asked.

"Wlodek sent him to Siberia." I wanted to snicker but held it back —the Gavin behind me didn't appreciate severe cold and I knew he'd have memories of it when this was over.

"Does this mean you're going to L.A. too?" Jayson walked in, dressed in a suit and tie.

"I will be going." Gavin's words were clipped.

"I'm ready," Merrill folded in, straightening a cuff on a snowy dress shirt. He and Gavin wore suits that cost a mint. I hoped the Rome lawyer was prepared to be intimidated.

"Me, too," Bill said, appearing beside Jayson. Dressed in a dark suit and tie, this wasn't Agent Bill I'd met in the field long ago. This Bill was in charge of a large intelligence organization and could strike fear in just about anybody. It wouldn't have mattered if he'd gone naked. I'd never say it to Tony, but Bill was better at this than Tony ever was.

"Are you ready for this, Lissa?" Trajan asked softly. He didn't say what all of us were thinking—that this could be a trap, just as Baetrah had been a trap.

"Yeah." I hunched my shoulders. Gavin pulled me protectively against him.

"The rest of us are just mindspeech away, don't forget that," Trajan said as Gavin kissed the top of my head.

"Swanky," I muttered as we walked past heavy glass doors and into the building that housed a prestigious law firm in Los Angeles. Trust James Rome, Sr. to hire the most expensive suits he could find. Polished marble was everywhere; the massive receptionist's desk was curved and made of solid, dark wood and fresh flowers filled tall vases on tables scattered throughout the foyer.

Our steps echoed as we made our way to the elevator—the offices we needed were on the tenth floor. With heavy shields surrounding us, we stepped onto a waiting elevator and pressed the button.

Here goes, Jayson's voice sounded in my mind. *Kal is bringing Mom, by the way.*

It's good that she's traveling with a Larentii, Merrill observed.

I'm glad Kal is making his presence known, I replied. *Connegar says that he disappeared for thousands of years because he and his father disagreed on just about everything.*

At least he's back, now, Merrill sighed mentally. The elevator dinged as we reached the tenth floor. Kathleen Rome, standing beside a shielded Kalenegar, stood there, waiting for us as the elevator doors opened. The surprise was this—Terry Johnston, Breanne's attorney, was also there, waiting.

"Yes, he left a third of his estate to each of you," the lawyer slid papers across his desk toward Kathleen, Jayson and Jamie, Jayson's brother. Jamie's wife, Laurel, fumed from a chair in a corner—Jamie left her there while he, his mother and brother tended to business.

"But," the lawyer continued, "Mr. Rome set up a separate account and placed the profits from the sale of *Torture in Texas* in it. That account holds his name, as well as Breanne Hayworth's charity. As Ms. Hayworth couldn't respond personally, I contacted Mr. Johnston as her representative. That account is in the charity's name and it is now the sole holder of those funds."

"How much?" Laurel stood and demanded.

"Laurel, shush," Jamie snapped.

"I just wanted to know," Laurel whined.

"Half a billion, I believe," the Lawyer replied stiffly. Laurel huffed as she sat heavily in her chair, arms crossed angrily over her chest.

I suppose one-and-a-half billion just isn't enough for her, Merrill offered dryly. That's what each of the three would get, when all was said and done. I wondered at the fact that Rome Sr. had even thought to put the money in the charity's name. The truth, however, was that he wouldn't have had a story, or his revenge against Joyce Christian, without Breanne's suffering.

"I'll see that the money is placed in Ms. Hayworth's charity account," Terry nodded to the lawyer. "And I'd like to thank the Rome family on her behalf—this money will be used to help children across the globe."

Laurel snorted at Terry's comment. I wanted to slap her for that.

"Laurel, Breanne saved my life. Where were you when I had a heart attack?" Kathleen turned hard eyes on her daughter-in-law. Yes, Kalenegar had made her appear older again before bringing her to the attorney's offices. Once she was away from there, he'd allow her younger-looking self to manifest again.

"Not worth it, Mom," Jayson placed a hand over his mother's. "Let it go."

"You're right," Kathleen nodded. "At least James found his heart before he died."

"Jayson, I can give you your job back," Jamie began.

"Jamie, I've moved on," Jayson lifted a hand to hold his brother off. "Let somebody else have that slot. I don't need it anymore."

"If that's what you want," Jamie sighed. "Are we done?" He turned to the lawyer.

"Yes. I'll have the funds transferred in two weeks. Let me know if you have questions or problems." The attorney stood and extended his hand to Jamie first.

"I'll never understand what Jamie saw in her," Kathleen muttered as we watched the couple walk away with a driver and bodyguard in tow.

"I'm surprised we didn't get ambushed by the enemy," I responded. "Not that I'm complaining," I added.

"I'm just happy we got out of there unscathed," Jayson said. "Relatively speaking."

"Pun?" Bill asked.

"Yeah."

"You made that lawyer nervous," Kathleen smiled at Bill. "He kept cutting his eyes toward you, and then he'd turn to Gavin and Merrill. I think he was sweating in that expensive suit."

"You know why the enemy didn't show up at a lawyer's office, don't you?" Gavin said.

"No, honey, why is that?" I turned to him—he'd remained silent and inscrutable during the meeting with the attorney.

"Professional courtesy," Gavin said. All of us burst out laughing.

Gavin actually told a joke? Winkler sent. He was back in Texas, taking care of Packmaster duties. He'd been on standby, though, in case he was needed.

Yeah. I don't know what's gotten into him.

Don't make a big deal out of it—you'll scare it away. I like this Gavin much better, Winkler said.

I think it's because of Breanne, I returned. *Ever since she gave him what she did, he's been more human than I've ever seen.*

I hope he doesn't go back, then. A joke from Gavin now and then can't be a bad thing, can it?

Nope. It was so unexpected, and that made it even funnier.

Lissa?

What?

You know I love you, don't you?

I do.

Don't forget that, all right?

I won't.

~

Campiaa—present

Tybus' Journal

"Take a look," Astralan pointed out the image.

"That's Rezil." Kay held a hand to her mouth as she, Reah, Aurelius and the reptanoids watched the live feed from one of the casinos. Thankfully, it wasn't one that now belonged to me.

"I assume," Stellan said, "that the one beside him is Sirenali. Whatever the difficulty, it prevents us from getting a lock on either of them."

"Look, there are three more behind. They don't appear at first to be with them, but they are," Aurelius pointed to three men who walked casually along, seemingly unconnected to Rezil Foculis.

"You're right," I agreed. "They are together. We know at least one is Sirenali. We have no idea what the others are. Kay, do you recognize any of them?"

"That one," Kay tapped the desk screen, indicating one of the three stragglers. "That one is a wizard. I saw him a few times, but I don't know his name."

Kay's face was pale as she studied those who'd come for us. Since

I'd made the engagement announcement, I'd been bombarded with requests for interviews—with my new intended. I'd brushed all of them off; Kay would never survive such scrutiny. I'd kept that information from her, too—it would only upset her more.

"Are you sure about this?" I asked her.

"I'm sure," she replied, her voice and hands trembling.

I admired her courage, because I wasn't sure at all.

Earth—past

Adam's Journal

"Have you watched any of this?" Kiarra tossed the television remote onto the coffee table in disgust after turning it off.

"The news?" I asked, surprised that she'd even bothered.

"Yes. Adam, I remember how everything was before. I have those memories. This isn't what I remember."

"What's going on? That didn't happen before?" I asked.

"Politicians and others in power are calling for a war on the poor. They're saying they're only parasites and deserve to die. They've already defunded programs to feed poor children. I suppose this was the logical next step."

"Politicians are doing that? Are you joking?"

"I'm not joking. Three people died yesterday in New York, because somebody took those words to heart. Three homeless people—two men and a woman, were killed. One was shot, the other two beaten to death. People watched, Adam, and nobody did anything about it."

"That's happened in the past," I sighed, realizing that this sort of thing upset my mate a great deal. "Is this all politicians, or only a few?"

"That's the trouble, Adam. When I go *Looking* to find the sources of this hate, the information is blocked."

"You're saying Sirenali may be involved."

"I'm saying that, yes. They're interfering with governments now, Adam. If they do that, there's nothing beyond them. I can only imagine that anyone from another country might become a target, or those from another religion—basically anybody who isn't like the one holding the weapon might be vulnerable."

"Kiarra, we're talking chaos. We know who wants chaos, don't we?"

"Saxom and his brother." Kiarra snorted in disgust.

"Then we need to find them fast," Merrill walked in. Kiarra had obviously linked him to our conversation.

"We have no real clues as to where to begin our search," I pointed out. "Martin sent mindspeech earlier—he says Shaver Lake has been abandoned by the enemy. He and several wolves from the local pack found the cabin where they were staying, but it's empty, except for the stench of Sirenali. He says he detected three distinct scents, and one of those was the creature I killed. Who knows where the other two are now?"

"They're causing trouble, you can bet your life on that," Kiarra snapped and stalked toward the bedroom.

Lissa's Journal

"Cara, this is wrong."

"What's wrong?" I mumbled. Gavin and I were in bed. I was half-asleep while he watched the late news. I'd placed a shield so I wouldn't hear it, but Gavin shook me anyway.

"I don't recall these events," Gavin muttered.

"Honey, things are changing." I curled into a ball and placed a pillow over my head. I was tired and Gavin wanted to talk.

"No, Lissa. Not like this."

"All right," I sat up in bed and blinked in an attempt to clear my head of sleep. At least enough so that Gavin might make a smidgen of sense.

"Politicians are behaving irrationally," Gavin said.

Yeah, I stared and shook my head. "You woke me up for that?" I squeaked.

"I realize that your opinion of any politician runs to the negative, but this is even more irrational than normal. They're advocating the killing of the poor. What might be next, Cara? Tell me."

"Have you *Looked*," I began.

"Cara, I found something blocking the information. You know what that means."

"It means chaos." I chewed my lip as horrifying thoughts chased one another through my mind. Moments ago, I'd been comfortable, warm and sleepy. Now, I was starkly awake and shivering.

Lissa? Mindspeech came from Kiarra. *Are you awake?*

I am now, I flung blankets aside.

Everything is going batfuckshit crazy, Kiarra said.

I hear that, I said and folded Gavin and me to Kiarra's house.

"Ah, Calhoun. What do you have for me today?" Senator Blake Folie asked. Folie sat in his office at the Hart Senate Office Building, waiting for his scheduled appointment with the one who simply identified himself as Calhoun.

Folie couldn't say why, but everything Calhoun said seemed to be a truth from God. Calhoun's assistant, whom Calhoun referred to as V'ili, walked in behind Calhoun and sat when Calhoun sat.

"As you know, the Senate election is coming up." A slow smile spread across Calhoun's face. "V'ili, tell the Senator what he should do."

"Rigo?" Kooper looked up to find the ancient vampire-turned-Mil'Karha in his office at Lissa's palace.

"I have information through my spy network," Rigo placed a comp-vid on Kooper's desk and sat on a guest chair with a sigh.

"What's this? It looks like financial records," Kooper thumbed through lists on the first comp-vid.

"It is. Lissa contacted me last night. I've been working on this since then."

"What do these have to do with anything?" Kooper asked.

"On Earth in the past, it seems the rogues are taking over governments in unusual and subtle ways. They're starting with a war on the poor and some minorities. Lissa asked me to check other worlds where I have contacts, to see whether the same thing is occurring during this timeframe."

"And is it? These seem to be reservations for large venues," Kooper scrolled through the second comp-vid.

"They are. So far, we haven't determined what the connection is, but on the worlds where the venues are reserved, there are also abnormalities occurring within the governments. The poor are targeted. The weak or those belonging to minorities are targeted. Those with ties to lesser known religions are targeted."

"There's a pattern on all these worlds? You have more than forty listed here," Kooper muttered.

"Those are the worlds where I have reliable contacts," Rigo pointed out. "There are many others where I do not have contacts or sources of verifiable information. Those worlds are where I've seen troubles arise in the past. I concentrate my efforts there. Who knows whether others might be targeted? This enemy is unpredictable, Director. I feel we must unravel this mystery before it is too late."

"I'm with you on that," Kooper agreed. "Will you transfer these records to me? I'll get someone to help me investigate. Trevor is out with Nefrigar's sons, looking for rogue gates with Elizabeth, Macy and Luanne. I've heard rumors of disappearances on several worlds, so they are investigating."

"I will volunteer, as will Anthony Hancock," Rigo said.

"Good. How soon can you be ready? Where do you think we should go first?" Kooper stood and stretched.

"Yalles would be first on my list. I haven't slept in more than thirty hours, Director. Give me six. I'll be ready to go after that."

"Good. Thank you, Rigo. Your help is greatly appreciated."

Noppen—present

Luanne's Journal

Jerigar had a large blue hand on Macy's shoulder as we stared at the rogue gate. It vibrated within a dangerous, purple cloud as we regarded it. Macy still hadn't recovered from Norian Keef's disappearance and death. I was grateful Jerigar stayed with her constantly—he cared for Macy; that was evident.

This gate had swallowed more than two thousand people—it appeared near a sporting event on a small planet located near Wyyld after the event started and before it finished. So many had been swallowed up as they'd emptied the arena afterward.

"This really sucks," Elizabeth told me quietly. Liz was so different from the person she'd been at sixteen. I suppose centuries of being dead had taught her a lot.

"Yeah. Trevor?" I turned to the one who'd been vampire for more than three thousand years.

"We've already tried putting the barbs around it. The gate expanded past them," Trevor turned to me with a sigh. "They've gotten wise to our tactics already, and they're taking steps to prevent us from doing the same thing again."

"How big do you think it will get?" Macy asked her Larentii guardian, peering up at his concerned blue face.

"My dearest, I know not. After learning of the energy expended upon Kifirin not long ago, I worry it could swallow the entire planet and we would be powerless to prevent it."

"All we can do at this point is put up normal barriers and hope the curious don't ignore them," Trevor shook his head.

"How stupid would you have to be?" Liz turned to me, her blue eyes puzzled.

"Liz, stupidity is more common than most people think," I replied.

"Bring the barriers," Trevor spoke into his wrist comp-vid. "Set them up in a click diameter around the site."

"What about the arena, sir?" a voice asked.

"Find another place for sporting events—this one will kill you."

"Local law has changed just this morning, sir," the voice replied. "All ASD commands must be approved by the legislature first before they can be enforced."

"Is this planet still a member of the Reth Alliance?" Trevor barked.

"For now," the voice sounded worried.

"Then the ASD commands the local constabulary until further notice. Do you want the Founder to declare this a rogue world and send in troops?"

"I'll pass that along to the president," the voice said and cut off.

"I will set up barriers," Jerigar sighed. "Kalenegar seemed concerned that something such as this might occur."

"I'll help," Trevor nodded. He'd been invited to join the Ba'Mirha and had power at his command. Raising his hands, Trevor set about putting up an outer barrier while Jerigar employed his power to set up a second inside it.

~

"Lendill?" Ildevar looked up from the comp-vid message he'd received from Trevor. Lendill Schaff, Prince of the Elves and heir to his father's land of Gaelar N'Seith, walked into Ildevar's study.

"I heard," Lendill raised a hand. "Kooper sent mindspeech. He heard it from Trevor, too. If Noppen goes rogue, it's too close to Wyyld, Founder."

"They have no weapons at the moment, but that could be easily remedied, should the enemy choose to arm them."

"My father worries that the enemy could devise a weapon from the entire planet."

"What does your father suggest?" Ildevar rose—Kaldill Schaff was never one to spread fear or wild speculation. If the King of the Elves was concerned, then Ildevar would also be concerned. "Willem?" Ildevar spoke to empty air.

"Here, Deonus," Willem appeared inside Ildevar's study, noticeably shaken. Apparently he'd gotten the same information.

"My father says to remember what Lissa did at the enclave years ago," Lendill said. "He says to consider it soon."

"What—ah. That. Does he have suggestions?"

"He says there is a place in the orbit around Falchan's sun."

"I heard that Dragon moved the High Demon army to Falchan to train," Ildevar said.

"All the better, according to my father. He is prepared, Deonus. We must prepare as well."

"Then we will." Ildevar's mind was made up. "Alert the twenty, Willem. Wyyld will relocate shortly."

"I suggest leaving a shell in its place," Lendill said. Ildevar stopped for a moment, considering Lendill's words. "Yes," he nodded. "I have sufficient power to do that as well."

"Do you have enough to shield Wyyld after its relocation?"

"If I don't, I'll ask for assistance from Li'Neruh Rath."

"Do it. Father says it's the only way," Lendill sighed.

Ildevar sent rapid mindspeech.

CHAPTER 6

"We barely got away before we were attacked," Trevor handed his comp-vid to Kooper. "They meant to kill us. I recorded everything from the time we landed there."

"Even with a Larentii present?" Kooper stared in disbelief.

"Even with a Larentii with us," Trevor said. "Who knows about that rule? Is it anybody who kills a Larentii, or only gods who kill a Larentii?"

"I never thought about that," Kooper growled, rising from his chair. "This is fucked up in every way it can be fucked up. Isn't it?"

"I have to agree, Koop."

"I heard from Lendill, too. Things are about to change for Wyyld, since Noppen is prepared to go rogue."

"No surprise," Trevor said.

Campiaa—present
Tybus' Journal
Don't argue, just let them through the gate, I instructed. I had four

former Saa Thalarr stationed at the entrances to San Gerxon Palace. *Pretend the obsession works.*

Will do, Brock replied. He manned the main gate with Stephan, his mate.

"Are you ready?" I turned to Reah and Kay.

"I'm ready," Kay said.

"As much as I can be," Reah replied.

"Then all we have to do is wait a little longer," I said. "They'll be here in ticks."

~

Breanne's Journal

"Rezil Foculis and his entourage just gained access to San Gerxon Palace." Charles sat beside me at a kitchen island designed to seat more than twenty people. The kitchen around us looked big enough to hold a cricket match. Beyond the kitchen, in an open floor plan that any architect might be proud to call his own, lay a football-field-sized common area with seating groups scattered throughout. Along two, very tall glass walls, I could see the ocean below, where high waves crashed and broke against rocks jutting up from the ocean floor.

"I'm connected with Kay," I nodded. "She thinks the notion to change the Sirenali and wizard's lines is hers, but I sort of nudged her in that direction." I lifted my cup of coffee—when Charles designed this place, he'd seen to everything, including the food and other necessities we'd need.

Built into a solid rock cliff, the house he'd constructed for me was perfect. Up a nearby staircase lay thirty-five bedrooms. Enough for all of us, our mates, a few guests and sufficient room to construct more if it were necessary. Charles and I shared a bed, but there'd been no coupling—we still didn't have enough energy for that. All we could do for the moment was what we'd done already—send mental nudges or mindspeech here and there, where it was most needed.

Ashe was the one who'd instructed Nefrigar to take Kifirin's Thifilathi to the Larentii Archives—a choice would have to be made eventually as to what to do with it. I intended to traverse time the moment I was able, to ask a question. The answer to that question would decide many things for the future.

Lissa grieved for Kifirin—I could feel it if I reached out to her mentally. There was no question he'd loved her, and the blame for so many things he'd done couldn't be fully attributed to him.

We knew Quislus was partly responsible for Kifirin's actions. He was also responsible for Kifirin's death. That alone would gain him an audience with at least one of the powerful—eventually.

"My love, I can feel your thoughts," Charles's hand covered mine. "This is why I enjoy corporeality," he lifted my hand to his lips and kissed it. "This isn't possible while we're energy."

"It adds another dimension, definitely," Ashe walked in and sat on my other side.

"You look tired," I reached out with my other hand and smoothed light-brown hair off his forehead.

"I made my bed," Ashe offered a wry grin. "It wore me out."

"We're a mess," I sighed.

"It'll get better," Charles observed philosophically. "Besides, I have a plan."

"What's that?" Ashe asked.

"Think about this," Charles began. I looked from Charles to Ashe as Charles outlined a course of action, and watched as Ashe began to smile. Something about Charles's suggestion triggered an almost-memory for me, however. It bothered me, too, so I'd have to consider it further as time allowed.

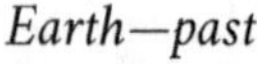

Earth—past

Lissa's Journal

"Sixteen people gunned down in an L.A. slum," Bill shook his head. "I'm afraid to contact the President. He may be obsessed."

"I worried about something Quislus said," I responded.

"What's that? I wasn't there," Bill reminded me.

"He said that Gavril's mind cloud was transferred onto him, I figure from Gavin. Quislus told us that mind clouds can take over a weakened mind."

"You just described many politicians in Washington," Bill snorted.

"I figure it's Calhoun," Trajan wandered in and nodded to me. "The one Hank pointed out in that photograph." Trajan lifted the photograph in question off the kitchen island and waved it at me.

"Not much to look at," I shook my head.

"Probably a purloined body, don't you think?" Trajan asked. "I get the idea that a lot of the enemy have bodies that way."

"Yeah." I took the photograph from Trajan and studied Calhoun. He had dirty-blond hair, a slightly crooked nose, brown eyes and a medium build. "So you think Calhoun has been visiting politicians, likely with a Sirenali in tow?" I said, setting the photograph on the island again. "Once a handful are obsessed, all they have to do is convince others that what they're spouting is the truth or the right way to go and here we are. This is only going to get worse," I rubbed my forehead, where tension was building and threatening to become a full-blown headache.

"We've said all along it wouldn't take much to nudge some people in this direction," Trajan said. "What can we do about this?"

"I have no idea," I sighed.

⁓

Campiaa—present

Kay's Journal

The Sirenali's lines were a jumble, but eventually I selected the proper ones to change. "What will he be after you're done?" Reah asked softly at my side.

"Mostly human," I replied, setting to work. "He'll still be able to change to look like a Sirenali, but his ability to place obsession will be cut off."

"Too bad," Farzi muttered. "He bother, he die, now."

I wanted to smile—the reptanoids were quickly becoming friends.

There was no deviousness or insincerity about them—they spoke plainly about everything and I appreciated that.

All eight of them had provided backup for the Saa Thalarr at the gates—as snakes hanging from trees and hiding in flowerbeds or ornamental shrubs. Rezil had no idea how much danger he'd been in when he strolled casually past the humanoid-appearing guards and into San Gerxon Palace.

Tybus placed compulsion on Rezil while I'd changed the wizard's lines—none of us were susceptible to the Sirenali's obsession, so I'd waited to change his lines after the others were taken care of.

Aurelius had seen to the other two humanoids—both acting as bodyguards for the wizard. He wouldn't need them any longer, but it was wise to return them to Hordace the way they'd left—intact and seemingly normal.

"You know, I like you so much better this way," I said softly after finishing my work. This Sirenali could no longer obsess anyone.

I liked Rezil helpless and quivering beneath Tybus' relentless glare, too, but I didn't voice that opinion aloud. Rezil should be afraid—I didn't think Tybus or Aurelius planned to let him live after we were led to Hordace Cayetes.

"You will contact Hordace now, and inform him that you have killed the target and taken the other captive," Tybus hissed as he gripped Rezil's shirt in strong, capable fingers.

"Yes," Rezil nodded like a bobble-head doll.

"Kay, come," Tybus held out a hand to me. "You will pose with Master Rezil, to convince Cayetes that all is well."

I had no difficulty expressing my fear as Rezil held me against him —I was trembling and the image transmitted to Hordace recorded my pale face and wide eyes. He'd believe it—because it was real.

Wyyld—Present
Hank's Journal
"I like this idea," I nodded toward Lendill Schaff. Ildevar had

reached out to me, so I'd arrived immediately. He and Lendill Schaff explained what they intended to do, and apprised me of the situation on Noppen.

"I can arrange to place you in an orbit close to that of Falchan's. Your seasons will remain much the same," I added.

"Good," Ildevar breathed a sigh. "I worry about the people here. If we can make the transition relatively painless, they will adapt quickly."

"Adapting is better than perishing," Willem Drifft observed. "What can we do about Noppen?"

"I've already cut off all shipping and interstellar travel," Lendill said, tapping the last of a message on his comp-vid. "I have something to show you as well." He handed an envelope to me, which bore his name. I already recognized the stationery; I merely wanted to read the offer inside.

"Pan'Warha," Lendill said before I could slide the card from the envelope. "Father received one as well. His was Al'Riyu."

"So it wasn't only those invited to the Archives." I nodded to Lendill. "This increases your father's gifts greatly, does it not?"

"He says as much," Lendill agreed. "He tells me that he sees better and farther now, when he applies his abilities. He says at times, he can even see past the clouds surrounding the Sirenali, but he imagines that these are the younger and weaker ones of that race."

"That may be of enormous help," I said. "Ask him to track as many of these as he can and pass messages to those who need the information. Ildevar and I will set about moving this world and leaving a decoy in its place."

"Father is linked with me—the message has been received," Lendill said.

"Good," I nodded at Lendill before studying Ildevar's power and linking it with mine.

Falchan—present

Torevik's Journal

Ry was always the one who kept records and journals. A good thing, as it turns out, since he's King of Karathia. It was odd that I had the sudden desire to write things down, although Mom would be proud of me for it.

We were currently training with Falchani blade masters on their world; Jayd sent most of us to learn what we needed to know to become the elite fighting force required by Li'Neruh Rath. So far, he hadn't told us what he meant for us to do.

Dragon actually grinned when I stepped up to spar with Drake—Drake and Drew taught Ry and me years go. My skills were rusty at first, but they improved before the bout was over. It turned out that I lasted longer than any other High Demon who'd sparred with a Falchani, so Drake put me with the small class assigned to Caylon Black.

Caylon's assistant turned out to be a werewolf—Salidar DeLuca. He checked and measured before ordering two blades for me from the Falchani smith who'd been assigned to Caylon's contingent.

"How does a werewolf end up a blademaster?" I asked as I sat beside Salidar during the midday meal.

"Ashe," Salidar shrugged. "Call me Sali—everybody does."

"Ashe—the Mighty Hand?" I asked.

"Yeah. We were best friends when we were young. Ashe understood me, even when I didn't understand myself. He contacted Dragon years ago, to get me lessons in how to fight with a blade. Dragon sent me to Caylon Black. If you haven't figured it out, yet, Caylon trained Dragon and his brother, Crane. Caylon will beat you into the ground if he spars with you. Thank him for the lesson afterward."

"Will that make him go easier on me the next time?"

"Nope." Sali grinned and sipped his cup of Falchani black. "That means he'll spar with you again, and you'll stay where you are, learning from the best. Fail to appreciate that and you'll likely be sent elsewhere."

"Has anyone ever beaten Caylon?" I asked.

"Once," Sali nodded.

"Who?"

"Your mother."

After our midday meal, those in Caylon Black's contingent were set to exercises. We practiced drawing blades and going into the middle position. Sali watched us closely as we pulled blades in unison. He barked or growled if any one of us was too slow. By the end of the day, my shoulders sore from the training, I walked toward the bathing tents to clean up before going back to the cooking tents for the evening meal.

~

Noppen—present

Reah's Journal

You're where? I thought Lendill might explode when I informed him where Rezil had taken us.

We thought Hordace was on Du'Ferias. We're on Noppen. Rezil and his Sirenali directed us here instead, I returned Lendill's mindspeech.

Reah, I can't think of a more dangerous place—Noppen has gone rogue and we're in the process of moving Wyyld into an orbit around Falchan's sun. Noppen's president informed Ildevar a click ago that they're pulling out of the Reth Alliance.

That's not good. How much influence do you think Hordace might have over the local politicians? I asked.

If the enemy has taken over, they're likely bowing and scraping to that bastard now, Lendill said, his mental voice expressing anger and disgust. *Are Jett and his crew there with you?*

Not yet—when we found out that Du'Ferias wasn't our first stop, we asked them to wait until we had a better handle on a final destination.

Good. I'll ask them to keep me informed, and I'd appreciate it if you sent regular mindspeech, too. I love you, Cheah-mul. Don't forget that.

I won't, I acknowledged.

What are you doing at the moment? he asked.

Waiting for transport. I assume we're being taken somewhere. The others are shielded and invisible to all except each other and Kay. She's terrified.

No surprise, Lendill said. *I would be as well, if I were being taken to my torturers. Do you know where you are?*

At the space station for the moment. Most inbound travel has been diverted—I assume you had a hand in that?

With Ildevar and the twenty, yes. Outbound travel is also put on hold. I can only imagine that your craft was unregistered?

Unless it's registered to the Cayetes Alliance, I replied, my mental voice dry.

Let's hope that Alliance doesn't expand, Lendill's sending was just as dry.

I worry that it will, I responded. *Look, a hovercar just arrived. I'll contact you later.*

See that you do, Breah-mul.

~

Tybus responded to the limited space inside the hovercar by turning all of us to mist. We fit into a small space overhead as Kay was herded into the vehicle with Rezil, the Sirenali who went by Fe'rangl, plus the wizard and two bodyguards.

I felt Farzi and Nenzi's discomfort—they were coming to like Kay very much and both wanted to eliminate those who now sat around her while she trembled.

"Hordace is waiting for you," Rezil grinned at Kay, making her shrink away from him. With Tybus' apparent disappearance and Rezil's belief that Tybus (as Teeg) was dead, he'd reverted to himself in most respects. Tybus' last command, however, was that neither Rezil nor anyone with him would harm Kay.

Aurelius and I helped in that respect—we watched closely and sent mindspeech to Kay whenever she seemed overwhelmed. Farzi and Nenzi watched even closer—Tybus and Aurelius might not have to destroy Kay's guards—the reptanoids would likely get there first.

Tybus kept us as mist when the hovercar pulled to a stop outside

Noppen's Presidential Palace. Covering nearly a city block, it housed the President, his family, the servants and his advisors.

Architecture is nice, Tybus sent as he surveyed the building. Of course he'd notice—he'd designed many palaces in his day. His work was so much better than this, however.

You think President Utrill will allow Hordace to take over, or will he be Cayetes' hand puppet from now on? Kevis asked.

It doesn't matter at this point, I said. *Noppen has pulled out of the Alliance. They're on their own, now. Wait until the population figures out that Noppen is mostly industrial, with very little agriculture. If Cayetes and the enemy don't kill them, they'll likely starve, especially since their president has threatened Wyyld—enough that Ildevar intends to move the planet.*

Where Wyyld moving? Farzi asked.

Into an orbit around Falchan's sun, I said. *Li'Neruh Rath says that he can place them in an orbit to keep their seasons much like what they have now. They'll adapt easier.*

Understand, Farzi replied. *Look—they move.*

He was right; Rezil moved Kay toward a side entrance; the Sirenali and the others followed. Tybus moved us overhead, in case we were needed quickly. With another Sirenali likely blocking any information, I had no idea what we'd find once we passed through the guarded door.

Noppen—present

Kay's Journal

You can do this, entered my mind. One of those with me was offering encouragement, but my mind was so frozen with fear I didn't recognize which one. The door was getting closer—the door that would lead me to Hordace Cayetes. I shuddered and found myself hoping that Q'Ind Ribalo was far away. That hope was probably an empty one—Hordace kept Q'Ind close most of the time.

The guard at the door opened it for us and I was ushered inside.

We're right over your head, Reah soothed as I stepped timidly across the threshold.

The interior was dim but warmer than it was outside—Noppen was currently in its third season, which was fall-like with lower temperatures. I shivered anyway as warmth from solar-heated panels enveloped us.

The walk was a long one, down the initial corridor to a set of stairs normally used by servants or employees, away from the public eye. Unless I missed my guess, the public would no longer be welcome inside the Presidential Palace.

We climbed three flights of stairs as increasing dread threatened to still my numbed feet. That meant Hordace was waiting on the top floor—likely in the President's lavish suite of offices. If he wasn't sitting in the President's chair already, he would be there soon enough.

When we arrived outside the wide, double doors leading into the President's suite, my breath threatened to stop altogether. I was petrified. *You can do this,* the voice came again. A male voice. At least I knew that much. Rezil nodded to the guards who stood at the doors, and they were opened to allow us inside.

Reah's Journal

Kay muffled a scream and struggled in Rezil's grip—she wasn't thinking clearly, else she might have blasted him with a thought. Hordace Cayetes, Q'Ind and Q'And Ribalo, a Sirenali and several others waited inside the Presidential offices.

"Ah, Kalia," Hordace smiled. That smile was vicious, conniving and murderous. "Come in. I have questions. Q'Ind will see to it that you answer all of them."

Q'ind's smile was just as horrifying as Hordace's, as he drew a thin-bladed knife from a leather holster clipped to his belt. Kay cringed as a sob escaped her lips. Hordace's Sirenali stood nearby, waiting for a command to place obsession on Kay.

Kay, change the Sirenali's lines, Tybus coaxed, attempting to draw her attention away from those who only wished to torment her. Hordace was shorter than I'd imagined—the few photographs available on the ASD websites were poor, as Hordace often killed anyone who held an image of him. I didn't wish to speculate on his sexual preferences, either.

My love, Aurelius' mindspeech drew me to the one actually sitting in the president's chair—it was neither Hordace nor Noppen's president. The president stood behind this one, obviously obsessed.

Had I not been mist, I would have gasped aloud. A rogue god rose and stared directly at Tybus' mist before raising his hand. If I hadn't seen what happened next, I'd never have believed it.

The rogue god screamed before his body dropped, face-first, onto the President's desk. Hordace shouted for his guards to protect him as the rogue's body began to shrivel.

Kay? I shouted mentally. Was she doing this?

What is happening? Kay's mental voice trembled. She wasn't the one responsible for sucking the power from a rogue god. I understood what was happening, now—Kevis had reached out to the shrinking body, before providing us with the knowledge of exactly what was occurring.

Matters became complicated when Ranos pistols were drawn and Hordace's guards fired at everything surrounding them. Chunks of plaster flew from walls and windows shattered around us. Everyone who was mist wasn't in danger, but Rezil dropped beside Kay—dead before he hit the floor, his head blown apart.

Aurelius and I shielded Kay from the pistol blasts as both guards at the door died behind us. Kay screamed, then screamed again as blood, wood, plaster and glass rained around us.

It time, Farzi snarled as he and Nenzi dropped from Tybus' mist. Both whipped their lion snakes toward Hordace and his crowd. As it turned out, it only took the space of two blinks for the worst criminal in either Alliance to die from lion snake bites, and his guards, minions, the president of Noppen and the Sirenali died with him.

~

Tybus' Journal

It was more than fortunate that Ildevar and Li'Neruh Rath moved Wyyld when they did. The shell they left in its place was blasted to atoms when the Ranos cannon fired following the President's death on Noppen.

Somehow, that act was triggered by the President's death and not the demise of the rogue god. I felt the Sirenali had placed obsession on those whose fingers were on the trigger, but that was no longer our concern. Part of our target had been eliminated, but Song and Serenade were still out there.

"We'll still have to travel through the jungles of Du'Ferias," Aurelius said as we surveyed the bodies littering the floor around us. None of them were whole—Ranos fire will destroy most anything when shot from such close range. Farzi and Nenzi didn't care that our next destination was Du'Ferias; they'd shielded themselves and dispatched an enemy who deserved a far worse death, and jungles were no obstacle to them—their lion snakes could comfortably move through the worst any jungle had to offer.

"You think we'll find the contact information there? For Song and Serenade?" Kevis asked.

"I believe so; I'm sure Hordace left someone in command," Reah said. "We'll ask questions later, when Kay feels better," she added. We needed information from her as to who might be left in charge of Hordace's empire. It was my guess that there were plenty of pedophiles in Hordace's ranks, since he was Song and Serenade's best customer.

"I want to know what happened with the rogue god," Aurelius said. "That was completely confusing. Helpful but confusing," he amended.

"Let's make arrangements to get to Du'Ferias," I suggested. "We can talk about fortuitous events as we prepare for jungle travel."

"I'll contact Jett," Reah offered.

"There's something I have to do before we go," Kevis said. We all felt it when the Ranos cannon supplied by a rogue god became dust—

Kevis didn't want it used again. Noppen had played its hand —and lost.

"Good," I nodded at Kevis. "Let's get out of here before all of Noppen arrives on the doorstep," I said and folded us back to Campiaa.

Ashe's Journal

"That seems to have worked," I offered dryly as Charles stood and stretched, a lazy smile on his face.

"It did. I don't feel half bad. Power is power, it doesn't matter where it comes from," he added. "Not with us, anyway."

"Thank goodness for that," Breanne shook her head at Charles. He leaned forward and kissed her.

"I need to contact Kaldill Schaff," Charles said, after pecking Breanne a second time. "We'll track others, and Kaldill can help with that."

"You shouldn't let anyone else know we're back," I pointed a finger at Charles. "We're not ready for a war, yet."

"I know that," Charles chuckled. "That's why I'm going like this."

I blinked at what was suddenly before me—a hooded figure with no discernible features inside the hood.

"Weird," Breanne mumbled, hunching her shoulders.

"Call it anything you like," Charles said. "This will work." He disappeared before either of us could stop him.

Calhoun worried that the General would destroy everything around him. That included a planet that Calhoun and others were carefully preparing to take, but the General was angry and held little regard for anything or anyone else.

"One of mine, shriveled and dead, even the spirit obliterated," the General shouted. "Find out how this happened. Immediately!"

"As you desire, General," Calhoun bowed and folded away, afraid of what the General might do next.

~

Quislus studied the body. He'd searched the area surrounding the Noppen Presidential Palace, but found no evidence anywhere that the spirit inhabiting the body still lived. The holes from Ranos pistol blasts would have been held at bay with the normal power of even the lowliest of gods. This one—one of the Hidden—had been of the Pan'Warha and quite powerful in his own right. Quislus had supplied the body only a day before.

Yes, Acrimus had created Quislus, and made him capable of killing, just as the Koh'Ahmari had suggested. Mortal spirits were so simple to dislodge and send on their way, leaving a viable body for a rogue god to inhabit. So much more could be accomplished that way—if the races believed they were made in the gods' image.

He couldn't help but recall what the Koh'Ahmari had told him, too —that he would trap him as bait to call the General forth. Quislus had been just as shocked to have the General show up as he had, but as a result of his actions, he was now under the General's scrutiny and Kifirin was just as dead.

"I will not say I grieve for you, Kifirin—as that would belittle your existence and assign the lie to your reality," Quislus whispered. "I will only say that I regret your death."

~

Wisdom's Journal

Kaldill Schaff? I sent mindspeech as I wandered through the Elf King's private quarters.

"I am here," he appeared and bowed before me. "I understand the secrecy and why I and my son were not at the meeting on the Larentii homeworld."

"Then I don't have to explain it," I lowered my hood and smiled at him.

"Ah. I see you as you really are," Kaldill smiled back.

"There are many things we must do, and we must do them swiftly," I said. "That means I need your help."

"Anything you need," he acknowledged.

"Good. We'll start by tracking the Sirenali you detect, then we'll go from there."

"I have anticipated this," Kaldill said. "Here is what I have." He handed a paper to me. Seemingly blank, the moment I touched it, words formed upon it. Kaldill had been casting spells and living in secrecy for a very long time. Breanne was wise to choose him as a member of her army. She might be angry with Lendill, still, for his treatment of Reah. I chose him, instead. The Elves had kept to themselves for so very long, gathering power and searching for secrets. It was time to employ those hidden talents.

"I need someone to go here, here and here," I began selecting targets. "I will be seeing through their eyes. Don't worry," I held up a hand. "They'll never know I'm there."

"Then I may have some suggestions," Kaldill smiled widely. When the Elf King smiles in that way, his enemies should tremble.

~

Campiaa—present

Tybus' Journal

"I think we should stay together, now," Jett suggested. "Cayetes is dead, but we have enough among us to track his replacement and those who serve him."

"We find them," Nenzi huffed. "They die. We get what we need. Track others."

"We need to hurry," Kay said, her voice trembling. "If Song and Serenade think Hordace's information is compromised, they'll kill all the children and escape."

"We'll try to keep that from happening," I pulled her against me. "I promise."

CHAPTER 7

Adam's Journal

"All of these events—whatever they are—are roughly a week apart for twenty weeks, beginning in three weeks." Joey tossed a comp-vid onto the kitchen island. "And they're all scheduled in the largest cities and the biggest arenas. I just wish I knew what this is about."

"As do I." I rubbed Joey's shoulders affectionately.

"You know, Adam, I really liked this house. I liked the strawberry farm better, though." Joey gazed about in nostalgic appreciation.

"At least Lissa relocated the strawberry farm—it's on Le-Ath Veronis, now. Justin and Mack spend a lot of time there."

"I go now and then," Joey grinned. "Erland likes it."

"How is that wily warlock?" I asked.

"He's fine. Still in a male phase, though," Joey shook his head. I understood that to mean that sex from Erland wasn't as forthcoming as Joey might like.

"Let's look at this from our angle," I suggested, changing the topic and steering away from sex. "I believe we need to take what we know of Saxom and begin our search for him and his brother by tailing his habits."

"I don't know much about him," Joey shook his head. "I only saw him a time or two, when he was still on the Council."

"I recall him when he was on the Council," I said, "but that pretty much covers what I knew of him—we had no interaction outside the Council—until Corpus Christi, that is."

"Then what do we have to go on?" Joey gave me a puzzled look.

"You're forgetting about before he was vampire, and who knew him then."

"What?" Joey didn't understand. I did—all too well—and it would make things uncomfortable for several of us as soon as the words left my mouth.

"We don't know much about him, that's true. But for nearly a hundred thousand years, Saxom acted as Griffin's healer in the Saa Thalarr."

Joey's breath caught and his eyes widened. "Oh, my gosh," he eventually whispered, a hand partially covering his mouth. "This won't make Merrill or Lissa happy, will it?"

"Not at all, but if we're going to track the bastard, we need information. And to get information, we need the one who knows the most about him."

"We have to track Griffin down first," Joey pointed out.

"I don't believe that'll be a problem—we have access to his grandson, the current King of Karathia," I replied. "Ry probably knows where Wylend is, and Wylend likely knows where Griffin is."

"I have one other suggestion," Joey said.

"What's that?"

"Thorsten. Well, Thurlow, now. Didn't he have a hand in making Saxom Griffin's healer?"

"It had to meet with his approval, yes," I agreed, but the idea suddenly sent a shiver up my spine and a suspicion began to form. "We need Belen," I muttered. "And anybody else we can gather to sort out this mess."

"You got that right," Joey agreed. I had a feeling his mind was now traveling in the same direction, and the uncertainties we were uncovering weren't pretty at all.

~

Karathia—present

Rylend's Journal

"I heard from Adam," my father said.

"What did he say?" I asked, removing the gold circlet from my head. I hated wearing the thing, but it was expected on full court days. Mom likes to tease me and call it a full-court press, but basketball references never amused me as much as they did her.

"We had a lengthy mental discussion," Dad informed me, taking one of the chairs in my private study with a troubled sigh.

Setting the crown on my desk, I looked at my father for a moment before nodding. It was something I expected, actually. We'd have to find my grandfather and great-grandfather. They were needed in this war, but bringing them in wouldn't be easy. Neither wanted to involve themselves in anything, nowadays.

"I sent mindspeech already. No reply, but that's no surprise," Dad added.

"They're still citizens of Karathia," I said.

"You can try, Son, but I can't guarantee results. I'm sure they've heard by now that all the Saa Thalarr received promotions and are now more powerful. As did we." He motioned toward me before tapping himself on the chest. "They were left out. Everybody knows that."

"So they don't want to come slinking back with their tails between their legs, is that it?"

"That's how they'll see it."

"So it won't matter that people may die, as long as their pride doesn't get squashed?"

"That's how they'll see it."

I cursed. Yes, my mother can curse with the best of sailors, as she always puts it, and so can I, if the situation warrants. "Fuck," I ended up muttering under my breath. "I'll have to send somebody looking for Wylend, then. He'll know where Griffin is."

"We need to do it now. Adam and his bunch need information from Griffin, and they need it now."

"It's too bad we can't play on his sense of duty. I believe he lost that, years ago."

"There is one thing we might try." Dad rose from his seat and swirled his court robes about him dramatically—with a wicked smile stealing across his lips.

"What's that?"

"Amara," Dad said and disappeared in a blink.

"Oh, shit," I slapped my forehead with a palm.

SouthStar—present

"Thurlow?" Amos and Flossie Thompson had gone looking for him. Both outranked him, now, and he understood that when he lifted his gaze to them.

He'd chosen the waterfall on the southern edge of SouthStar to make his home, and he lived there with very little in the way of comforts.

"Yes?" Thurlow sighed.

"You are needed," Amos Thompson said. "On Earth, in the past."

"I have very little power. You would be of more assistance now," Thurlow replied, defeat evident in his voice.

"That's not what is needed," Amos said. "They need information— that only you might have."

Thurlow's eyes widened in surprise.

"We will take you," Flossie Thompson spoke for the first time. "Now is not the time for pride or old feuds to stand in the way of progress. Or justice. Remember that."

"I will remember," Thurlow sighed again.

Adam's Journal

"You're the one who knows her best." Erland arrived, informed Merrill of his conclusions and sat back while he considered them. His suggestions made sense to me; we only had to make sense to Merrill, now.

"She and I talk," Merrill hedged.

"Look, I realize this could damage the friendship you have with Amara, but she's our best chance at reaching Griffin. Or Wylend," Erland pointed out. "And, as Adam so acutely observed earlier during our extended mindspeech, Griffin knows Saxom better than anyone, as he knew him longer than anyone."

"I understand the logic, but this has little to do with emotions—in either of our cases," Merrill said. "Amara informed me when she was leaving Griffin, and I was there in the meeting with her and Belen, when she asked him to separate her particles. I begged her to reconsider and she still asked. If you fail to understand how difficult that was for me to witness, then you know nothing."

Seldom had I seen Merrill ruffled over anything, but Griffin was the sorest of sore spots with him. Griffin had acted as a trusted friend and brother to Merrill for most of Merrill's life, and it had taken years for him to realize that Griffin had his own agenda all along. Merrill never said it, but lost time with Lissa was one of the worst offenses.

I'm sure Amara felt the same—she'd stayed at Griffin's side, childless for years uncounted, when he'd managed to father two daughters with other women while mated to her. Then, when Lissa made it possible for Amara to birth Wyatt, Griffin and Wylend had sealed Wyatt's fate with their meddling, leaving Amara childless once more.

It had taken that to force the breakup between Amara and Griffin, and we would be asking her to go to him now and demand that he help us. This wasn't going to be easy, regardless of how we approached it.

"Merrill, we need information from Griffin so we can track Saxom. That's it," I said. "This is the way to get it. Amara and Edan are Powers That Be, now. Surely they understand the need for help, no matter how difficult it might be for all involved."

"I still don't like it, but I do understand that my feelings don't matter in the larger scheme," Merrill grumbled. "I'll contact Amara. And I'll talk with Lissa. This will upset both of them, you understand?"

"I understand," I jerked my head in a curt nod.

Amara? The familiar voice sounded in her mind.

Merrill? She sounded happy to hear from him. *How are you, old friend?*

I'm fine. Actually, that's not true. Can we meet? I need to speak with you.

Of course. Where?

Lissa's palace? Her study is available.

I'll be right there.

Lissa's Journal

I wasn't thrilled with the idea, but it was all we had. Either we got Griffin to tell what he knew or we'd still be grasping at straws. Merrill arranged a meeting with Amara after explaining the difficult details to me, and I'd agreed (reluctantly) to meet with Amara about contacting Griffin.

What we didn't know—until the last moment—was that Thurlow, formerly Thorsten, would be joining us as well. I hadn't seen him since he'd been pulled away from SouthStar and Breanne ended up saving his life. Ashe must have taken him back there—I hadn't heard otherwise and he hadn't contacted me.

"Lissa?" Thurlow arrived first and held out his hand to me. He was accompanied by Amos and Flossie Thompson, who were now members of the Mil'Karha and outranked him.

"Thurlow?" I frowned at him—I couldn't help it.

Lissa, I can't feel her any longer. His mindspeech sounded thick with unshed tears. The depth of his distress upset me greatly. He meant Breanne, and that upset me as well.

It would be an attempt to locate the One, I replied. *Don't fret over it. What's done is done.* It wasn't difficult to tell that regret ate at him—he knew all along where she was and he could have stepped in so many times. He didn't, because of the long feud with Griffin. We could lay blame all we wanted but in the end, it wouldn't change one damn thing for her.

"Thurlow," Merrill nodded, breaking our mental conversation. "Amara should arrive at any moment."

She did, accompanied by Edan. "Lissa," she smiled and came forward to take my hands and kiss my cheek affectionately. Edan smiled and nodded to me. "What's this about?" Amara turned to Merrill, then.

"It's about Griffin." Merrill couldn't keep the rough sigh from escaping. "We're attempting to track Saxom and his brother, Moxas, but we need information. Griffin likely has what we need, but he hasn't answered mindspeech sent by others. We need your help, dear friend."

"I see this troubles you just as much as it does me," Amara touched Merrill's face gently. She'd been a healer for millennia uncounted and could read emotions as well as anyone. Merrill couldn't hide this behind the vampire mask—it upset him too greatly.

"Will you reach out to him?" Merrill pleaded, concern for Amara clouding his dark eyes and etching furrows around his mouth—this was extremely distasteful to him, as Griffin had misled him for so long.

"I will. I don't have to like it, after all," she murmured, taking her hand away from Merrill's cheek. "I'd say don't let this overwhelm you, but I'd need to take that advice as well." Her lower lip trembled slightly as she attempted a smile.

"Want me to sit with you?" Merrill offered.

"Yes. You on one side, Edan on the other." She gestured toward the comfortable sofa I kept along a wall of my study.

"Lissa?" Thurlow stepped behind me and slipped his arms around my waist. *I love you*, he said.

I know, I responded. *Do you believe you might still be in danger?*

I doubt it. I have no information to give, and if I did, which of them might confront the One? Acrimus' death was so easy to accomplish, was it not? He had no defense against that and the enemy knows it.

Thurlow? I sent.

What, love?

Who made you? Who is your parent?

That is difficult to say. I know who made me in the beginning, but when I was sent back, that changed. I cannot say, now, who was responsible for that change.

Who made you in the beginning?

Quislus.

"Thurlow," I gasped, turning in his arms.

"We no longer have contact, my love. When I returned, he and I— we were no longer connected. I can't describe how I know that, I just do."

"I can explain it." Someone else joined us. A shrouded figure, his face hidden behind a dark cowl.

"What?" Thurlow pushed me behind him, forgetting for a moment that I far outranked him, now.

"Don't get your panties in a knot, Lissa," the cowl was pulled back, revealing Charles as he really was—dark-haired and gray-eyed.

"What the bloody hell?" Merrill was off the sofa and staring at Charles—just as Thurlow and I were.

"Did you reach Griffin?" Charles ignored Merrill and asked his question of Amara.

"He is coming," she said, allowing Merrill to help her rise.

"Good. I need to see the old goat as well." Charles made himself comfortable by sitting on the edge of my desk.

"You were about to explain about Thurlow?" I said, crossing arms over my chest in a sudden fit of anger.

"I remade him," Charles shrugged. "Got anything to eat? I've had a busy day."

"Where are the other two?" I demanded.

"Ashe," he raised a hand. "Bree," he tapped his chest.

"I take it you're the One, then?" Merrill said.

"Take it any way you like," Charles said before waving the other hand and causing a tray of food to appear next to him. "This is good," he lifted a roast-beef sandwich and bit into it. It wasn't difficult to see he'd raided my kitchen with power.

All of us gaped as the One sat on the desk in my private study, consuming a roast-beef sandwich, potato salad and tea. When Griffin arrived, Charles licked a crumb off a finger, glared at Griffin and Griffin cowered.

$\sim$

Du'Ferias—present

Reah's Journal

"I thought the jungles at the edge of SouthStar were bad," Keith Caldwell stared at the mass of tangled vines, trees, brush and tropical flowers surrounding us. Tybus and Aurelius had shields up, keeping vermin and insects away, but I felt they wouldn't bother us anyway—they recognized us, whether humanoids did or not.

"Will we be able to travel through this mess, without using power?" Tybus pulled me into his arms and placed a kiss atop my head. I'd be lying if I said his touch didn't send a thrill through me, because it did.

He'd watched as I fed the baby earlier in the morning, and held her while I dressed for the jungles we'd be traversing to reach Hordace Cayetes' compound. I worried about leaving her behind, but Lexsi was in good hands. Edward always chose well when we hired anyone, but these—several women from SouthStar volunteered to watch her.

Tilting my head up, I offered Tybus a smile. He took advantage by leaning down to kiss me. There would be no subterfuge with this man. No withholding of information, as Teeg had done. I wanted to melt against him. We had no time for that.

"Kay, what do you recall about Cayetes' compound?" Tybus let me go—he'd come to the same realization I had—that our relationship must be put on hold while we concentrated on our mission.

"The buildings were in a clearing, higher than the surrounding trees," Kay said. "Because it rained a lot. I remember the smell, too, at times, like we were near a river or something."

"Here." Aurelius lifted a hand and formed a map from energy. It floated amidst us and depicted a wide, winding river that traversed the jungles of Du'Ferias. He added a three-dimensional, topical aspect and we all searched for higher ground near the Gul'ib River.

"Possible here," Jett pointed out. "And here." Both places were practically surrounded by the river, it curved so deeply around a circular portion of jungle. That left only a narrow space to drive land vehicles in and out, leaving the area easily defensible.

"We'll check both. How close do you think we might get without alerting them to our presence?" Edward asked.

"That depends on whether there are any waiting who outrank us, or worse," Kevis rumbled, examining the map carefully. "I just had mindspeech with Dad. He says to be careful—he asked Li'Neruh Rath to join the conversation, and he agreed. We all know what happened with Lissa and the others on Baetrah's edge."

We did know. While Li'Neruh could have defeated the one named Quislus, the General arrived and attempted to destroy all those present. Kifirin was already dead by that time, and I had mixed feelings about that. Now that I knew Quislus had influenced much of what had occurred, my anger with Kifirin had deflated greatly.

"Then let's land here by mist," Aurelius suggested, pointing to a likely spot near the first target, "keep our shields tightly about us and allow Farzi, Nenzi and Philip's animals to lead us in."

"I'm worried that they may already know that Hordace is dead," Kay sighed. "And that we may be too late, no matter what."

"We'll still be tracking them, even if the worst comes to pass," Edward soothed. "If we can't save all the children, we'll at least save those in the future."

"Don't forget, we can bend time," Kevis pointed out. "I don't have a problem doing that, if lives will be saved."

"Then let's do this," Kay said. "For Ashe and Breanne. For us. For those waiting for us to rescue them."

I knew without asking that she'd waited for someone to rescue her as well. I wanted to weep because it hadn't happened.

"Turning to mist now," Tybus said, and soon we were flying over the jungles of Du'Ferias as invisible, untraceable mist.

~

Lissa's Journal

"I don't give a damn whether you like it or not. He was your healer and it's the least you can do. Refuse and I'll have your power, here and now. It's as simple as that."

I'll admit, I'd never seen this side of Charles. He was always so accommodating—the one I'd known in the past. This one was telling my biological father—plainly—that he'd cooperate or he'd lose what he had.

"Look, I only know what foods he preferred, what sort of fabrics for his clothing, his preferences for housing, that kind of thing," Griffin complained. "I ought to—I fabricated enough of those things for him through the years."

"Griffin, do this," Amara snapped at him. "You may know more than you think," she added.

"I'll do it. You're right—I don't have to like it," Griffin offered a curt nod to Charles.

"The moment they find Saxom is the moment you can go back to wherever you were hiding and feeling sorry for yourself," Charles said and disappeared.

"Then let's go," Griffin muttered.

Merrill kissed Amara's cheek, nodded to me and he and I transported an unwilling Griffin to Fresno in the past.

~

Bill's Journal

I wasn't sure what was going on, but it didn't look good from my point of view. Griffin—Lissa's father—glowered, his arms crossed tightly over his chest as the rest of us were introduced to him.

"He may have vital information on Saxom," Adam said. "About personal tastes and things of that nature. As questions come up, Griffin is the one to ask and advise us. And, as Moxas is Saxom's twin, it seems logical that the two would have similar tastes."

"It's a safe bet that others are carrying in food and anything else they want," Trajan offered. "But we can place someone in the likely places, or divert security cameras. I assume that we'll have Sirenali or others we may recognize running errands for those two."

"Tell me this," Merrill began, "What kind of climate did Saxom prefer?"

"Cooler temperatures. Loves fog and mist, for some reason," Griffin shrugged uncomfortably. I could see there was a disagreement between them, but decided not to pry.

"You just described the bay area and much of the Northern California coast," Lissa said.

"That's a big area to cover," Adam said.

"Images?" I asked. After all, I'd never seen Saxom.

"Here." Griffin held out a hand and photographs appeared. I studied a photograph of Saxom that Adam passed to me. He was short —perhaps five-three or four, with dark, straight hair, hazel eyes and a straight mouth. Could they not see that it appeared cruel, that mouth? I wondered at the fact that he'd been selected as a healer for the Saa Thalarr to begin with.

"Prefers seafood," Griffin went on. "The more expensive kind. If there's a good seafood restaurant anywhere, you can bet he'll buy from there."

"He doesn't cook?"

"Very little. Hates it, actually," Griffin replied. "The few times he went on assignment with me, I did most of the cooking."

"There are hundreds of good seafood restaurants along the coast and in the bay area," Kiarra said. "He could pick and choose and still not go to the same one twice in six months."

"Then what to lure him in?" I asked.

"Something new," Lissa said. I could see that an idea was forming with her. "Merrill—can you send Amos and Flossie Thompson to Kiarra's planet to replace Fes? If we bring him here, it will almost be like putting Reah in a high-dollar San Francisco restaurant to cook fish for them. He does it almost as perfectly as she does, and that will bring in customers by the boatload."

"I think that might work," Trajan said. "We can put him up in Breanne's house—it's still there and waiting. A few of us can stay with him and work on that front," he added. "That way, somebody will be here, waiting, if he shows up, and some of us can be there, waiting to see if he sends somebody to the restaurant for Fes' fish. Either way, we may get him."

"Who's going to the bay area?" Opal raised her hand.

"I'll certainly go, I'm probably more familiar with the area than anyone else," Jayson volunteered.

"Then let's do this," Merrill suggested. "Lissa, Gavin, Kiarra, Adam, Joey and I stay here with Griffin, the rest of you go to San Rafael. Find a really good restaurant and convince them to hire Fes. Communication should be easy enough between us, and whoever locates Saxom first, the others will come running, guaranteed."

"Good enough," I said. "If you need local resources, let me know —I can make arrangements. Keep an eye on the political temperature, too. We may need to intervene if the situation gets worse. Those killings in slums and poor areas are beginning to bother me a lot."

"Me, too," Kiarra spoke up. "I'm afraid the local police may not investigate properly, either."

"Who can we put on that?" Lissa asked.

"How about Gracie, Devin, Fox, Radomir, Lisster and Chazi?" Kiarra said. "All of them can shift and get in and out of places without being suspicious," she grinned.

"You handle that," I said. "Get them on the job fast. I'm sick of hearing how people are being targeted like this, and you can bet it'll turn into the worst kind of class war ever."

"I will come with you, then," Thurlow volunteered with a nod in my direction. He didn't want to be near Griffin and the feeling was mutual, I could tell.

Lissa? I sent.

Yeah, she returned. *I don't want to hear any bickering, if you want to know the truth.*

Then we'll take him and put him to work, I agreed. "I'd like to bring some of the reptanoids with us," I said aloud. "Bekzi and Perzi want to help, I think."

"You take them, we'll take Darzi and Hirzi and send Yanzi to work with Chazi," Adam agreed. "Those men are more helpful than most people might imagine, and their snakes are even more effective."

"Never hurts to have their help," Trajan drawled. "Call Winkler, Trace and Weldon if you need help, plus Martin is here in town—the updated version—let him know if you need anything."

"Let's go pack," I nodded to my group. "Who wants to go after Fes?"

"I'll get Fes and we'll meet you at Breanne's house," Trajan said.

"This is almost like old times," Jayson looked around Breanne's kitchen. "Need groceries, too."

"Then you and Opal get on that, I have some calls to answer," I said. "Plus, the President and a few congressmen want a meeting, so I may be in D.C. the rest of the day."

"Call if you need help," Opal waved before she and Jayson disappeared.

Frankly, I was worried about what I might find when I reached D.C. That's why I sent mindspeech to Hank the moment Jayson and Opal were gone. Only Thurlow remained, and he moped on the back patio, which overlooked San Rafael Bay.

Bill? Hank returned my mindspeech immediately.

I may need a little help in Washington, I replied.

Worried that a few may be obsessed?

More than a few, I responded.

I'll be in your office there in ten.

Thanks.

Hank walked into the meeting room with me an hour later. He was just as concerned as I when I told him what was happening across the country. While there were always crazies who'd take any excuse to involve themselves in murder and mayhem, this was unconscionable.

The President, Joint Chiefs, three Senators and three Representatives were already there, seated and waiting for us to arrive. A Sirenali also stood beside Senator Blake Folie's chair. Folie had always been a thorn in my side, but a Sirenali advisor made things so much worse.

Hank didn't waste time, reaching out with a hand and releasing the Sirenali's particles before Folie could whimper in protest.

San Francisco—present

Terry Johnston read the note he'd pulled from an expensive, cream-linen envelope a second time.

You are a Nameless One now, the note read. *Trust me, you'll need it.*

Nothing else was written on the note, and only his name was spelled out on the envelope. He'd already asked his secretary who'd delivered it, and she couldn't remember.

Terry had no idea what a Nameless One was, so he opened his laptop to type in the words. Before he'd half-finished, information filtered into his mind, causing his eyes to widen in surprise.

Bill's Journal

"Thanks, Russell," I nodded to the former vampire. He'd arrived after I sent mindspeech, to place compulsion on those who'd witnessed Hank's separation of particles. I could have done it myself, but I knew a vampire would be much more adept at it.

The President still didn't have an obsession, but one Senator and two Representatives did. That wasn't good news. "The only way we can remove this is with Kay's help, and she's in the jungle on Du'Ferias, tracking Cayetes' bunch," Hank shook his head. "At least the President hasn't been affected—yet."

"Do you think the obsession can still be transferred?" I asked.

Hank frowned as he considered my question, while a curl of smoke escaped his nostrils. He, Russell and I were in my office after we'd taken care of business at the meeting, and it appeared that Hank was just as perplexed as I that the original obsession seemed to be tainting others.

"That prick Folie lied his head off the whole time," Russell growled as he settled on a guest chair. Russell had stayed for the meeting, shielding himself so he wouldn't be noticed. We listened as patiently as we could while the President asked for suggestions to quell the growing problem of shootings in poor neighborhoods and slums.

I'd told the President I was already looking into the matter and would let him know later what my suggestions were. It was a noncommittal answer and the best I could do with obsessed people in the room.

"It's possible the Sirenali was waiting for you to arrive before obsessing all of you," Hank said. "And if an obsession can be transferred once, it only makes sense that it might be transferred again. This is worse than I imagined."

"What are we going to do about it?" I asked.

"No idea." Hank breathed more smoke. "Send out messages to everyone. Ask for suggestions. If this grows like a virus, and I suspect that's what it is, in a way, then I'm not sure what we can do to stop it."

"Do you think there's power behind this—pushing an obsession to replicate this way?" I asked.

"No doubt," Hank replied.

~

Grey House—present

"The blades have to be ten feet long and fourteen inches wide at the base, in order for a Thifilathi to have any effectiveness with them," Nissa said, handing a drawing to Trik and Toff. "And they have to be fireproof. Even with power, this will be tricky."

"How many?" Toff asked.

"Drake says one hundred matched pairs for those who can wield two blades, and an additional four hundred single blades. We're making spelled swords for the Thifilathi; the Falchani sword smiths are making blades for their humanoid counterparts."

"I'm really glad we don't have other pressing business," Toff said.

"Breanne did that for us. She pulled us out of the blackmail mess Grey House was in," Trik responded. "Think where we'd be if that were still in effect."

"I'm happy that's over," Nissa sighed. "Let's get to work. We may have to bend time to get this done, but it will be done."

"Agreed." Toff smiled before leaning in to kiss Nissa gently.

CHAPTER 8

"Terry?" Jayson sounded surprised when he opened the door. I was, too—neither of us expected a visit from Breanne's attorney.

"I got this," Terry handed an envelope to Jayson as he stepped inside the house.

"Are you kidding me?" Jayson grinned and slapped Terry on the back.

"I assume this means we're on the same side now, Rome?" Terry asked.

"That's what it means," Jayson said.

"What is he?" I asked. Bill still hadn't made it back from Washington, and I'd considered sending mindspeech when the doorbell rang.

"Nameless One. Says he'll need it," Jayson waved the card at me.

"I worried about that. I didn't appreciate the way your sister-in-law was staring at Terry," Lissa appeared and lifted the card from Jayson's fingers.

"I didn't like the way she was staring at me, either," Terry agreed.

Terry was a tall, black man in his forties, although he was now immortal and could appear as young as he wanted.

"Mr. Johnston, I think we should move your family to a safe place," Lissa suggested, her blue eyes studying Terry with concern. "I don't want anybody getting to you through them."

"You think they might?" Terry sounded worried.

"We have to think of everything," she said. "Who wants to transport Terry's family to SouthStar?"

"I'll do it," I raised a hand. "It'll keep me busy and I can collect Fes on the way back. Lissa, if you could, check on Bill in D.C. Okay?"

"I will," she said. "Come with me, Terry. You'll get your first lesson in folding space."

Lissa's Journal

"How did you know to get there?" Terry asked.

"Thurlow sent mindspeech," I said as we walked toward Bill's office in Silver Spring. "We're putting a grassroots effort together to prevent the enemy from taking over."

"Where is Breanne?" Terry asked.

"She is and isn't anywhere, if that makes any sense."

"Tell me later, I feel a headache coming on," Terry sighed.

"I know exactly how you feel," I agreed.

Bill? I sent mindspeech as Terry and I walked through the outer doors and into the building that housed his and several other offices.

What's wrong? Bill's reply was immediate.

Nothing—Trajan was worried. I brought a friend—we're downstairs. Can we come up?

Sure. I'll call the receptionist and tell her to let you through.

Thanks, Bill.

Five minutes later, Terry and I walked into Bill's office. Russell and Hank were with him.

"Terry, welcome aboard," Hank held out a hand.

Terry shook and grinned at Hank. "Never suspected. Not even for a minute," Terry chuckled.

"I have a feeling this involves Jayson's family, and a money hungry sister-in-law," Hank said. "You'll have to protect yourself. Trajan says your wife, kids and your sister are safe at SouthStar, now."

"Thank you for that," Terry nodded. "I still have your apartment locked up in San Francisco. I run by and check on it twice a week. The bar property has been cleared, too."

"Hold off on building anything else just yet," Hank said. "Or on selling the property."

"Just say the word and I can make it happen," Terry shrugged. "You're the boss, in more ways than one if I understand correctly."

"You catch on fast," Russell laughed.

"And he smells nice," I agreed.

Trajan's Journal

"Our chef has to prepare the best fish in the city," the manager sniffed. Fes and I sat inside the manager's office at the Title Wave restaurant, while Fes applied for the position of head chef. I wanted to snicker but didn't—Fes could walk into any restaurant in two alliances and they'd beg him to cook. In this one, the manager wanted to be an asshole.

"Let me cook for you, and you can decide," Fes shrugged. Two hours later, after Fes made six types of fish, each with its own sauce, the manager tasted the turbot made with a sauce that Fes and Reah had designed together.

"You're hired," the manager mumbled and finished the entire plate of food.

"I want the money that went to Breanne Hayworth's charity," Laurel Rome huffed.

"I can get it for you," her attorney smiled. "With his help." He indicated the man standing beside his desk.

Laurel sat in her attorney's office, dressed stylishly in a navy dress with red designer heels.

"We want your husband's money," the man standing beside the desk grinned, revealing many sharp teeth. "You're going to get that for us."

Laurel's eyes widened and she nodded helplessly as the obsession soaked into her brain.

Trajan's Journal

Lissa came back with Bill, Hank and Terry. Terry, as a newly made Nameless One, was eager to learn everything he could.

Bill grinned as he showed Terry how to separate particles by destroying Breanne's TinyCar.

"She won't like that," Terry laughed as the car's sparks dissipated inside her garage.

"She doesn't need it," Bill sighed. "Besides, I'll buy her anything she wants if she manages to come back."

"What this is for," Lissa explained, "is separating particles of any Sirenali you come across. Don't wait to ask questions, because they may have more powerful allies nearby. Do it immediately, send mindspeech and get the hell away."

"You'll take mindspeech?" Terry blinked dark eyes at Lissa.

"Honey, you bet. Anytime. If you need help, send out blanket mindspeech. Anybody who can, will come."

"Damn, that's an efficient network," Terry breathed.

"It'll have to be," Bill agreed. "We may not be able to survive, otherwise."

"I can't believe this was going on under our noses, and we never suspected."

"You just watch for somebody to come into your office, asking for the money Breanne got for her charity," I said. "Check in with us often, and we'll do the same with you. Communication will be key, I think, in fighting this war."

"You got it," Terry grinned at me. "Damn, I always thought werewolves and vampires were fictitious."

"Wait till you see the Larentii," Bill grinned.

～

Du'Ferias—present

Reah's Journal

"Someone with power did this," Jett announced. He would know—he'd grown up in Avendor's jungles.

We stared at the tightly formed wall of roots and vines blocking our way. This wasn't natural—there was no way for the plants and trees before us to get sufficient light, as tangled as they were, to survive.

"So they have Sirenali and rogues with them," Aurelius rumbled.

"And we have no idea how many," Edward said. "This doesn't look good."

Farzi and Nenzi studied the tight, impenetrable barrier before us—just beyond, by a few Earth feet—lay the entrance to Hordace Cayetes' compound. At least that's what we hoped—we had no way to tell at this point.

"I'm concerned he may have more than one fortress," Tybus said.

"That's a frightening thought—and one we should have already considered," Kevis observed. "This is the wealthiest criminal in two Alliances, after all. Why wouldn't he have two fortresses here?"

"This certainly complicates things," Edward huffed. "Should we mist over this barrier, or check the next one first?"

"Let's fly over both," Tybus offered. "It won't take long—both areas are close together."

"We may not be able to see anything, if they're shielded," Aurelius said.

"True," Kevis agreed. "This makes it worse, doesn't it?"

"I'm terrified that they may already know we're here," Kay quavered.

"Kay, we're with you, don't forget that," Kevis rubbed her shoulders gently.

"I know. But we don't know what's on the other side of this," she flung a hand toward the thick, natural barrier. "Or who is on the other side. Just the humanoids Hordace has will scare anybody."

"Kay, whatever it is, we'll be here with you," Kevis soothed.

"Do you smell that?" Aurelius lifted his head swiftly.

"We smell," Farzi hissed. "Turn mist. Now."

"Just a little taste," Moxas smiled as he blinked hazel eyes at Calhoun. "On a small scale. You'll have believers ready to spread the word; you can trust me on this."

"Who will be the victims?"

"Target the poor or any minorities—it doesn't matter," Moxas shrugged. "Announce that they've committed crimes against the population. If you find the right venue, those people will believe it anyway, without the announcement."

"Make sure to have a camera crew there, for documentation. Put the video on the Internet afterward," Saxom said. "If you build a web page, you can make announcements there later, as to when and where to attend the next one."

"What about police intervention?" Calhoun asked.

"Then target them as well," Moxas laughed. "Teach all that none are immune, if they are disobedient or fail to believe."

"Terrifying and effective. I like it," Calhoun nodded. "Thank you. I'll solicit help in the construction."

"You keep forgetting about my love," Saxom pointed out as Calhoun made ready to go.

"I haven't forgotten. In fact, I'll put someone on that immediately." Calhoun disappeared.

Du'Ferias—present

Tybus' Journal

Where did they come from? Kevis asked as we hovered overhead. I hesitated to remain for very long—I could feel Kay's fear vibrating from her mist.

Below us, growling and snarling, lay a vast herd of hideous beasts. Chimeras snapped at kobolds. One-eyed giants shoved manticores aside as they stomped around the perimeter of seething monsters. Outside those, a group of rogue Copper Ra'Ak held themselves apart. While we watched, one of the Ra'Ak stretched out its deadly head and snapped up an unsuspecting minotaur, swallowing it in two gulps.

What are they waiting for? Philip sent.

Us, Reah replied. *Or anyone else foolish enough to breach that barrier.*

Let's check the next target, Aurelius' voice held a mental sigh. I was happy to mist everyone away from the creatures gathered below us.

Rigo stood in the Hraedan King's private library as the King studied him. "Rigovarnus," the King eventually nodded with a sigh. "I assume you don't have welcome news?"

"Sadly, I do not," Rigo agreed. "I have investigated that portion of the square where several have disappeared, as you requested."

"And?"

"That is a portal, built with dark power. It will engulf any who tread near enough," Rigo answered.

"Your painting that hangs in the great hall doesn't do you justice," the King said. "Had I not known that you counseled my father as well as you did, I'd have my doubts about you now. As it is," the King lifted a comp-vid to send a message to his guards and constabulary, "I will attempt to keep all away from this blight until a more permanent solution might be found."

"Check every day," Rigo warned. "In case the portal expands. We have seen this on other worlds already. Noppen is being consumed by such."

"And yet they managed to destroy Wyyld," the King's eyes hardened.

"Wyyld survives," Rigo said. "That world was moved, leaving a decoy shell in its place. It now shares Falchan's sun, and I charge you never to reveal that information."

"At least the Alliance knows Deonus Wyyld still lives. It was wise of him to announce that immediately after the destruction."

"Yes—Deonus Wyyld is very wise and has good advisors about him. He suggested the move and gained assistance to achieve it."

"I hope good advice will continue to come my way, should it be needed," the King said.

"It always has," Rigo offered a slight nod. "I and others continue to watch Hraede—as we have always done."

"Then I thank you—for myself and for the people of Hraede."

～

Du'Ferias—present

Reah's Journal

A teeming mass of creatures surrounded a circular area covered by jungle at both target sites.

We're seeing shielded and disguised areas, aren't we? Edward said.

It looks that way, Aurelius conceded. *I want to get closer, just to see if we can detect anything.*

I can drop lower, if that's what we all decide, Tybus suggested.

I want, Farzi said.

Nenzi, too, Nenzi added.

I'm willing, Kevis agreed.

I really want to, Philip growled.

The only two who didn't vote were Jett and Kay, although I felt Jett agreed. Tybus dropped gently toward the circle of trees below, while all of us searched with sight and senses for any hint or movement that might indicate subterfuge.

There, Nenzi shouted.

Where?

Somehow, Nenzi pulled our attention to the proper place. It looked to be an ordinary lion snake, hanging from a tree. Nenzi knew, as did Farzi, that this was no ordinary snake.

Change when you hit the ground, Tybus instructed. We were about to go to war, as none of us believed that a single lion snake shapeshifter guarded the area. We were about to discover just what it was that Hordace Cayetes' ghost might throw at us.

~

San Francisco—present

"Well, well, Mrs. Rome," Terry stood and nodded to Laurel, who was accompanied by two men. "What can I do for you today?"

"You can start by handing the money back that Breanne Hayworth stole from me," Laurel huffed.

"No deal," Terry grinned and separated the particles of one of the men behind Laurel, causing her to scream and the other man to curse loudly.

~

Trajan's Journal

Terry's office was destroyed. It took a concentrated effort on his part to save his secretary and assistant while his office building was leveled around him.

"Do you think he was more powerful? The rogue with them?" Bill asked, stepping through the remaining rubble.

"I think so," Terry said. "I didn't feel strong enough to stay and fight, that's for sure, and he got Laurel away after I destroyed the Sirenali."

"We know it took someone with power to get Laurel from L.A. to here," Jayson said. "I talked to Jamie. He says Laurel was home the whole time."

"I think Jamie ought to be warned that she has an obsession," Bill said.

"I don't know what to do about that. Jamie thinks she actually loves him," Jayson snorted.

"I suggest we freeze his accounts and get him out of there," Opal said. "Just to keep him safe."

"We can take him to Mom," Jayson nodded. "He won't understand, but he'll be safe. Somebody else can run the company while he's gone."

"I'm concerned that the enemy wants the money," Bill said. "After all, look who we've got involved—the Tanner brothers, Marc Cummings, several members of Congress and who knows who else? They all want money, as if that will save them from what they've allied themselves with in the end."

"Half of them obsessed, too," I said.

"Trajan?" Winkler appeared beside us.

"What is it?" The look on Winkler's face told me something was seriously wrong.

"You need to see this—it just went up on the Internet," he said, raking fingers through his hair in frustration. "I warn you—it's not pretty."

All of us, Terry included, folded space to Fresno, where we watched the video on the large screen television at Adam's home.

It looked to be an old-fashioned revival, with the pastor preaching hellfire and brimstone. That's when it got real, in the literal sense.

People taken from the streets outside the church were led in, chained together like slaves. All seemed poor or belonged to a minority group, and I could tell that several were gay.

"You're going to hell," the preacher roared and the floor opened before the chained group while monsters spilled from the opening, followed by fire. I imagined that a horrible stench arrived with the monsters, as the people were grabbed, bitten, some of them eaten while others screamed, and then bits and pieces of bodies were tossed into the fiery pit.

Lissa and Kiarra looked green as Adam turned off the television amid claims from the preacher that judgment was nigh.

"This is what they're planning, isn't it?" Joey muttered angrily.

"It looks that way," Merrill nodded grimly.

Bill's Journal

Oddly, none of the church members could be found after the debacle in Mississippi. Half the church was charred or burned inside and the brick on the outside showed evidence of smoke damage. I had local agents combing through the building for evidence, but they'd found nothing useful.

"I want anyone you can find, especially the preacher, brought in for questioning," I told the local police. "Do we have identification on any of the victims?"

"We only have the images from the video," the lieutenant said. "We've pulled it off the Internet, but enough people have seen it, and who knows how many copies have been made? I'll send information if we manage to identify anyone," he added.

"It'll go viral by tomorrow," I said. "You can bet on that."

"It's already on the news here, and probably traveling outside the country," he agreed.

"No answer at the preacher's house, and his wife is missing, too," another agent walked up and nodded to me.

"I'd sure as hell go missing after doing that," the lieutenant huffed.

"Be prepared," I said. "I think this is only the beginning."

"You mean there might be more of this shit?" the lieutenant blinked at me in shock.

"That's exactly what I mean," I said. "I have possible dates and locations, but after today, those may not mean anything, other than to provide a distraction while the real action happens elsewhere."

"This is fucked up," the lieutenant shook his head. "I've never seen anything like this. Do you think it's real, Director?"

"It's as real as you can possibly imagine, except for the reasons given," I replied. "Those people didn't deserve what they got. You see that no murderers disappeared from prison to get killed, don't you?"

"I noticed that," he said.

"You'll see it again, guaranteed," I said. "This is only the beginning. After a while, if we don't find a way to stop it, nobody will be safe."

"Who is behind this?"

"Somebody you won't see coming," I said.

Du'Ferias—present

Tybus' Journal

We fought them—a multitude of monsters attacked the moment we touched the ground with corporeal feet. Reah became Thifilatha, burning any Ra'Ak who approached her. Aurelius and I had claws out, decapitating whatever came near. Farzi and Nenzi bit anything they could reach while Kevis placed a shield around Kay, Jett and Keith. Edward's War Eagle screamed overhead, snapping necks of giants leaping from the ground in an attempt to grasp a claw and pull him down. Philip's mountain lion snarled as he fought an aggressive harpy that dived in and out, taunting him as she attacked from the air. For a moment, the balance teetered, as we were afraid to employ power and draw more powerful enemies to the fray. And then, just as suddenly as we'd been attacked, the battle ended and every creature we fought disappeared.

"What the hell?" Edward landed nearby, puzzled by the sudden disappearances.

"There," Kay pointed toward a bare spot not far away. "A gate. I see it."

"They gated out of here?" Reah became herself and stared at the area Kay indicated.

"I don't believe it was their choice," Philip said.

"I feel the same," Keith nodded. We had four with us who could see gates easily—two half Elemaiya, one more than half and one pure blood.

"So they were pulled away to cause havoc somewhere else?" Jett asked.

"It looks that way," Edward replied. "I worry that there may be more than one destination, too. Face it—that's a lot of creatures to send to one place. There were enough of them to cause havoc in several places at once."

"This is awful," Kay moaned.

"Agreed. And we still haven't approached the compound," I said. "Is anyone hurt?"

"I'll check everyone over, then we can proceed," Kevis offered.

∾

Le-Ath Veronis—present

"This is the tenth report, sir."

Weariness threatened to overwhelm Kooper as he studied the comp-vid handed to him. On ten worlds in the Reth Alliance, pits had opened in crowded areas, regurgitating strange creatures that killed anything they could capture, ate what they could and tossed remains into the fiery pit that had birthed them to begin with. The news vids couldn't keep up with the multitudes of images pouring in from citizens who'd recorded the debacles from a safe distance.

"Koop, the worlds that believe in hell or a version of it are saying it's the end times," Trevor arrived in Kooper's office and tossed his comp-vid on the desk. "I hear Noppen has practically imploded through a massive pit, and the population has almost been destroyed or devoured."

"And nobody there to save any of them," Kooper sighed.

"Earth got hit," Grant rushed in and dropped another comp-vid on Kooper's desk. "Is anybody doing anything about this?"

"We've got people in the field, but this looks to be a hit-and-run type of offensive, and all we can do is react when an attack happens,"

Trevor said. "We have to be better than this or we'll go down with the rest."

"Any ideas?" Kooper turned pleading eyes toward the old vampire.

"None at the moment," Trevor shook his head. "Right now, I'm willing to entertain any suggestion, no matter how far-fetched or from what source."

"Can we get a meeting?" Kooper asked. "Bring in as many as we can muster?"

"I'll send messages," Grant offered.

"Can you send mindspeech?" Trevor asked.

"Hey, Lissa gave me blood. Of course I can send mindspeech." Grant was offended by the question.

"Then get on it," Trevor snapped. "We can't afford to waste any more time."

"On it," Grant said and rushed out of Kooper's office.

Breanne's Journal

"How many?" I pleaded with Ashe to tell me—after a while I couldn't stand to *Look* any longer.

"More than fifteen thousand, total," Ashe sighed and sat beside me. I'd dropped to the floor beside the kitchen island, and ended up with my back pressed against the base while I hugged myself.

"This is just an opening volley, isn't it?" I chewed my lower lip while studying Ashe's face. He was pale—that was easy enough to see. This had shaken him, too, but he'd faced it while I'd shrunk from the visions.

"Those creatures are being sucked back into the pits before anyone with weapons can arrive," Ashe added.

"Are the pits left behind?" I asked.

"Oddly enough, no," he replied. "They're opening to let the creatures out, and then sucking them back in after they've caused their chaos, leaving nothing of the crater behind."

"Fucking Acrimus," I muttered.

"Fucking Quislus. Fucking General," Ashe agreed with a decisive nod before pulling me onto his lap and wrapping his arms around me. "Baby, you're shaking," he sighed against my neck before planting a kiss there. "Just relax and let me hold you," he breathed. "Nobody's here to hurt my girl."

~

Tybus' Journal

"We have to stop. We're not getting anywhere," Reah brushed tendrils of pale hair back and shook her head. We'd passed the area housing the herd of creatures and through a tunnel formed of trees and vines. Darkness pressed about us as we walked farther and farther down the path, but we should have reached our destination long ago.

"What this?" Farzi grumbled. "Maze?"

"That doesn't sound good," Kevis whispered. "I think the trees are listening," he added.

This is scary, Kay's voice entered my mind. *I want to leave.*

The tunnel is gradually narrowing, Edward pointed out. *We think we're traveling in a straight line, too, but that's just not possible.*

Reah backed against me and my arm went around her protectively. We'd walked into a trap without bothering to consider that it might be such.

Farzi and Nenzi moved to flank Kay—I could tell both were prepared to protect her with their lives if necessary. None of us could tell anything about our surroundings by *Looking,* and we'd suspected it was because it was protected by the presence of Sirenali. Fear grew in my mind and I struggled to push it away.

We get out now, Nenzi's voice rumbled in my mind.

I think you're right, Aurelius responded.

We'll have to use power, Reah said.

I think we'll have to combine power at this point, Edward advised.

Do it now, Kay shrieked.

~

"Director Griff, half of Du'Ferias just exploded," Kooper's assistant was back and handing a comp-vid to Kooper with shaking fingers.

"What in the name of," Kooper snapped as he studied the vid in shock.

"It's all over the news vids, right beside the reports on the monsters," Kooper's assistant explained. "Director, what is happening? Is it really the end of the universe?"

"Dene, calm down, all right?" Kooper growled. "There's an explanation for all of this, we just don't know what it is, yet."

~

SouthStar

"Mom, I don't understand any of this." James Rome Jr. paced inside a massive kitchen, after Kathleen informed him he was no longer on Earth in the past.

"Jamie, if you'll sit down, I'll pour both of us a glass of wine and we'll talk," Kathleen coaxed.

"You look twenty-five," Jamie exploded. "This is ridiculous."

"Not from my end of it," Kathleen snapped. "James, sit down this minute and shut up. I have to tell you what's going on, and you're not going to like it."

~

Lissa's Journal

Even across time, I knew. Aurelius and Tybus had called out just before I felt the explosion around them. Then silence came and I was screaming mentally for help as I folded space and bent time.

CHAPTER 9

"What the hell happened?" Kyler asked. She and Cleo appeared shortly after Gavin and I arrived at my palace. That's where they'd been transported—by Larentii.

Karzac and most of the healers, including Cleo, worked frantically over mangled bodies, putting them back together as quickly as they could. Several Larentii, including Renegar and Lenigar, were helping. Surgical tables stood in a row inside my arboretum, each bearing a burned and broken body while several worked around every table.

"They got caught in a trap on Du'Ferias. Somebody expected them to come hunting Hordace Cayetes' stronghold there, and planned this attack carefully." I shook my head as I stared at Aurelius' body—he, Edward and Tybus had taken the brunt of the explosion, combining their shields to protect the others.

"Will this make Kay's situation worse?" Kyler drew me toward the doorway as she spoke.

"I hope not," I said. "We'll see how she is when they're done."

"I was hoping to get her help with a few politicians on Earth," Bill appeared beside me and shook his head. "They have obsessions, and Kay can change that."

"Is it worth wasting her time?" I shook my head at Bill.

"No idea," he shrugged. "Maybe it's selfish of me to even think about that. The same is likely going on elsewhere."

"Noppen," Kyler agreed. "That planet has almost been consumed."

"We need Breanne so badly," Gavin came to stand beside me.

"How is he?" I asked. Gavin knew I meant his vampire sire, Aurelius.

"Better, but Karzac says that it may take some time to make them whole again." I knew he meant that Breanne could *Change What Was* for all eleven who'd traveled to Du'Ferias.

"We only thought the God Wars had come before, didn't we?" Kyler shook her head. Flavio appeared and pulled her against him.

"It looks that way," I sighed. "I'll ask Cheedas to find rooms for these, once the healing is done."

～

"They're all healed and sleeping quietly." Karzac settled on a guest chair inside my study after spending hours healing bodies. I could tell he was exhausted—he'd used up everything he had to work as quickly as he could to bring them all back.

"You think it was a power trap, too, don't you?" I asked.

Lines formed around Karzac's mouth as he considered his reply. "Yes," he said after a moment. "They were wise not to use power in the beginning, but something happened and they felt the need for it. That triggered the trap."

"It sounds as if they're taking a page from the Copper Ra'Ak playbook," Dragon appeared and settled on the chair beside Karzac's. "You remember how we couldn't employ our power on any world where the Ra'Ak were, for fear that they'd destroy the planet because they knew we were there?"

"I remember," I said, giving Dragon a nod. He, Karzac and I had worked together to save Refizan long ago. I'd employed my abilities as a Vampire Queen, as those wouldn't appear on the Ra'Ak radar. Tybus' mist wouldn't have caused a stir, either.

"Were there Ra'Ak in any of those vids?" Dragon asked. "Where those gates appeared?"

"I saw a few," Kyler said. She and Flavio folded in to join the conversation.

"Have you contacted Youon?" I turned to her and asked.

"Yes. He says that no Ra'Ak from this time period is involved. That means they've collected others from the past."

"And that is the worst news of all," Karzac muttered. "Infected populations will fall quickly, and we have no way to fight all of this."

"We need a meeting." Kooper Griff walked in, closely followed by Trevor and Stellan.

"Ain't that the truth," I agreed.

~

Adam's Journal

"Ready?" I asked.

"Yeah." Kiarra sounded depressed, and that wasn't a good thing. We'd gotten the news regarding the explosion on Du'Ferias. We all worried over the same thing, we just hadn't voiced it aloud. Twice, now, the power we had hadn't been enough. Not even close, if anyone took time to study it thoroughly. It looked as though those thoughts were about to be discussed, only I feared that no solutions might be found to counteract what we faced.

"I'll drive," Merrill offered. I was willing to allow anyone else to fold us to Lissa's palace—it gave me more time to consider other things.

~

"This is where the woman is," Quislus informed Jarnis. "Take her and destroy the home. Immediately."

Jarnis glowered. He'd been involved involuntarily with too much of Quislus' dealings, and he hated his superior for it. Jarnis knew, too, that if the General ever discovered that Quislus could have done better research and destroyed Breanne Hayworth while she was still humanoid, he would be furious. Without her interference, much of their troubles could have been avoided and many of his colleagues would still exist.

Quislus hadn't thought to keep tabs on her, however. All he'd known at the time was that Breanne was half-sister to the Vampire Queen, and he'd laid a mind cloud on several to cause mischief for Le-Ath Veronis. Jarnis was instructed to bring the woman to Le-Ath Veronis and give orders to one of those affected afterward.

Jarnis felt anger at Quislus for treating him as an errand boy, as he was capable of so much more than what was reflected by his assignments. He'd offered a threat against those pathetic humans Breanne cared for, when she refused to come with him. She hadn't known at the time that he could be punished for harming them, and the threat had been quite effective, as it turned out.

"Get it done," Quislus growled. "You have two things to do. Get the woman and destroy the home. Go."

Jarnis went.

Lissa's Journal

My library was full. All the Saa Thalarr and anyone else with power, including several from Grey House, arrived. I hid my surprise when Kaldill and Lendill folded in with Ildevar and Willem Drifft.

Jayd, Glinda and Garde came as well, then Tory came with Salidar DeLuca. They appeared to be getting along, and that was a good thing. I'd worried that Tory would resent anyone who tried to teach him after learning from Drake and Drew.

"Mom," Ry leaned in to kiss my cheek when he, his father and Corolan appeared. A host of Larentii folded in last, with Kalenegar and the Wise Ones at the front.

"Quiet, please, we have much to discuss," Belen said, blowing out a flash of light to get everybody's attention.

"Good," someone said from the back. "What are we going to do?" he added. "We don't have enough power to do anything, or so it seems."

~

Adam's Journal

I shouldn't have been surprised. Joey was the one who spoke, and he spoke plainly.

"We've lost two rounds, and now they're opening their version of the gates of hell and spewing out monsters to kill anyone close enough and terrorizing the rest," Lisster said. "Devin and I went through the neighborhood on Earth and we have the names of those who died there, but there are ten other worlds in the Reth Alliance that were hit harder."

"We're talking two timelines," Dragon pointed out. "Only Earth in the past has been hit, while ten worlds in the present have been attacked. Eleven, if you count Noppen."

"Hordace Cayetes was involved on Noppen. I hear he died for his troubles," Grace said. "And then ours were hit trying to reach his stronghold on Du'Ferias."

"The creatures used in the attacks were housed in both places on Du'Ferias," Reah said. Nefrigar held her in his arms when they appeared, and I knew this early appearance by her was painful in many ways.

"They have disappeared from there," Nefrigar said. "Since they were discovered, another hiding place has been found, no doubt. Some of ours are watching, but the area has been abandoned."

"We never had an opportunity to destroy them," Reah's voice was rough, her words forced. "If we'd used power, we'd have been attacked sooner. The enemy was waiting for us."

"Have they gone to the past to collect these creatures?" Lisster asked. "If so, then it had to be before the Ra'Ak destroyed their worlds. The same goes for the Sirenali, does it not?"

"Selecting a time and place in the past to meet up with them and attempt to prevent the collection of these creatures would be like choosing one cherry from a tree full of them, and hoping to get the right one with no clues or evidence," Pheligar said. "You could be off by a single day, and be just as wrong as missing it by a century."

"Is he giving a cherry picking reference?" Gavin whispered in my ear.

"He probably came up with it to begin with," I muttered. "He's nearly three-quarters of a million years old, you know."

"Then we're no closer to a solution than we were when we got here," Kiarra said, frowning at Pheligar. She, like most of us, was clearly upset by this kind of attack by the enemy. Pheligar responded by lifting her in his arms and trilling softly.

"Is there any way we can track the enemy? Any at all?" Crane asked.

"All we can do is what they've done—search for expenditures of power. We'll only be reacting at that point, but at least it's something."

"Can we employ nexus echo for that?" Opal asked. I jerked my head in her direction—she stood in a corner, flanked by Jayson Rome and Bill Jennings. She'd only learned recently how to employ nexus echo, but the question was a valid one.

"That bears consideration," Kalenegar said. "I will put a team of Larentii on this and advise everyone if we arrive at a viable solution."

"We'd have to tune the net to fire at the first sign of power," Renegar observed. "And to filter out power that comes from wizards, warlocks and such."

"If we manage to do this—then we need a response team," Merrill pointed out.

"Like a fire department?" Joey asked.

"Yes—something like that. The Saa Thalarr had something similar, whenever a spawn attack warning went out." Kiarra, her arms wrapped around Pheligar's neck, was still listening carefully to the conversation.

"Tracking spawn was so much easier than tracking these will ever be," Belen said. "As well as being far less dangerous."

"Every Liaison knows how to track Ra'Ak and their spawn. Perhaps we can build on that premise," Renegar offered.

"We will employ every option," Kal agreed. "I have already sent mindspeech to the homeworld. Larentii are gathering to discuss the problem."

"If the Larentii employ nexus echo, will their power still be invisible?" Lisster asked.

"It should be," Pheligar gave a thoughtful answer. "As the Ra'Ak could never detect it before. We have those with power, here and now. Can you detect our power when we act?"

"Honey," Kiarra patted his face, "I can't feel your power. Even now."

"Awesome," Joey lifted his hands in the air and sighed happily.

"What can we do in the meantime?" Grace asked. "Anything?"

"Respond if you can and don't get killed," Hank growled. How had I missed him? He'd arrived as Grace asked her question.

"We have an announcement." Dragon and Crane rose, both nodding to Hank after Dragon spoke. "We've moved the High Demon army into the past to train them. They should be ready to go the next time one of those rogue gates opens. We'll see how those creatures match up to those designed to take them down in the beginning. Provided we get enough warning to get them there," he added.

"Then I believe the High Demons, led by the Falchani here, should be the response team, combined with any others they might choose to assist," Hank said. "I will be there as well, whenever possible."

"I'll be happy to help," Caylon Black rose to stand beside Dragon and Crane.

Tory? I sent. *How long did Dragon and the others train you?*

A year, he replied.

Holy cow, I responded.

Mom, we're as ready as we can be, he said. *I have a new respect for the Falchani, believe me.*

Tory, you have to be careful—you and your father. You know what happened to me and the others.

I know. We can fight the creatures they have—no problem. It's what came after you that I'm concerned about. I want to visit with Reah for a while, he nodded to me and walked toward Nefrigar. Reah slept in the Larentii's arms.

❧

Ry's Journal

"Hey, bro." I slapped Tory on the back. We'd had the same idea—to see Reah.

"Come with me," Nefrigar nodded to us. "I'll put her in bed so you can spend time with her."

"We're coming with you," Amara and Edan walked up. I nodded—Reah was asleep and likely to stay that way, so it wouldn't trouble her if her father visited for a while.

"What was she doing on Du'Ferias?" Edan asked after Nefrigar folded us to Reah's bedroom and placed her gently on the bed.

"Chasing after Hordace Cayetes' bunch so she could track Song and Serenade," I said.

"Who are they?" Amara turned dark, lovely eyes in my direction.

"Those child traffickers—the ones who bought, trained and sold Kay as a child sex slave," I replied. "Cayetes was one of their best customers."

"They buy children for this?" Amara asked. This information upset her; that was easy to see.

"Or steal them," Tory said. "They look for the pretty ones—girls and boys. At least that's what I heard from Sali."

"Any idea where they get these children?" Edan asked.

"None. That's why they wanted to reach Cayetes' hideaway—to find contact information on those two women. They likely have Sirenali there with them, so we can't get information on their location."

"The ASD and CSD can't help with this?" Edan asked. "By providing reports on missing children?"

"Edan, children go missing all the time," Reah spoke weakly from the bed. We all turned in her direction immediately.

"Baby, we're here," Edan sat on the side of the bed and took her hand. "Do you need anything?"

"Song and Serenade on a platter, and all those children in your care," she rasped, turning sleepy green eyes on Edan.

"I wondered what Aurelius meant when he asked if we could take some in," Amara placed a hand on Edan's shoulder.

"We don't know how many, even if we find them." Reah shifted, attempting to sit up in bed.

"Just lie still, we're fine," Edan stroked platinum hair away from her forehead. "If we need help to care for them, we'll ask. I'm sure there'll be plenty of volunteers. Now, I believe your mates want your attention." Edan stood to allow Tory and me to reach the bed.

Reah's Journal

The word *Daddy* almost escaped my lips as Edan moved away. He squeezed my fingers before letting them go and allowing Tory to take his place.

"Baby? How are you feeling?" Tory leaned in to kiss my forehead.

"You have more muscles," I blurted. He did. His shoulders looked wider and his upper arms strained the fabric of his shirt.

"I do." He leaned farther in and took my mouth with his. "I learned a lot from the Falchani," he said after pulling away. "How's Lexsi?"

"Good," I croaked. "Can I have some water?"

I had water in almost as much time as it took to blink, and Amara checked me over after Tory lifted me so I could drink.

"Are the others all right?" I asked after emptying the glass and handing it back.

"They are; most of them are still asleep," Amara smiled at me. "Karzac and several healers are watching them carefully."

"Farzi and Nenzi?"

"Want me to bring them?" Ry asked with a grin.

"You can put them in the bed with me—there's plenty of room," I pointed out.

"Then I'll get them," he said and disappeared. Two lion snakes came floating in moments later, Ry appearing with them and lowering them carefully onto the bed with power so they wouldn't wake. I smiled—I couldn't think of a single one of my mates who didn't love both of them.

"We've come up with a couple of solutions, but those are temporary fixes," Ry sighed, leaning over Tory to give me a kiss.

"Ry, go ahead and say it," I said. "With the level of power aimed at us, we're being backed into a corner. I was there when the blast hit, and it came as soon as we employed power. I thought we would be blown apart, but somehow, Tybus and Aurelius managed to keep their shields up while I held the rest of us together. We were still knocked around. I have a feeling Karzac had major reconstruction to do, too."

"That's no longer your concern, baby. We're all here, and that's all that matters," Tory soothed.

"Tory, I still want to find Song and Serenade. Breanne asked me to do that."

"Then go at it from an angle nobody expects," Tory grinned. "I learned that from Caylon Black."

"Edan?" Fes walked into the room, surprised to see his brother.

"Fes," Edan rose and surprised Fes by hugging him and clapping him on the back. "Still cooking?"

"In San Francisco in Earth's past. We're trying to lure Saxom and Moxas into a trap with seafood," Fes laughed.

"Ry, Tory, get Kay. Right now," I said.

"Why?" Tory stood, his mouth etched in a frown—he had no idea what I'd realized.

"Because Kay knows Song and Serenade, that's why. She may know where they go, what they do, their eating habits," I said. "Unless I'm wrong, they have plenty of money. That means they eat very, very well."

~

"Tell us everything you know about them," Lissa said. "No matter how insignificant it seems. Favorite foods, what they talked about, clothing they wore, everything."

She'd arrived with Gavin and Kay. Kay was still very weak from our ordeal, but she wanted to help.

"They're really particular about their clothes," Kay said. Nefrigar lifted a hand and made a comfortable chair appear so Kay could rest while she spoke. "They always talked about Drian."

"That's an expensive designer. Been around a while," Lissa said. "I have some of his things in my closet."

"We can approach from that direction, certainly," Amara said.

"What about food?" Fes asked.

"They always talked about going to Tulgalan to eat," Kay said. "I don't know which restaurants."

"Did they ever talk about a particular meal they ordered?"

"They always talked about an ox-roast they could get, and complained that reservations had to be made far in advance."

"They came to Dee's," I covered my mouth with a hand. Dee's still served my ox-roast recipe—it was always popular. "What do they look like, Kay? Describe them."

"I need power to show you," she said.

"I'll lend you some," Lissa declared and grasped Kay's hand in hers while light formed around her.

In very little time, we had three dimensional images floating in my bedroom while we studied Song and Serenade. Song was shorter, with dark hair stylishly caught up in a twist atop her head. With dark eyes, she wore makeup meant to lend mystery to her features. Wearing designer clothing, she looked to be a wealthy socialite instead of a child-selling criminal.

Serenade was a hand taller, with golden-blonde hair, likely dyed, and blue eyes that Kay claimed were enhanced with lenses. Also dressed very well, Serenade's image stood next to Song's as they seemed to silently discuss something.

I saw quickly that this image came directly from Kay's memory—

both images turned and beckoned someone to come to them. Neither of their expressions was kind. Kay shut the images down immediately.

"I've seen them at Desh's," Fes declared as we all sighed at the sudden disappearance. "Several times a turn, actually."

"Do you recall the names they use?" Lissa asked.

"Not those Kay has given us," Fes said. "It's something like—oh, Serena. Yes. Serena Mallus and Melody Molster."

"Malice and molester? That's appropriate," Lissa muttered. "When are they scheduled to come back—either to Desh's or Dee's?"

"I'll go check," Fes said.

"I'll come with you," Tory stood and stretched.

"I'll come," Lok appeared. "Do you think they'll have noodles?"

Fes' Journal

"I have to work tonight," I said. "Or I'd cook here for everybody." We stood in the kitchen of my restaurant, studying the comp-vid that held all the reservations. We'd found Song and Serenade easily enough —they had a table for four reserved in two eight-days. Dee's showed a reservation in a moon-turn, so they were alternating between Reah's and my restaurant quite frequently.

"Just think, those bitches have been coming here for years," Lok muttered. "Too bad we didn't know to look for them then."

"At least we know to look for them now," Tory observed. "And we'll be waiting, be assured of that."

"My question is this—who are the other two? The table is for four," I tapped the comp-vid.

"Probably one is Sirenali, and the other some sort of power wielder, to hide them and to shuttle them around," Lok said.

"That makes sense, but we have no idea who or what the power wielder might be," I agreed.

"We'll plan for the worst and hope for better," Tory said.

"Not bad for a trainee," Lok grinned and slapped Tory on the back.

~

Reah's Journal

"We have two eight-days," Kevis said, slipping into bed next to me. Farzi and Nenzi's snakes slept peacefully on the other side, oblivious to the parade of people in and out of my bedroom. "Fes says those women have a reservation at Desh's then. Lok, Tory and several others are having a planning session in Lissa's study right now."

"We can't let them be waiting for us, like they were this time," I agreed, settling my head on Kevis' shoulder. "We have to take them by surprise and take them quickly."

"We have two eight-days," Kevis repeated. "We have to plan this carefully. Young lives are in the balance."

"What's for dinner?" I snuggled against Kevis.

"I believe you might get anything you want," he kissed my forehead.

"I want Yaris fish," I sighed and closed my eyes.

~

Adam's Journal

"Do we have enough High Demons who know how to wait tables?" Lissa asked. It was a valid question—I'd never seen any of them perform menial labor.

We'd come to the conclusion that a High Demon waiter wouldn't be susceptible to a normal power wielder, such as a wizard or warlock.

"We have sixteen days to teach them," I said.

"But will they learn to serve or will they become belligerent with a grumpy customer?" Lissa asked. "Will we be able to utilize the reptanoids?"

"I can work with them," Kooper offered. "They can serve drinks and pour water, then be there at the proper time if someone needs to be bitten."

"I don't want any regular employees on duty that night," Merrill said. "Reah can cook, and we have enough among us who can assist. Franklin and Shane can come. Bill can cook, Flossie Thompson can cook—there's quite a list, actually."

"I'll be there," Lissa declared.

"Cleo, Kyler and I can help," Kiarra offered. "That ought to be enough."

"Just don't use power—for anything," Lissa said. "We can get caught that way. We've seen that already."

"You don't have to convince me," Kooper rolled his shoulders uncomfortably.

"Vampires can be standing by, in case compulsion is needed," Merrill suggested.

"I think that's a good idea—memories may have to be modified as well," Lissa agreed. "We just have to make it look like we're all supposed to be there. Anything out of the ordinary and we'll spook 'em."

"And possibly bring on another attack," Lok said. "That's the last thing we need or want."

"At least they won't question the quality of the food," I said, rubbing my forehead. We'd had a long day already, and it was approaching the dinner hour.

"Let's finish this discussion over dinner," Lissa said. "I'm starved and I'm getting mindspeech that food is ready."

"I can't help it if they're not here," Jarnis mumbled as he stared at the empty house. "There's no woman to take, but there's a house to destroy." Holding out a hand, he sent a bolt of energy toward the structure, smiling at the firebomb that erupted as it exploded. Plumes of black smoke reached skyward as he watched.

"I see you enjoy your explosions," a figure robed in dark gray appeared beside him. Jarnis attempted to step away—none except the most powerful might see through his shield.

"What?" Jarnis began, discovering that he couldn't move.

"Oh, I just want your power," the hooded one said. "And your death. In that order."

Jarnis opened his mouth to scream, but found he couldn't. Mindspeech was blocked, too, as his body shrank and his power left him in a rush.

~

Le-Ath Veronis—present

Lissa's Journal

"Kiarra," Flavio knelt beside her chair. "I'm afraid I have bad news." We'd gotten to the dessert course while still discussing how to take Song and Serenade. Until Flavio arrived, anyway.

"What is it?" Kiarra placed her napkin over her plate, her fingers trembling slightly. Adam and Merrill were already on alert, ready to react to whatever Flavio had to say.

"Your home in Fresno has been destroyed," Flavio reported. "Pheligar asked Daragar to watch it, but he has no idea what caused the explosion."

"Was anyone inside?" Kiarra gasped.

"No. Don't concern yourself with that—Joey was having dinner with Kyler and me when we got the news. Daragar asked me to convey the message."

"Where is Griffin?" I asked.

"Talking with Amara and Edan," Flavio replied.

"Let's go," Adam rose and tossed his napkin on the table. "We'll look at the damage and see what needs to be done."

"Take Larentii with you," I warned.

Without asking, several Larentii, including Pheligar and Renegar, arrived in my dining hall, ready to transport us back to Earth in the past.

"I'm ready," I said, standing and nodding to Merrill, who stood with me. Gavin was already up, preparing himself for whatever we might find when we arrived.

"We go," Pheligar nodded and transported us to Fresno.

~

Bill, Trajan, Jayson and Opal met us at the property. Local law enforcement had arrived, so we had to conceal our unusual arrival and come in by more mundane methods.

Several cars arrived within minutes of each other—Gavin and I were in the second car, behind Adam, Merrill and Kiarra.

"You the owner?" A police officer walked up to Adam.

"Yes," Adam replied. "Can you tell me what happened?"

"Explosion. Haven't determined a cause," the officer replied briskly. "Anybody home?"

"No. We were out having dinner," Adam replied, shaking his head at the pile of rubble beyond. "With a few friends. We came home as soon as we received word."

The pile still smoked and burned in a few spots, and I could see the twisted metal that used to be the refrigerator poking up amid a pile of burned cabinets and exploded canned goods.

Heading back to the car, I got inside, shut the door and turned to mist before going through the windshield. It was easier this way—I could go through the site without getting yelled at by the police and fire department.

All of Kiarra's things can be replaced in one way or another, I thought as I scanned everything carefully. That's when I saw it. At first, I imagined it was a piece of clothing that hadn't burned—it looked brown and flat to me as I misted toward it. It lay in the backyard, near the door. The scent reached me first—it smelled of death and disease.

What the? I attempted to puzzle this out in my mind. Reaching out with a tendril of power, I gently flipped it over before mentally screaming—it had a fucking *face*.

CHAPTER 10

*J*arnis, Gavin's mindspeech permeated my mind. He recognized what remained of the face. Adam and Merrill dispensed what might have been the fastest compulsion on record to get rid of the authorities on the scene, the moment they'd heard my scream in their minds.

I was still mist, so I sent my question back—*Jarnis?*

The one who brought Breanne to Le-Ath Veronis. Told me to turn her and then left with no explanation. You see where that got us, he added.

I know exactly where that got us, I replied stiffly. If Jarnis had bothered to explain, so many problems could have been avoided.

Rogue. Belen arrived in a corporeal fashion, and walked up to us. Lissa, Gavin and I will shield you if you wish to turn back.

I became myself and stared at the leathery pile of skin that still bore a face—Jarnis died in corporeal form, and that might present a puzzle to all of us. Not to mention how the hell he'd died to begin with—none of us were capable of doing what had been done to Jarnis, rogue or not. Not only had he been drained—his bones and internal organs had disintegrated, leaving only a puddle of skin behind. No matter how you looked at it, it wasn't pretty.

"I'll transport the body to the Larentii archives and allow them to take a look—this defies logic," Belen shook his head.

"It looks as if he were sucked dry," Gavin muttered.

"That's exactly what it looks to be," Belen allowed. "Yet I have never heard of such happening to one of the powerful. The body might be destroyed, yes, but this—I believe what he was no longer exists in any form."

"I saw something similar to this on Noppen," Kevis arrived, looking the worse for wear after folding in.

"On Noppen?" Adam, Kiarra and Merrill joined us, but Merrill was the one who asked. Kiarra looked ill as she studied the pile of skin lying on the ground.

"A rogue god was sitting in the Noppen President's chair. Something similar started happening to him, but I didn't see the whole thing—Cayetes and his guards started shooting Ranos pistols and destroyed the office around us. Things were so chaotic, I couldn't tell what eventually became of the rogue."

"So we're two rogues down, then," I blinked at Kevis. "Do you need to sit down or something? You look exhausted."

"I came as soon as I heard. I didn't even think about being this weak," Kevis replied.

"He's going home now," Karzac appeared and frowned at his son.

"Thanks, Dad," Kevis nodded. "I need the help."

"Then I won't yell," Karzac smiled and disappeared with Kevis.

"Belen, let me know about this," I toed the rubbery skin at my feet, "after the Larentii perform their examination."

"I will," Belen agreed and studied the pile distastefully before disappearing with it.

"My guess is that this rogue destroyed the house, and then something else destroyed him," Merrill speculated.

"Then he either messed up or pissed somebody off," I said. "Or both."

"If they wanted us to know they were after me, they certainly have my attention now," Kiarra mumbled. "Usually it's wise not to let your quarry know that you're hunting them."

"And you can't announce it any louder or more directly than this," Merrill said. "Is there room at your compound for all of us, Lissa?"

"Yes. Ashe's shield is still up, thank goodness."

"I wholeheartedly agree," Adam said.

~

"Quislus told him to take the woman and destroy the house. It appears as if he left his assignment half done and disappeared." Calhoun growled as he paced. He knew it was an extremely human thing to do. He did it anyway. "She has since relocated, and I cannot trace her."

"This is unacceptable," Moxas huffed. "We were given a promise. We are waiting for delivery on that promise. Did your experiments we suggested not go well? Is the population not sufficiently panicked? Tell me, how have we failed you?"

"It is merely a matter of time—she cannot hide from us forever," Calhoun snapped. "I suggest you recall to whom you speak."

"I have not forgotten," Moxas fumed. "We will wait patiently—for a little while."

"Good. I have planning to do," Calhoun said and disappeared.

~

"I can't find Jarnis," Calhoun complained to Quislus.

"I have not been able to reach him either, and that is most unusual. He has always followed through before, even when he found the assignment distasteful."

"What about the other Hidden—can you reach them?"

"Of course. Jarnis is the only one who has disappeared. No, that is not true—Hydel was destroyed with Cayetes on Noppen, and I have not heard from Morren or Ploddas."

"I know Hydel and Cayetes are dead," Calhoun reminded Quislus. "Killed by those we destroyed on Du'Ferias. Have Morren and Ploddas not been seen since then?"

"Not to my knowledge." Quislus felt a bit of fear before releasing it

—the Three were gone and the One had never destroyed any except for Acrimus, and Acrimus had defied the decree and murdered a Larentii.

"Keep looking—they'll appear," Quislus commanded. Calhoun nodded and disappeared.

~

Lissa's Journal

All of us had a bad night. Connegar eventually arrived and tapped my forehead, sending me into a healing sleep. I hadn't been able to get the vision of the rogue god's body out of my mind.

When I awoke in the morning, the same visions clouded my mind as I shuffled to the kitchen for coffee. Merrill was there ahead of me. "Come," he held out a hand after I poured a cup for myself. I went. He seated me on the barstool next to his and wrapped his arms about me.

"You smell good—like fresh coffee," I said as he kissed the side of my neck.

"You smell wonderful—like Lissa." I could feel his smile against my skin.

"How's Frankie?" I turned in his arms and kissed him.

"Frankie, as you put it, is just fine. He and Shane are chasing Farzi and Nenzi about this morning. He says he can't keep them in bed and they insist on crawling all over your palace. I believe they've scared half the vampires in the Council."

"Probably the wrong half," I said.

"You're saying half of them deserve to be scared?" Merrill asked before kissing me again.

"Maybe more than half," I shrugged. "But only by snakes. Big snakes."

"I hope they know not to attempt to harm those two."

"If they don't, they'll find out soon enough. I imagine Kooper would turn with them, and they'd have a vampire hunt."

Merrill smothered his snicker against my shoulder.

"Cara," Gavin touched my shoulder gently as he walked past. He was heading to the coffeemaker, just as Merrill and I had done. How happy was I that there was no jealousy between these two?

Kiarra and Adam wandered in next, closely followed by Joey. "I'll start breakfast," I said and pulled away from Merrill, who seemed reluctant to let me go. Kiarra and Joey helped me put biscuits, eggs, bacon and ham together while Merrill made more coffee and Adam and Gavin folded to the grocery store for milk, orange juice, jam and honey. Norton and Bearcat, two of Joey's mates, showed up as we sat to eat.

"I like this—having breakfast this way," Joey said, stuffing half a biscuit coated in butter and strawberry jam in his mouth.

"I like cooking in the morning for people I care about," I said. "Instead of being queenie pants every day."

"Queenie pants?" Adam almost guffawed.

"Grant and Heathe," I muttered. "They call me that."

"Not in my hearing," Gavin growled.

"Honey, nobody says anything in your hearing," I patted his back affectionately.

Norton slapped Joey's back when he choked on a mouthful of food.

"We have to make it look as if we suspect nothing," Adam sighed as we studied fixtures at a local home improvement warehouse. "I'll start rebuilding, so they'll realize we're still here."

"Then you'll need to get a temporary home and make it look as if you're there," Gavin said, lifting a faucet and studying it carefully.

"We have one in mind, and we'll make arrangements," Merrill said. "I just don't want to stay there often. Not after what happened to the last one."

"I'm just glad we weren't home," Joey shivered. Bearcat responded by hugging him.

"We only had a minimum of shielding in place," Adam took the faucet from Gavin and nodded at his choice. "The rogue tore through it as if it were tissue paper, and we didn't even get any alarm bells when the house blew."

"That's odd," I said. "We always know when our shields are breached."

"Not this time," Adam shook his head. "Merrill and I received no warning at all."

"I think I want wood and tile in the whole house," Kiarra said, handing paint chips to Adam.

"Good choice," I said, giving her a smile. "It's easier to change an area rug than carpet."

"Exactly what I was thinking."

"Martin can act as my construction manager," Adam said, tapping product information into his cell phone and then taking a photograph of the faucet. "I can be on the worksite most of the time and let my current construction manager handle other projects."

I kept forgetting that Adam was taking his own place in the past, when he owned a construction firm. He had work to do, just to make everything appear normal. At least Aryn and Rigo could take care of things for me on Le-Ath Veronis, which included stepping over lion snake shapeshifters inside my palace.

"Somebody say my name?" Martin walked around a tall shelf. Mack, his son, followed close behind. This was the adult Mack instead of his nine-year-old former self. That one was on Kiarra's private planet, playing with a young Justin.

"Good to see you," Adam grasped Martin's hand immediately and smiled at the werewolf-turned-Saa Thalarr. "We haven't built anything together in a long time."

"Hey, Dad," Justin stepped in behind Mack. "Thought we'd show up and help."

"Good," Adam grinned before hugging Justin. "I'll put you to work right away."

"I'll buy lumber tomorrow," Martin said. "I'll take these two with me." He nodded toward Justin and Mack.

"It's better, seeing Fresno from this height," Justin said. "Just wish the circumstances were better."

"Honey, I think we all feel that way." Kiarra put an arm around her son and hugged him.

~

Hank's Journal

"I heard you'd shown up," I grumbled. I almost couldn't look at him —to me, he was still Wisdom. Somewhere within him, Breanne lay. All I could think of—all I wanted—was to pull her away. I knew better than to try.

"It wouldn't do you any good, she isn't here," he said.

"What the hell are you talking about," I snarled, my response tinged with smoke.

"I mean she's safe elsewhere, that's what I mean," he snapped. "You could be a bit more respectful, you know."

"I want to see her." Yes, anybody could have guessed what my reaction would be. I loved her. Would never give up on that love. If she were alive and elsewhere, I needed to know where that was. *Now.*

"You'll see her, but we need to take a short trip into the past, first," he said, studying his fingernails absently. "I wouldn't look this healthy if I hadn't taken power from a few rogues recently," he added, lifting clear, gray eyes to study me.

"How is she?" I began. If this one wouldn't be healthy without acquired power, what would Breanne's condition be?

"She's fine—better now, actually. We're weak when we come back to corporeal bodies. It's like moving everything from a vast castle into a small tent. The power has to slowly accumulate or the body is destroyed. I'm pushing things at the moment, because so much needs to be done."

"You say I can see her?"

"If you come with me first. There's something we need to do— together. It affects our futures."

"Lead the way." I blew more smoke. I'd do almost anything if it got me to Breanne.

"I hoped you'd see things my way, instead of just being pissed," Wisdom grinned.

"How far into the past?" I asked.

"Not far." Images filtered into my mind and I stared at him in surprise.

~

Trajan's Journal

"They offered me a raise, and three other restaurants have called to hire me," Fes placed the rolled case containing his knives on the counter and blinked tiredly at me.

"Sit down and have a drink," Bill offered, rising to pull a bottle of expensive bourbon from the counter behind him.

"I could use it—the owner is talking about expanding the restaurant," Fes shook his head. He'd been on the job for ten days. Not much had happened in that time—Adam and his crew had made strides on rebuilding the house. The foundation and framework were up and construction crews were busy as ants putting the house back together. We'd gotten no obvious nibbles on Saxom or Moxas, however, while Lissa, Karzac and I were still waiting for word from the Larentii about Jarnis' remains.

Fes, however, was building a following for the restaurant, and an article was scheduled to appear in the newspaper in two days—the food critic had raved about the fish choices on the menu. "Thanks," Fes nodded to Bill as he accepted the generous portion of bourbon in a glass.

"Killings in Atlanta, Paris and London," Opal walked in and placed a tablet in front of Bill. Bill took his seat and flipped through the information. The homicidal virus had spread throughout Earth and people were dying everywhere.

"What will they do when they run out of poor people?" Fes asked, shaking his head. That was the one thing that continued—the senseless killings. At least we hadn't seen the apparent gates of hell open up again to swallow people—in the physical sense.

The video was still on the internet and many were screaming that it was the end times. In a way, they could be right. The same was happening in the Reth and Campiaan Alliances; images continuously shown of people dying when attacked by hellish creatures. Everybody was afraid.

"Grace and Devin say they can't get information fast enough when the killings take place," Jayson shuffled in, raking fingers through his hair in frustration. "They've saved a few, and the lion snakes have taken down several killers, but that seems to be too little too late."

"I heard from Trevor and Kooper," I said. "More gates are cropping up. Macy, Luanne and Elizabeth are finding them everywhere. Jerigar and several Larentii are ferrying them around, but they're getting tired."

"Any sign of where those creatures are now?" Opal asked, taking a barstool next to mine.

"None," I shrugged. "Du'Ferias is just a shell, now. Kooper has his agents searching for other likely spots, and Reah and her crew are following leads, but so far there's nothing. They could be going back and forth in time and we'd never know it. I have no idea how many Sirenali they have, but it has to be quite a few."

"Meanwhile, Song and Serenade are scheduled at Desh's in two days and the first of those arena events is in four," Bill shook his head. "So far, nothing has been announced for the arena in Chicago, but it will only take a blast on the internet to bring people in for whatever sick activities they have planned."

"Or whether that's only a diversion from the real activity," Jayson said. "I hate this. I hate not having a clue what's going on."

"How's Terry?" Opal asked.

"He's fine—I took him to the shooting range today and then handed him his Ranos pistol afterward—he's pretty good with a gun."

"I worry that he's not safe staying at his home," Bill sighed. "He could stay here or at Hank's place."

"I'll mention that to him," Jayson agreed. "He's working with the insurance company to rebuild his office. I told him not to worry about money."

"He's keeping in touch with Marco at SouthStar—Marco lets him know how his family is doing. They like it there. It's sort of a vacation for them."

"I'm glad they're away from this," Opal grimaced as she studied the tablet over Bill's shoulder. "It says here that people—the ones who can, anyway—are walking or driving out of New Orleans in droves. Campsites are overwhelmed with people trying to get away from poor areas. They're terrified the killers will show up at their doorsteps."

"The area has been hit twice already," Bill said. "They're not waiting for a third strike, but that doesn't mean that those bent on killing won't follow them."

"More than two hundred thousand dead worldwide, that can be attributed to this 'cleansing effort,' as the politicians are calling it," Opal said. "With more strikes coming in regularly. The news has even stopped talking about the latest celebrity scandal and concentrated on this genocide instead."

"I hear some of them speculating on where the next mass murder will take place," I muttered. "How sick is that? Websites are set up for that, with people prepared in certain cities to drive to the scene and watch the carnage. Sales of bullet-proof vests are through the roof, gun and ammunition sales have skyrocketed and who knows where the population is getting weapons in countries where they're not readily available?"

"Somebody will always look for a way to profit," Bill muttered. "Guns are likely coming from Russia and the U.S. A nine-millimeter submachine gun was used today in Paris to kill twenty-six people. That one came from Russia—no doubt about it."

"The police are slow to respond—I hear some of them have either been shot trying to defend victims or, in a couple of cases, joined in the massacre."

"It only takes a bit of obsession on those who are so-inclined," I said. "They act on their fantasies and with politicians backing them, few have been apprehended."

"You discussing the state of the nation?" Lissa folded in with Gavin and her Larentii.

"And a few other things, like where the weapons are coming from," Opal nodded.

"I've been hanging around the arena in Chicago the last few days, hoping to get information," Jayson said. "Nothing. The office has information on the reservation and payment, which leads back to Zeke and Obediah Tanner, but we already knew those things. There's nothing else, and the folks in the office don't care, as long as the money's good."

"Sirenali," Lissa shook her head. "Normal protocol flies out the window if they're involved."

"What are you doing up so late?" I asked, turning to Lissa. "I hear people call you queenie pants."

"I hear that's making the rounds," Gavin grumped. "I heard you were having drinks. I suggested we drop by."

"Then have a seat," Opal said. "I'll pour."

~

Reah's Journal

"Tory, is this going to work?" I blinked up at my High Demon mate. He and several other High Demons had been training at Desh's for the past three days so we'd be ready when Song and Serenade arrived in two days for dinner.

"I sure hope so," he replied, tucking my hair behind an ear and leaning down to kiss me.

"We've already sent your father home—he was ready to decapitate a customer," I pointed out.

"Dad has never had to work in the service industry," Tory grinned. "Ry, Nissa and I worked occasionally at Niff's. We know how to be nice to people, or at least pretend to be nice."

"This is our chance to take those women, save the children they've enslaved and give Kay closure," I pointed out. "We can't fuck this up."

"I want this almost as much as you," he kissed me again. "Nissa tells me they have the first batch of spelled Thifilathi swords ready."

"I sure hope they work instead of melting when you get your hands on them," I said. "A Thifilathi has never handled weapons before."

"They weren't needed before."

"I get that. We've never faced rogue-backed creatures before."

"Nissa says they've tested these in the hottest fires, and they've maintained integrity. She says they'll stay sharp and can't be used against the High Demon wielder."

"Let's hope you don't get overwhelmed anyway. How are the Larentii doing on the modified nexus echo net?"

"Sali says that they've done a few test runs and things are looking good," Tory said. "I hope they get it in place soon—I'm getting itchy about this."

"Like the other shoe is about to drop, as your mother says?"

"Yeah. Exactly."

"How many Thifilathi would it take—in your estimation—to combat what showed up via one of those gates?"

"Dragon, Crane and Caylon have discussed this with us. It looks as if twenty or thirty High Demons might handle that many monsters, as long as we're prepared and have some backup in case some of them try to get past us."

"Who is set up for that?" I asked.

"Trevor and Kooper have a bunch of Saa Thalarr who aren't working elsewhere. They're armed with Ranos pistols and rifles in case rogues show up. A couple of healers will be there to ferry civilians out of the way if things get nasty."

"And they can provide medical care if it's needed," I said. "We just can't use power the enemy will recognize."

"That's what Dragon thought," he agreed. "I'm worried about what the rogues might come up with later if our plan works."

"Tory, that's frightening," I shuddered.

"Baby, stop worrying, okay?" He pulled me against him in a tight hug. "Just promise me you'll head to SouthStar if things don't go well."

"I can't just run away," I muttered.

"Karzac has already put you together once. That scares me. I need you. Lexsi needs you. Ry and the others need you."

"Tory, the people who are dying need me, too." I watched as his face turned grim and he looked away to hide the curl of smoke drifting from his nostrils. "Look, it can't be helped. We are what we are and we were asked to do what we could."

"And yet the Mighty Heart almost got you killed," he turned back to me. "What has she done for you? For us?"

"You have a short memory," I pulled away from him. "If she hadn't intervened, we'd be overrun by rogues already. She bought us time, Torevik Rath, and I hope you remember that." I stalked away without a backward glance.

Tory's Journal

"Way to mess up, dude." Sali shook his head later as we shared a beer at a tavern in Cedar's Falls.

"I always mess up," I said. I wasn't drunk yet, but I was working on it. "I don't mean to—it just happens. Ry says all I have to do is open my mouth and the wrong shit comes out."

"Your brother may have gotten all the diplomacy," Sali agreed. "You seem to be all raw dumbfuckery."

"Thanks for taking my side of things," I growled. Smoke followed the comment and I didn't try to hold it back.

"Dude, you need to slow down. Your emotions come to the fore whenever you're with Reah—you can't help it. Just remember to think before opening your mouth."

"Aurelius says the same thing," I nodded after a moment.

"Aurelius would know," Sali said. "I figure he's seen just about everything by now. Besides, I was an idiot once. Took the Falchani ten years to beat it out of me."

"You mean you never make a mistake?" I offered Sali a skeptical frown.

"Oh, I make plenty, but they're calculated mistakes," he grinned.

"Come on, let's loosen you up with half an hour of blade practice."

"Fine. We can discuss how to apologize to Reah while we're at it," I said.

"And I'll have an apology for your gibe about Breanne," he pointed a finger at me. I'd forgotten she was Sali's mate.

"Fuck," I muttered.

~

Hank's Journal

"Just keep this between us," Wisdom advised.

I nodded—how could I do otherwise? A visit to Breanne was in the offing and I wasn't about to spoil that. What we—*I*—had done, I almost couldn't comprehend. "You'll know when the time is right," Wisdom said, as if he were reading my thoughts. Likely, he was. I didn't care.

"Ready, then?" Wisdom smiled. He knew, the bastard.

I nodded and he folded us away.

~

Breanne's Journal

I felt better. Ashe was certainly feeling better. He'd built a fire in the fireplace and lounged in a comfortable chair in front of it, reading a book. He'd even *Pulled* a cup of coffee to him, the schmuck. I was still working on things like that.

Coming home, Charles announced in mindspeech. I'd lost track of how long he'd been gone, but it was days in my estimation.

About time, I returned. I got a full-blown mental laugh back. Somebody was definitely feeling better.

Keeping my seat at the kitchen island, I waited for Charles to arrive while I sipped coffee. Someday, maybe I'd learn to read him better. Maybe. I wanted that information, and time wasn't on my side. Charles wasn't alone when he appeared—Hank stood beside him. My coffee cup shattered on the floor as I stood abruptly, but Hank was already there, pulling me into a hug I might never escape. I didn't want to. I drowned in his kisses.

~

"Baby?" Hank's voice was soft. Gentle. A hand smoothed my hair back when I opened my eyes. "Wisdom said you were weak. Sorry."

"Worth it," I stretched beside him. I'd lost consciousness when I climaxed. No surprise.

"I sure thought so." He grinned. I reached out to trace fingers over his mouth.

"I love you," I said.

"And I'm thankful," he leaned in to kiss me. "You ought to know I love you."

"After you said it about a hundred times, I sort of got the idea," I said.

"I wasn't sure how many times it would take," he said, nuzzling my neck.

"I'm glad you brought us here," I said, patting the mattress.

"Better than the kitchen floor," he agreed before kissing my collarbone.

"That floor is cold and hard," I said as he locked onto a nipple.

Not the only thing that's hard, he sent. Well, it was difficult to speak with your mouth full, I suppose.

~

Ashe's Journal

"He's giving her energy," Charles shrugged. We sat in front of the fire I'd built, considering our options. Charles had already given me as much energy as I could handle. I felt good—the best I'd felt since we'd separated.

"We're not strong enough to take on the General, but we're good enough now to cause havoc elsewhere," Charles said. "We just have to leave here in disguise."

"And make sure nobody can reveal us," I agreed.

"You can do that," Charles grinned.

"Yeah. I probably can. Where are we going first?"

"How about San Francisco for Breanne, Fresno for me and Le-Ath Veronis for you? Hank and the High Demons will be watching for the Gates of Hell to open."

"Have the Larentii perfected their nexus echo variation?"

"I had Hank send mindspeech. They're almost done implementing his suggestions. It'll be ready soon."

"You mean you told him what to say," I pointed out.

"Maybe." Charles shrugged modestly. "We had a discussion. He drew the proper conclusions."

"If we do this right, we can disguise ourselves to everyone except those we trust," I said.

"True. I'll vote for that. I'm not going as the old Charles, though. This is better. I like being myself."

"Why the disguise, then?"

"Less threatening. Harmless enough—in appearance, anyway. I'm thankful Flavio took the bait, though, and pulled me out of the Thames after I attempted a stunt dive."

"Flavio was a good choice."

"The best—as far as a vampire parent who was high in the vampire hierarchy went," Charles said. "I had to position myself close to Wlodek, so when the time came, I could nudge him toward the peace agreement with the werewolves."

"It wouldn't have happened, would it?" I blinked at him—only now realizing how much of a role he'd played.

"No, it wouldn't have happened. Wlodek is more than stubborn, as you already know."

"I know you sent me the complete file on the Elemaiya," I acknowledged.

"I kept Lissa alive—twice. Wlodek would have voted for her death without my intervention, and then, when she attempted suicide on Merrill's rooftop, I asked Wlodek for permission to go see her. When I arrived, she was floating in a bathtub. It took just a moment of time and bit of power, but she came out of it."

"And then you made the vamps forget her after Griffin pulled her away."

"It was prudent to do so."

"Yeah. I'm not sure she appreciated it so much at first, but I believe she sees the sense in it now."

"That was hard for her," Charles observed. "It's a testament to her strength that she made it through."

"What about Breanne?" I asked.

"Unforeseen—most of it," he shook his head. "I hope things smooth out eventually. Breanne's memories are horrible. Her inner strength is astounding."

"You got that—her memories?" I asked.

"I went looking for them while we were together. None of that was pleasant." Charles seemed troubled by what he'd seen, and I understood—what little I'd gotten from Breanne had frightened me horribly.

"What did you and Hank have to discuss?" I changed the subject. "Other than nexus echo?"

"This, among other things," Charles smiled and touched my arm. I blinked as the vision hit me.

A car drove along a street in a small Texas town. My breath stopped. The woman inside shrieked at what appeared in the street before her—an enormous High Demon stood there, his wings outspread, breathing clouds of smoke while stars fell through his eyes. Without a doubt, I knew she believed that the devil had arrived to collect her soul in exchange for her sins. Hank's presence caused the driver to skid to a stop, then back up and turn around quickly, her car tires screeching loudly as she sped in the opposite direction.

She didn't bother stopping for the traffic light, running right through it and into another vehicle. Joyce Christian died quickly. I knew the driver of the other car, who was drunk, would take the blame for her death—the local sheriff would see to that. Hank's Thifilathi had already disappeared when the sirens sounded.

CHAPTER 11

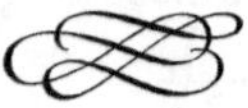

*B*reanne's Journal

"Ready to go see Bill, Trajan, Jayson and Fes?" I watched as a corner of Hank's mouth curled lazily when I opened my eyes.

"I'm hungry," I complained.

"You think Fes will let you starve?"

"No."

"Good. I think a quick bath is in order, then we'll go. Feel better?"

"I feel great." I surprised myself with the truth of my statement—I hadn't felt this good since before Charles, Ashe and I separated.

"It's amazing what a little sex will do." Hank gave me a mischievous grin before sliding off the bed and offering me a hand.

"Is sex the answer for everything?" I asked innocently.

"It doesn't hurt." He pulled me up and settled my body against his.

"You're so warm," I mumbled, my cheek pressed against his chest.

"To keep you warm." His arms tightened around me.

"You're doing a mighty fine job, then."

"Anytime." He grinned and pointed me toward the bathroom. "Shower. Now."

"Going. Will Bill be mad?"

"Bill will do handstands. Trajan will likely start howling."

"What about?" I couldn't finish because his hand went over my mouth.

"They'll be so happy to see you that anger won't be a consideration. Get clean and we'll go."

Trajan's Journal

"We'll have a visitor," I said. I'd just gotten word from Hank, and I almost couldn't contain my excitement. He was bringing Breanne to us first. I didn't bother asking questions. I knew Ashe and Charles were back as well, but Breanne was my first priority.

"Who?" Fes had risen late after a long night working at the restaurant. He was having difficulty getting days off—the owner wanted him there constantly to oversee the food preparations and to cook specialty dishes.

"It's a surprise. A really good one." My wolf wanted to howl, and it wasn't anywhere near the full moon.

"When?"

"Soon." I couldn't stop myself from grinning.

"What are you hiding?" Bill's eyes narrowed in speculation.

"The best secret ever. I'd tell you, but then Hank would kill me."

"What the hell are you talking about?" Jayson stalked toward me, wearing a heavy frown.

"This." Hank appeared, grinning foolishly. Jayson whooped when Breanne stepped from behind him, an uncertain smile making her lower lip tremble.

As a werewolf, I wouldn't have thought it possible, but Bill beat me to Breanne. He held her in a tight embrace and whispered tender words while the rest of us stood there, waiting for our turn.

Breanne's Journal

Tears came—I couldn't help it. Bill whispered how much he loved me while holding me and rocking my body. That felt so good. I understood, too, that he'd imagined he might not see me again.

"I'm sorry, honey," I apologized when I was able to pull away. "I wasn't in control to let you know otherwise."

"I know." Bill leaned in to kiss me. "That's in the past. I'm just glad you're here now."

"Bree?" Trajan's deep brown eyes seemed concerned as Bill moved away to allow my werewolf to step in.

"Trajan?" I sniffled when his hands cupped my face.

"I missed you so much." I was lifted, carried and settled on the kitchen island, where Trajan accepted a tissue from Fes and tended to the tears tracking my cheeks.

"She's hungry," Hank said.

"We can fix that," Fes declared.

Ashe's Journal

"Baby?"

"Huh?" Kay was sleeping and I'd woke her.

"Sweetheart, I'm back."

"Ashe?" One eye opened, revealing the startling blue that I'd loved the moment I'd seen it as a thirteen-year-old. I grinned at her. What I wasn't expecting happened next—she was in my arms and pressing kisses to every part of my face and neck she could reach.

"Slow down," I teased as she pulled away to touch me with trembling fingers—as if she were making sure I was real and not a dream.

"Bree?" She whispered a plea.

"Fine. Visiting with her other mates at the moment. We'll catch up to her soon. I just wanted a little time with you—alone."

"I want that, too," Kay nodded. "Things are different for me now. Do I thank you for that?"

"Thank Breanne. She changed things for you. I hope you don't mind."

"I love her for it," Kay nodded emphatically. "Everything is so much better—easier for me to deal with."

"I know you got hurt," I pulled her into a tight embrace.

"But Karzac fixed us. I'm fine. The others are, too."

"Charles said so." I kissed her. Then kissed her again. She didn't protest when I gently lowered her body and followed it down.

Lissa's Journal

"I heard you wanted to yell." Charles appeared inside the kitchen at the Fresno compound. Adam and Kiarra were there with me and both stared as he'd made his appearance.

"I don't want to yell—not exactly," I said. "This is you, right? And not the One?"

"It's me," he nodded. "Go ahead, say what's on your mind."

"Charles," I shook my head, not sure where to start. "Look, let's table this for now. You knew so much all along, and there I was, fumbling my way through everything. Thinking that you were merely Wlodek's mild-mannered assistant and the vampire who was so organized he could do sixteen things at once."

"Think of this from my point of view," Charles said, sliding onto a barstool and accepting a glass of orange juice from Kiarra. "How hard it was for me to bite my tongue and keep that information to myself—to save both of us." He drank half the glass before sighing and going silent for a few moments.

"Moxas was connected to Xenides, did you know? Saxom made sure of that," Charles said.

"What the hell?" Adam, his brow furrowed in consternation, spoke for the first time.

"They always had mindspeech—the special kind between twins. The Ra'Ak couldn't shut that down, even when they held Moxas captive for so long."

"Are you saying that Moxas may have been pulling some of

Xenides' strings—after Saxom's death?" I almost held my breath, waiting for the answer.

"I believe so," Charles said. "Nearly every move the vampires made was marked by Xenides and transferred to Moxas. The only thing that he had difficulty tracking was anything to do with you, Lissa." He nodded dark eyes at me. Yes, this Charles hadn't bothered to disguise himself. This Charles was taller. Stronger. Held a presence that would cause most to back away. The other Charles? He'd seemed so approachable and nonthreatening. If I'd met this Charles the first time, I'd have backed away. Instead, I'd been comfortable with him before. Found it easy to talk with him. I'd been so afraid in the past of sharing secrets with him—afraid they'd go straight to Wlodek. Charles would have only shared what he deemed necessary for Wlodek to know. My most personal concerns he would have kept to himself.

"I missed you," I stepped forward and surprised him with a hug.

"And I missed you." He offered a lopsided grin when I pulled away. "Sorry about all the subterfuge. I had to do what I felt was right to protect everybody involved."

"I sort of understand. I think," I replied. "What worries me is what we're supposed to do now. The General can wipe all of us out. I'm not sure we have enough in our arsenal to defeat him."

"That's why we have to be creative," Charles shrugged.

Breanne's Journal

"I'm stuffed," I waved away a third helping of mushroom soup. Fes had taken care of me—and then some. The mushroom soup he'd made the day before was exceptional, and it had taken no time at all for him to heat it with power so I could eat.

"How do you like being you now?" I smiled at him.

"I love it. It came as a huge surprise, but I'll admit that I got used to it quickly."

"I love that you love it," I shrugged. "And I love your soup. I just can't eat anything else right now or I'll explode. Really."

"Then I'll cook something else later. I have to go to work in an hour."

I don't suppose you'd consider coming to bed with me before that? he sent mindspeech.

Uh, okay, I responded. *Sorry, that hesitation is nervousness, and not because I don't want to,* I added.

I know. Come on. We'll do this together. Don't feel uncomfortable, love. We'll find our way.

Finding our way was exactly what we did. Fes was a considerate (and extremely passionate) lover. He let me know what he wanted. Asked me what I wanted. I fumbled my way through that, eventually losing the embarrassment and telling him what made me feel good and what brought me to climax. Fes made sure I got those things. And then some.

Later, I watched him dress for work. We talked as he moved comfortably through the bedroom, slipping into a shirt and choosing a pair of shoes to wear in a busy restaurant kitchen.

"We're attempting to lure Saxom in," he explained as he sat on the side of the bed to put on socks and shoes. "Griffin said the bastard loves seafood. I'm cooking the best seafood in San Francisco. Reah is waiting for Song and Serenade to show up at Desh's in Targis," he added. "For years, they've made regular reservations. Those bitches have been right under our noses and we never knew."

I watched Fes' hands clench—I knew that disturbed him. I knew that Reah's abuse at Edan Desh's hands troubled him, too. He'd been unaware of it, as he'd worked the restaurant in Targis while she was sent to Edan in Shirves.

"Edan isn't the same man you knew as your brother." I rubbed his back gently.

"I know. I like this one. Edan now would never consider a jealous contest of wills or a foolish competition for our father's approval."

"I realize Reah was uncomfortable at first with this, but Kifirin actually did a good thing when he exchanged this Edan for the other."

"Kifirin's dead."

"I heard. I have to talk to my sister about that." I swung my feet off the side of the bed and stood to stretch.

"You're beautiful." Fes pulled me to him and planted a kiss on my lower back.

"And so are you." I leaned down to kiss him. "Plus, you make awesome mushroom soup."

"I have to go to work." He patted my bottom gently. "Although I'd like to stay home and keep loving you."

"Go to work. I'll go talk to Lissa."

Jayson followed me around after Fes went to work and I showered and dressed. "Jayson, I'll get to you, I promise," I said after he lifted my top to play with my nipples.

"We uh, have something to tell you," Bill walked in with Trajan.

"What's that?"

"When Terry was brought over, well, we taught him how to separate particles. It was a good thing, too—a Sirenali and a lawyer showed up at his office with Laurel Rome."

"So, which one got separated? The lawyer or the Sirenali?"

"The Sirenali, silly," Bill grinned. "But that's not what we have to own up to."

"Then what have you done?" Yeah, I was waiting for the big reveal.

"Your TinyCar is toast crumbs. Terry separated its particles."

"You did not separate my TinyCar. I liked my TinyCar."

"Sweetheart, I'll buy you something else," Bill soothed. "That wasn't really a car anyway. If it'll fit in a pocket, it's not a car."

"Seriously?" My hands were on my hips and I was feeling more than a little miffed. "You destroy my stuff the minute I'm gone?"

"Baby, I'll take you out and buy whatever you want," Jayson broke in. "As long as it's big enough for a normal person to fit inside."

"So I'm not normal?"

"Jayson, shut the hell up," Hank walked in. "Stop digging a deeper hole. If she wants her TinyCar back, you can reform one. And make it strong enough to withstand almost anything."

"I'll do that," Jayson stalked out of the room.

"Look who I brought." Hank grinned when Chazi, Bekzi and Perzi walked in behind him.

"Hey, you!" I held my arms out. I was covered by lion snake shapeshifters in no time.

"We go with you. Wherever." Chazi grinned after I'd kissed all three of them.

"That will be awesome," I said. "Want to take me to Fresno? I have to see Lissa."

"We go." Bekzi agreed.

"I'll come, just in case," Trajan said.

"Thanks, honey."

～

Lissa's Journal

Charles tapped me on the shoulder—he was having a late lunch that Kiarra and I had thrown together for him, and I'd sat beside him, a glass of tea in my hand while he ate. "She's coming," he said.

"Who?" The question was automatic.

"Me." Breanne appeared beside me, with Chazi, Bekzi, Perzi and Trajan right behind her.

"Bree." I stood and hugged her, fighting back tears as I did so.

"Good to see you, too," she whispered before kissing my cheek. "We need to talk. In private."

Five minutes later, we left Trajan and Bree's reptanoids in the kitchen with Adam, Merrill, Kiarra and Gavin while she and I went to the media room to talk. I had a guess as to what she wanted to talk about, and I didn't have any good answers.

"Kifirin," she sighed once the door was shut behind us.

"Yeah." I flopped onto a nearby chair with a sigh.

"What do you want?" she asked.

"I do and I don't want him back, and I know that's not an answer."

"If I bring him back, he won't be tied to Quislus any longer. He'll be my child, just as Thurlow is Charles's."

"You'll be Kifirin's parent?" I stared—I know I did.

"If I bring him back. I just wanted to make sure you were okay with that. If you absolutely don't want him back, then I'll leave him dead, but honestly, he could be a big help to us."

"I don't want him gone forever," I mumbled.

"You just have to get past a few hurts; I understand that," Bree said. She sent me *Love*, then, and it drove a shiver through me as I reveled in it.

"Look, I'll use up the energy I have to do this, but I'll stay on the Larentii homeworld for a few days with my Larentii and my lion snakes, until I build my strength up again. Coming back to a corporeal body sucks."

"I understand," I said. I did. I'd come back to a corporeal body before after leaving it behind for a while. It had taken time to get my strength back. I also recalled who'd lent me strength then—Kifirin.

"Then let's do this," I said, suddenly determined to see it through. Kifirin and I still had things to discuss.

"Great. Let's get the reptanoids and go. Kal will probably be pissed, but that won't be any different from how he usually is," she said philosophically.

Breanne's Journal

"Shall I keep the decoys in the archives?" Nefrigar beamed at me when Lissa and I arrived in the Archives.

"Sure. You never know when those things might come in handy," I said.

"My Love, you could have sent mindspeech."

Just as I expected, Kal was pissed when he arrived. His red hair crackled with the energy of his annoyance, and it would likely fry any normal person if they happened to touch it.

"Kalenegar, rejoice that she came to us," Barrigar and Graegar appeared together. Barrigar was the one handing a lesson to the new Head of the Larentii Council, however.

"I am rejoicing," Kal snapped.

"Good lord, I'd hate to see what happy looks like," Lissa muttered.

"Honey, you can yell later," I pointed out. "Lissa and I have things to do, first."

"What things? Li'Neruh said you were weak."

"Remind me to kick Li'Neruh's ass—later," I said. "I have enough energy for this. And then you get to put up with me and yell as much as you like until I'm strong enough to kick your ass."

"You will stay with me?" Kal expressed disbelief.

"I said that. Although I'd like Graegar and Barrigar with me, too."

"Then you will stay here and the Larentii will protect you."

"There's something I'd like to discuss with the Council, when you meet next time."

"I will put your request forward," Graegar nodded, after offering me a sly smile.

"We also protect," Chazi announced.

"You absolutely will," I agreed.

"Poison does not affect Larentii," Kal huffed.

"I can change that," I pointed a finger at him.

"I think we should leave things as they are," Lissa intervened.

"True. Stop pissing me off," I waggled my finger at Kal.

"I can't help it," he mumbled, before lifting me and kissing me soundly. "There. That is for making me worry."

Honey, I'm sorry about your father. I stroked his cheek to convey my sincerity.

Keep touching me and I will fold you to a very private place, he kissed me again.

Let's save that for later, okay? I kissed him to seal the deal.

I will not forget.

"Nefrigar, Lissa and I need to see Kifirin's body," I said aloud.

"We will come with you," Kal announced. He wasn't done handing out orders, looked like.

~

Kifirin's black scales were tinged with gray in death, and it was sad to see such a vibrant Thifilathi devoid of life and energy. I'd never really met him—what I knew I'd read from Lissa.

"You should move away from Breanne," Kal cautioned my reptanoids. "The backwash of energy will be enormous."

I waited until Chazi and the others stood at a safe distance before lifting my hands and pulling in every ounce of energy I could muster.

~

Lissa's Journal

The Archives filled with light—the brightness even penetrated opaque walls as Bree worked her miracle. I had no idea how Kifirin might be or feel when she brought him back, but I imagined he'd demand many answers. What surprised me was this; when the light dissipated and Kifirin's Thifilathi opened its eyes, a slow smile curved his lips before he changed back to humanoid.

We'll need time alone, my sister sent mindspeech. *And then I'll need some sleep.* I folded the reptanoids away while Kal and the other Larentii reluctantly followed.

~

Breanne's Journal

"This is how it should have been in the beginning, isn't it?" Kifirin lifted an eyebrow at me. My sudden exhaustion forced me to take a sitting position on the floor so he followed suit, watching me carefully.

"Yes," I nodded wearily. "I don't have a lot of time—I was forced to use up everything I had to bring you back," I said. "But you're stronger, now. I made you Ghi'Yisi."

"Why?" He lowered his head, afraid to look at me suddenly.

"To make you strong enough to rule the Dark Realm," I replied with a shrug. "It would have been done in the beginning when you volunteered, had anyone besides Quislus been your parent."

"You knew?" His head jerked up at my answer.

"Wisdom knew."

"Of course. But you are my parent now? I cannot express my gratitude for that."

"You don't have to. Bear in mind that you are new, too. All your old promises are gone. Li'Neruh will still supervise, but it is my hope that his supervision will be light in the future. And you may always approach me or the others, if you want."

"What about Quislus?" The question was a growl and a curl of smoke drifted away with an angry breath.

"We have to kill him. You know that, don't you?"

"I do." He didn't sound upset.

"Separate his particles if you see him. Don't bother to talk. That's what got us in trouble last time—we stayed for a chat and the General appeared."

"I understand. I will deal with any of the other Hidden the same way."

"Only a few of them might be stronger than you are now," I pointed out. "What they know—or think they know—is that you're dead. If they see you again, they'll expect you to be the same—a Nameless One. They won't expect this." I held out my hands tiredly. "So don't let any of the others know what you are now. Even Lissa. I think she's willing to forgive, especially since you can show her you've changed."

"It will help a great deal for her and the others to know that you are now my parent."

"Yes, but make sure that stays within the confines of our allies. The enemy doesn't need to know."

"I understand that." He smiled, which caused his dark eyes to light beautifully.

"Great. Let's go. I'm exhausted."

~

Lissa's Journal

A wave of emotion hit me when I saw Kifirin walk in with Breanne in his arms. Already her eyes were closed—she was beyond tired. Kifirin offered me a dazzling smile as he handed Bree to Kalenegar before stalking in my direction. I didn't try to stop him. When he leaned in to kiss me, love enveloped me such as I'd never felt from him before.

Yes, I knew it was from Breanne and I blessed her for it.

Ashe's Journal

"You're going after Song and Serenade, plus anybody else they bring along?" Kay rested in the crook of my arm in Lissa's arboretum while Edward, Reah and I spoke of their current mission.

"Yes. They have reservations at Desh's. For four," Reah said. "We arranged to have High Demons waiting on tables while they're there, and more than enough in the kitchen to take care of the situation. I hope," she added.

"I'll help," I offered. "I'd like to see them go down myself."

"Tomorrow night," Reah sighed. Kay huddled tighter against me. We had to be extremely careful—if the General was keeping a watch over Song and Serenade, we stood to lose a lot if we caught his attention a second time.

"I'll contact Trajan and we'll start shielding the restaurant," I offered. "To keep damage at a minimum, if it comes to that."

"Good idea. Let me know if I can help," Edward agreed. "We don't need to be obvious," he added.

"We can do this invisibly—as mist," I said. "Nobody will know we're there."

Are you sure? Kay's mental voice was small and tentative.

As sure as I can be in such unstable times, I assured her. *Nowadays, nobody can be one hundred percent certain of anything.*

I can't lose you again.

I know, baby. Don't ever forget that I love you. Okay?

I won't forget. Ever.

"How good are you in a kitchen?" Reah asked.

"I can boil water," I grinned. "Scramble eggs. Peel potatoes."

"We'll let you wash dishes," she grinned.

"Sounds about right," I laughed.

"I'll help. Wash dishes, that is. I can do that, no problem," Kay said.

"Are you sure?" Reah asked.

"Yes. I want to be with Ashe and the rest of you. This is important to me."

"Baby, hide in the kitchen if it gets to be too much," I said.

"I know that I need to be as calm as possible," Kay replied. "I swear I won't give us away."

"Then we'll do this," I agreed, leaning in to steal a kiss. "Those women won't know what hit them."

⁓

Lissa's Journal

"Do you love me still?" I snuggled in Kifirin's embrace atop my palace as he asked the question.

"Yes. You ought to know better than that," I mumbled. Rain threatened on a cool day in Lissia, although it hadn't fallen as yet. "I just have some issues regarding Gavril and Reah."

"I know. I should have considered other options. I did not."

"At least Tybus holds my son's soul."

"At least something went right," Kifirin agreed while nuzzling my neck and collarbone. "Tybus was more than honorable. He died defending his daughter, the former Queen of Le-Ath Veronis. *You.*" Kifirin's mouth took mine in a breath-stealing kiss. "I loved you then, but I was foolish and slept, leaving you unguarded."

"I believe Quislus may have had a hand in that, at Acrimus' command," I said when he pulled away. "This may be hard for you to hear, honey, but I think they were pulling subtle strings all along, and as long as your actions didn't interfere with their plans, you had some measure of free will."

"But it angers me that they were pulling my strings, but that is a weak description of what they actually accomplished."

"I agree," I said. "They were fucking everybody, we just didn't know it."

"They deserve the fucking this time," Kifirin blew a cloud of smoke. It drifted away on the breeze as he pondered his life and previous fate.

"Honey, I don't ever want to see you dead again," I sighed.

"I never wish to be visited by that condition again," he conceded. "I really was dead. I recall nothing after the initial pain."

"How do you feel about Breanne being your parent now?"

"I am more grateful than I have words to describe. When I woke this time, I knew I was loved. Quislus always said he loved me, and perhaps he did in an extremely warped fashion, but it was never like this. Not even close."

"Breanne has that way about her," I said, nodding. "She sent *Love* to Gavin and me after Gavril died. I can't begin to describe that feeling, or how it helped us. Gavin is a different person, now. I can't ever repay that debt. He mistreated her horribly and she still did that for him."

"She saved Gavril's life on several occasions. She just wasn't familiar enough with her abilities to read what was happening to him until it was too late. Either way, an innocent would have died. It would have been a choice between Gavril and Tybus."

"I know."

"Avilepha? Will we live through this?" Kifirin gathered me closer to him. His warmth enveloped me as the air became cooler and raindrops fell.

"I don't know," I replied. "I just don't know."

CHAPTER 12

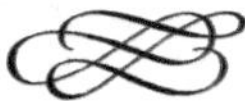

*B*reanne's Journal

"Many will be at the Desh restaurant in Tulgalan's capital tonight, waiting for those terrible women to arrive for dinner," Kal informed me when I woke.

"How long have I been out?" I rasped, rubbing my eyes to clear them of sleep.

"Nearly a day," he replied. "Graegar and Barrigar are nearby—they have taken turns watching you when I wasn't available."

"That's nice," I said. "Is there anything to drink?"

"We have anything you might want," he smiled.

"You have a nice smile," I said.

"You give me a compliment?"

"I'd give you a lot more if you weren't so grumpy most of the time."

"I'll work on that."

"I sure hope so. I might tell you how handsome you are—when you're not being an ass."

"You're calling me a member of the Equidae family?"

"Okay, you're being an ass again."

"I cannot be again what I already am."

"So you're saying once an ass, always an ass?"

"Please, no convoluted logic," he pleaded. "Come with me, I'll offer you food. I won't even place caterpillars in it."

"Didn't you have a childhood?" I asked as he lifted and carried me toward a very tall doorway. "That's what kids do."

"I had a very strict and public upbringing," Kal declared.

"Oh. The preacher's kid. I get it now."

"I fail to understand the ref—ah. Never mind."

"Just don't put caterpillars in my food. I like caterpillars. Just not to eat."

"I understand that. I was merely teasing."

"Awesome."

"How feeling?" Chazi, Bekzi and Perzi appeared inside what looked to be an enormous kitchen. The room had been sized for humanoids, too, and I was grateful as Kal settled me on a barstool at the island.

"I feel better," I said. "What do we have to eat?"

"All things," Bekzi grinned. "We make guacamole. It good."

"You made guacamole? Do we have chips?"

"We do," Perzi smiled shyly. "That why we make guacamole. We have cheese. Fruit. Pasta. All things."

"You are amazing. I love you."

"That good. We want love from you. We give love back. It work."

"Eat first," Chazi ordered with a grin.

"Yeah. Eat first," I confirmed with an answering smile.

Lissa's Journal

"I'm worried about tonight."

"Cara, it will go as it will. Stop second-guessing yourself." Gavin's arms went around me, settling me against his chest. We were still in Fresno, but planned to leave for Le-Ath Veronis in less than an hour. Everyone going to Tulgalan would gather in my library, and several

Larentii would fold us to Desh's in Targis. Adam, Merrill and Kiarra intended to go, leaving Martin, Mack and Justin behind to watch things in Fresno. Bill, Trajan, Jayson, Opal and Terry would keep an eye on the Bay area while all of us remained loosely connected by mindspeech—everybody was spooked about the upcoming raid and its potential consequences.

I knew where Bree and Ashe were—Ashe intended to help at Desh's. Nobody knew where Charles was and I didn't want to disturb him with mindspeech—I had no idea what he might be doing and if he wanted me to know, I figured he'd tell me.

Charles's Journal

"Those locations you gave me were quite productive," I said. Kaldill and I shared a glass of wine inside his private study.

"I have several more, if you're interested," he smiled.

"Of course. That's why I dropped by. For information and the wine." I held up my glass. "This is excellent."

"A thousand-year vintage," Kaldill informed me. "As the future seems somewhat uncertain, we may as well drink it."

"A good enough reason," I agreed. Kaldill sent information as we sat in companionable silence and drank.

Reah's Journal

"Stop fretting. We'll be with you," Tory soothed.

I was going through lists on my comp-vid, making sure everything was in place for the dinner menu. We were scheduled to arrive two clicks before the dinner rush, send the regular employees home via Larentii and take over the restaurant.

"I have to make sure everything is right. We can't make them suspicious for any reason," I mumbled. The High Demons we'd trained to wait tables stood nearby, talking quietly. Mostly, I worried about them and their ability to show deference to wealthy clientele.

"We're here." Grace and Devin appeared, accompanied by Renegar. Lissa folded in with Connegar and Reemagar, and was accompanied by Adam, Gavin, Merrill and Kiarra.

"Kay and I are ready," Ashe folded in with Kay. I studied her briefly —she was pale, but her hands were steady.

"Then let's go," I sighed.

Desh's kitchen was a hive of activity when we arrived. As planned, Connegar and Reemagar folded the employees away from the restaurant. They'd been given the night off—with pay—at Fes' direction.

The rest of us went to work—the doors would open shortly and diners would come in for the evening meal at one of the two best restaurants in Targis. I tasted and studied what had already been prepared—the fish would be last on the list to get ready.

"Things will go as they will," Aurelius leaned in to kiss my cheek.

"I know," I nodded, tossing spices into a saucepan and stirring vigorously. "That doesn't keep me from worrying about it anyway."

"I know. Tybus is quite concerned about you, but won't approach as he doesn't want to distract you more than you are already."

"I love him," I said simply.

"I know. He is a patient man. That is a good thing."

"Auri," I mumbled softly.

"Reah, we love you. That's all that matters."

"That, and getting through the night unscathed," I replied.

"Agreed."

Bill's Journal

I knew what was happening on Tulgalan. Everybody was treading softly, worried that the General was keeping tabs on Song and Serenade, after the debacle with Hordace Cayetes. After all—those women had a Sirenali with them, and likely power wielders as well. Those power wielders might be rogue gods—one of those had been with Cayetes.

Oddly enough, Kevis had seen that one shrivel, much like the one we'd found at Adam's home in Fresno. I had no explanation for that, and the Larentii hadn't revealed any findings after examining the body. The truth might be that they had no better idea than the rest of us, and were still attempting to solve the puzzle.

Bill? The sending came from Fes, who was working at the restaurant.

Fes?

We may have a hit, Fes sent. *I can't say for sure, but the reservation seems suspicious.*

What is it?

A reservation for Bayar and Rayab.

A name reversed? Like Saxom and Moxas?

Exactly.

When are they scheduled to arrive?

At eight tonight. I looked over the reservations list yesterday, and these names weren't there.

Definitely suspicious, I agreed. *I'll inform Trajan, Jayson and Opal. We'll be there, shielded if necessary.*

Perhaps a Larentii escort? Fes suggested.

Probably a good idea. I'll see who's available.

Thanks.

"Just what we need," I muttered after Fes ended our communication. "Two hits at the same time."

Breanne's Journal

"I have sent two Larentii to San Francisco," Kal informed me. "To transport and shield Bill and the others."

"Something happening?" I sat up—with help from Chazi. I'd been lounging lazily on Kal's wide veranda in the afternoon sunlight.

"Fes' gamble may pay off—there is a suspicious reservation at the restaurant where he works."

"And the one at Desh's happening at the same time?" I was on my feet quickly, my weariness forgotten.

"If you count two timelines as the same time, then yes."

"You know what I meant—that this is happening and dividing our resources," I said.

"We ready to take you. You want?" Chazi asked. He was willing, but his frown expressed concern—for me.

"Honey, I don't know," I moaned. "I'm not very strong, right now."

"It may only be coincidence," Kal pointed out. "I can transport you, should the need arise."

"I really hate not being able to help much," I grumped.

"You should wait," Kal advised. "I will take you and your lion snakes, should it prove necessary."

Lissa's Journal

"That's them."

Kay stood beside me as we watched Song and Serenade walk into the restaurant, accompanied by two men.

That one's Sirenali—the one on the left, I sent.

What about the other one?

Rogue. The word filtered into my mind and I knew that voice—Charles. *I'll take care of that one, you worry about the others.*

Wonderful, I responded. *You gonna tell us when?*

I will. I'm sending Ashe and Kay to San Francisco, he added.

Because?

Because they're needed there. Things are going down in both places.

You know Kay won't like that. I studied Kay, who still stood beside me.

We'll let her see what's left, if we're successful.

Now I'm really worried.

Why?

When one of the Mighty says if, I'll definitely worry.

I am prepared to transport, Connegar's hands gripped my shoulders for just a moment before he disappeared with Kay. I heard her mental squeal as she was taken away.

Ashe will be forced to explain, Charles said with a mental shrug as he appeared at my side.

I wasn't sure she was prepared for this anyway, I replied as I watched a High Demon waiter seat our targets.

Bill's Journal

"Just remember, they may be disguised," Trajan pointed out. "Especially if they have a rogue with them."

"Can anyone see through that?" I asked.

"Bree can," Jayson said. "We just don't have her with us."

"Ask." Chazi, Bekzi and Perzi appeared, followed by Kalenegar, who held Breanne in his arms.

"I deemed it prudent," Kalenegar announced as he set Breanne on her feet. I could see that she was still tired and likely didn't have much power as a result.

"I can see through any disguise," Bree said as I pulled her into a tight embrace. "They can't fool me."

"I know, sweetheart," I murmured against her hair. "I'm concerned about you."

"Don't worry," she rubbed my back gently. "I just need to identify these people for you, and then Kal can whoosh me out of there if it becomes necessary. If you need Chazi and the others, they can stay."

"We'll see. I'm hoping this won't be a difficult takedown, if it is Moxas and Saxom."

"It's probably a good thing Kiarra isn't here," she said. "She looks green every time somebody mentions Saxom to her."

"We're here," Ashe arrived with Kay and Connegar.

"But," I stared at Ashe. Kay seemed angry, but I wasn't willing to delve into the source of her irritation.

~

Breanne's Journal

Charles thought it would be better for Kay, Ashe sent.

I agree. Those women, I shook my head. *I'm not sure Kay could deal with that emotionally.*

I understand. We have to convince her to help us here, instead.

You know, I have an idea, I returned.

~

Lissa's Journal

They ordered Yaris fish, Tory sent. He'd taken their order, while Aurelius and Tybus watched discreetly from a distance. I'd already gotten a message from Tybus, saying that all was well so far. Our guests suspected nothing.

I'm working on it now, Reah reported. *Along with four other orders for the same thing.*

Make it come out at the right time, Avilepha, Tory replied to Reah's statement. *We shouldn't make the other customers angry by serving our target first.*

Tory, I know that, Reah snapped.

Everybody remain calm, Charles interjected. *Now isn't the time for this to fall apart. Proceed with the plan. We'll take them after they eat and are too full to move quickly.*

I didn't say anything, but my heart skipped when Charles said *now isn't the time for this to fall apart.* Perhaps I'd read his statement incorrectly, but I felt he meant it—that at some point, it *would* fall apart.

~

Breanne's Journal

"They're late."

"Stop worrying," I nudged Jayson in the ribs with an elbow. Bekzi stood nearby, eyeing Jayson as if he were studying what part of him would be easiest to bite. Jayson's worry was increasing everybody else's apprehension, and that wasn't a good thing. Kay was ready to hyperventilate as it was, and I was very grateful Charles had sent her away from Tulgalan.

They may fold in—they're not all that worried that we'll be here, waiting, Ashe pointed out.

They just checked in, Bill announced. *I can't tell—they don't look like the description I have, but they're definitely twins. Two more with them, too.*

I'm going, I said and turned to mist. They wouldn't detect me that way. I zoomed toward the front of the restaurant, where Bill sat at a corner of the bar, in disguise and seemingly waiting for a table.

～

Lissa's Journal

They ordered the chocolate cake with gishi fruit ice cream, Tory reported. The fish course had been consumed, and I could tell they'd enjoyed it immensely. All of us were on edge, waiting to see if they wanted dessert. They did, and ordered the most expensive dessert on the menu.

Plating it up now, Reah responded.

～

Breanne's Journal

It's them. It was—there was no doubt. I stared at Saxom and Moxas, both disguised by the rogue god who accompanied them. They imagined they were protected by the rogue and the female Sirenali, whose hand was on the rogue's arm, as if they were together.

Hank calls that one Calhoun, Trajan informed me.

Gotcha. I'd already seen that, in addition to other things as I studied

181

Calhoun. His death now could impact future events. My plan would definitely have to work or we could all be screwed.

Ashe, we need Kay to be functioning and coherent for this to work, I sent. *If she's both those things, it'll go without a hitch. If she's not, we could be in trouble.*

On it, Ashe responded. *I'll let you know.*

Lissa's Journal

They went through that fish like seagulls on a beach, and now they want to take their time with tea and cake, Reah grumbled. She, Grace, Devin and Kiarra had worn themselves out in the kitchen, filling other orders while waiting for our targets to finish dinner. A second shift was scheduled to come in for clean up, and it was nearing closing time as it was. Song and Serenade were making an evening of their outing —they'd already been at the table for nearly three hours.

They're signaling for the check, Tory announced.

Breanne's Journal

They ordered four different kinds of fish, Fes informed me. *We're working on it now.*

Kay? Ashe asked.

I'm fine. Just a little queasy, she replied.

Let me know if that changes, sweetheart, Ashe coaxed.

I will.

I was listening to two conversations—that of Moxas and Saxom, plus the one in my head.

"This had better live up to the hype," Saxom grumbled as he sipped an expensive glass of wine.

"I heard very good things about the chef." The Sirenali examined her carefully manicured nails absently.

Moxas toyed with his knife and soupspoon, clinking them

together in an annoying fashion. He'd already finished one glass of wine and waited impatiently for another to be brought. Obviously, he appreciated the wine selection Fes suggested.

"You prefer raw fish," Saxom lifted his wineglass to her. "I prefer mine cooked, although I do like tuna and salmon sashimi."

"Squid is better," the Sirenali countered.

"I'm not that fond of squid."

"Octopus," the Sirenali baited Saxom.

"Absolutely not."

"Your wine," the wine steward arrived with a clean glass and a bottle of wine. Moxas went through the motions of sniffing a sample and tasting it before nodding approval. The wine was poured, the steward disappeared, Moxas drank and Saxom and the Sirenali continued their dispute.

Friendly argument? Jayson joined Bill at the bar, but sent mindspeech to me.

Sounds that way. Don't know how well they know each other, I said.

Maybe he wants her real claws to come out, Jayson mused.

That wouldn't clear the restaurant or anything, I replied sarcastically.

I'm sending out a complimentary appetizer of several types of fish, including tuna sashimi, Fes sent.

You listening in? I asked.

Of course. I set this up early on. I know what all the customers are saying, Fes sent a mental grin.

Kay, are you ready? If they get into this appetizer, you can do your thing without their suspecting. Just leave the rogue alone. He'll never know.

I'll do this, Kay sounded determined.

Lissa's Journal

The only reason the other restaurant guests didn't scream or panic was that Reemagar held a shield around our targets' table. My breath stuttered and stopped as the rogue god collapsed inward, as if everything inside his body was being siphoned away.

I wanted to gasp—this was how Jarnis died. I didn't make a sound as I watched a rogue god die while the Sirenali and two sadistic women stood and screamed. I wanted so badly to tell them that their screams couldn't be heard; the other guests continued eating as if nothing were happening.

Get the Sirenali, Charles's voice entered my mind. I separated particles in a blink, causing Song and Serenade's screams to reach a higher frequency.

Time to force them to tell us what they know, Tybus, followed by Aurelius, made his way toward the two women.

They're shielded, Renegar said as the two vampires reached the table and each grasped a woman by the throat, issuing mind-bending compulsion.

We're going, Charles announced, pulling us away before Desh's exploded.

"Don't worry, the Larentii got the people out of the restaurant," Charles sighed as I dropped to a tiled floor somewhere.

"Who?" I blinked up at Wisdom. Aurelius and Tybus were working on getting information from Song and Serenade nearby, while Grace, Devin, Reah and the others watched.

"Who do you think? If my guess is correct, he has some connection to all the Sirenali. When they die, he knows. I figure Quislus set it up, somehow, after the one in D.C. The only good thing is this—if Quislus did it, he may not have had time to get to all of them yet, or only booby-trapped likely targets—the ones who might come in contact with us."

"But we still don't know how many Sirenali are out there. Even if he's got them stashed away somewhere, we'll never find it by *Looking.*"

"I know. All we can hope for is to get lucky on that quarter."

"What about those children? Will he?" I began.

"We know where their compound is," Tybus walked toward me

and extended a hand. I allowed him to lift me to my feet. "I just hope they're still there and alive," he muttered.

"Larentii will take you," Renegar offered. He and Reemagar folded us away.

Breanne's Journal

Change the lines, sweetheart. Do you see them? Ashe asked. All of us listened in while Kay attempted to carry out my plan—the one where Saxom, Moxas and a Sirenali would be disarmed of their abilities and rendered mostly useless. Ashe, looking through Kay's eyes, directed her as she attempted to change lines.

Saxom and Moxas' lives would hang in the balance if the rogues ever learned they'd been tampered with, but with so many deaths attributed to them, I had no problem with that.

All of us held our breath while I received mindspeech from Lissa— the General, with probable help from Quislus, had destroyed Desh's number one in Targis.

I'll let Fes know—we're in the middle of something here, I replied.

Understood. We are, too. Her mindspeech cut off, so I went back to concentrating on Saxom, Moxas and a Sirenali, whose lives, hopefully, were just about to change.

Lissa's Journal

"Gassed. It was the quickest way. At least they didn't suffer long." Aurelius shook his head at more than forty small, crumpled bodies, scattered about a windowless room. Some had clawed at the door, hoping to escape. The walls were steel and concrete. They never had a chance.

"We can't stay—someone may be laying a trap," Charles announced. "Leave these. They are past our help."

I hadn't realized I was weeping until then—when my vision

blurred with tears and a sob escaped unchecked. How? How had this come about? I failed to understand such cruelty.

"Cara, no," Gavin pulled me against him as Reemagar folded us to Le-Ath Veronis.

~

Breanne's Journal

Are you sure?

As sure as I can be. We watched as Saxom, Moxas and their two guests walked out of the restaurant, seemingly unscathed. They'd never known that Kay adjusted their lines, rendering them nearly helpless.

They'll know the moment that Sirenali can no longer place obsession, Trajan declared.

Then let's hope that happens far away from here, so they won't suspect, I said.

Fes, is it time to turn in your resignation? Bill asked.

I'm ready, Fes responded. *I'll do it after my shift tonight.*

I'll hang around, just in case, Jayson offered.

Me, too, Bill said.

~

Lissa's Journal

"I would very much like to draw out your deaths," Aurelius growled at Song and Serenade. We'd transported them to my dungeon and placed them in adjoining cells.

"We know the laws," Song sniffed. "You can't kill us without a proper trial."

"Then you know little about us," Ildevar appeared, his arms crossed angrily over his chest. "If we were merely humanoid and you an ordinary criminal, that might hold true."

"I'm not afraid of you, Founder," Serenade spat, gripping the bars of her cage.

"You should be afraid of me," Tybus hissed before misting inside Serenade's cell and decapitating her the moment he reappeared.

Song screamed as Serenade's head rolled across the stone floor, leaving her body to drop in a heap near the bars.

"You get the same," Aurelius folded inside Song's cage and relieved her of her head. I watched with a bit of satisfaction as their blood pooled on the floor. No more children would die at their command. We couldn't save the ones we'd found, but those would be the last taken by these two bitches. I wiped away more tears as I contacted my sister.

~

Breanne's Journal

We took down Song and Serenade, Lissa reported. *They're all dead,* she added. *All the children—dead.* I heard the mental sob accompanying her words.

Oh, no, I replied. *Look, I'll try to get Kal to bring me there.*

Oh, lord, Lissa said, and then went silent.

What? What happened? I sent, suddenly terrified.

Bree, get here as fast as you can, Charles said. I gave a mental shout for Kal.

~

Harm mine, you pay.

"A message from the General?" Ashe asked, anger vibrating from his body.

"A message spelled out in children's bodies," Tybus growled beside me as we stared at the vid screen in shock. The message had been left outside the Reth/Campiaan Embassy building on Tulgalan.

Already the news agencies were reporting on the incident. Wild speculation as to how the children died had everyone in a panic.

"Kay's sleeping," Kevis appeared beside me and put an arm around my shoulders.

"Thank you," Ashe muttered absently, still staring at the screen.

"These aren't the ones from Ooblerik," Charles said.

"What?" Lissa grasped his arm. She was still brushing away tears. I held out a hand to her; she came and hugged me. I gave her as much *Love* as I could. I'd have to take care of Kay later—when she woke.

"These are from Yalles—the General destroyed the entire planet."

CHAPTER 13

Breanne's Journal

"What can we do?" I asked. We sat inside Lissa's private study and pondered the situation over a cup of tea. Most of the others were in her library, likely doing the same thing.

"At least Song and Serenade are dead—Tybus and Aurelius decapitated them," Lissa sighed. "We promised Kay, so we didn't separate particles. We needed bodies."

"She'll really be upset about the children," Kevis said. He sat next to me, my hand firmly held by his, as if he were afraid I'd disappear again.

"I'll try to fix that," I said. "When she wakes."

"Take it easy, baby," Kevis whispered. "You're not responsible for fixing everything."

"I can't fix anything right now," I pointed out. "I'm too weak and that's a real pain in the ass."

"Kay really changed Saxom and Moxas' lines? The Sirenali, too?" Lissa asked.

"Yeah."

"Kiarra is hoping that worked. Do you know if Kay got rid of that obsession they had for Kee?"

"That was part of the plan. I hope it worked, too."

"I feel like crap," Lissa muttered, rubbing her forehead.

"I hear you," I said.

"Lissa?" Karzac walked in.

"Honey, what's up?" Lissa blinked wearily at her physician mate.

"I think you need sleep. It's three hours before dawn, love."

"Karzac," Lissa muttered while hunching her shoulders.

"Come. I'll take you. Leave Kevis to talk with your sister."

"Karzac, do you think he'll do this from now on—destroy a world whenever we have any sort of victory?" Lissa mumbled as Karzac steered her through the door.

"A valid question," I sighed, covering my eyes with a hand that wasn't completely steady at the moment.

"Come," Kevis repeated his father's words, only he folded me away instead of walking with me through the doorway.

Ashe's Journal

"You think Quislus found a way to booby-trap the Sirenali?" I asked.

"It makes sense," Charles said. "It was a relatively new development, don't you think? Terry Johnston's office exploded when he separated a Sirenali's particles. That was the first incidence. Now it happens again to Desh's. Notice that only the building around the Sirenali explodes—not the entire planet. The General chose a seemingly innocuous target after that to destroy."

"That's fascinating," Hank said. He and Kifirin had joined us in a corner of Lissa's library, so we could have drinks and discuss recent events.

"We're here," Trajan arrived with Bill, Jayson, Opal and Fes.

"I think you went the better way," Charles nodded to Bill. "Changing lines instead of separating particles. The longer the enemy doesn't know they've been affected, the better off everybody is."

"That was Breanne's idea," Bill pulled out a chair and sat. The others followed suit—we were all tired, we just hadn't gotten the night's events out of our systems yet.

"Then we need to give Breanne a big kiss," Charles said. "When she's awake. Kevis is quite handy with a healing sleep."

"So it doesn't register if a rogue god dies—only the Sirenali?" Opal asked.

"That's what it looks like," I nodded to her. "Charles believes Quislus set up some sort of alarm within the Sirenali. If they die, the building around them explodes."

"Hell of a theory," Jayson muttered. "How did he manage to accomplish that?"

"By subverting cells," Kifirin growled. "Placing microscopic explosives inside those cells—sufficient to destroy a building, but a Sirenali isn't big enough to carry enough explosives to destroy anything larger, such as a planet."

"Holy shit," Bill whistled. "That takes a devious mind."

"Quislus has that, most certainly," Hank said. "It is likely that he holds a separate key to setting off those explosives, in case the Sirenali displeased him for any reason or becomes too demanding."

"Or if he discovers one is close to any of us, perhaps?" Bill asked.

"Also possible," Charles agreed. "He should know that it won't penetrate a good shield, however."

"So he can only catch us off guard."

"It's moot, we know of his game, now," Kifirin blew smoke.

"True. So Sirenali can only blow up buildings and any people inside them, if they die."

"Have we explored the notion that it may only occur if the Sirenali's particles are separated?" Renegar and Pheligar folded in to join our conversation.

"Another theory to test," I sighed. "Kay's asleep or I'd ask her if she saw anything unusual in the Sirenali's lines that she altered."

"You know Calhoun and a few others will be pissed if they learn we fucked with Saxom and Moxas," Trajan pointed out.

"I don't care how pissed he is. I'll take him on," Opal muttered.

"There's something you should know about Calhoun," Charles said.

"Bree knows. The rest of you may not. He's important to maintain the integrity of the timeline. Don't kill him unless it's your life or his."

"Fuck," Jayson mumbled.

"Is there anything we can do in the meantime?" Opal asked. "How many died on Yalles?"

"Three hundred million, but who's counting?" I said. Just the sound of it depressed me. And then the General had the temerity to spell out his message in dead children. I wanted him gone. He was an evil and deserved to be destroyed.

"Kooper, Lendill and Trevor are taking care of the situation on Tulgalan," Charles said. "As much as they can. Obviously, they can't announce on the vids that rogue gods are attempting a takeover. That would result in even greater panic. As of now, people are speculating that Ranos technology was used in Yalles' destruction, but what they can't determine is the reason, or the intent behind the message."

"We have the first of those arena rentals in two days," Bill said. "We still have no idea what that's about."

"Where are we with the power version of nexus echo?" Charles lifted an eyebrow at Renegar.

"It has been successfully tested," Ren replied. "The net is ready to implement."

"Great. Do it immediately," Charles said. "Ask them to form High Demon squads, no more than thirty to a squad, and have them ready to go if there's a hit."

"I will carry that message," Pheligar said and disappeared.

"Good. At least something's going right," Charles huffed.

Breanne's Journal

"Hey." Kevis brushed hair off my forehead with gentle fingers.

"Huh?" My eyes work first. Doesn't mean my brain is connected. Not after a sound sleep, anyway.

"I love you," Kevis leaned in to kiss me.

"Where are we?"

"At EastStar. Mom, Aunt Devin, Dad and Lissa are here, too."

"Why here?"

"Because it's shielded against the General," Kevis grinned. "I don't want you worrying about getting blown up while we're fooling around."

"You know, that hadn't occurred to me until you said it just now. I'll worry about it from now on," I said.

"Stop." He kissed me again.

"Are we fooling around now?"

"I'm getting to that. First, I have to undress you."

"Okay."

"Then, I get to kiss whatever I want."

"Okay."

"Then, well, hopefully you'll be asking for it by that time."

"I'm asking for it now."

"Seriously?"

"You're not undressing me yet."

"Where did this forwardness come from?"

"Fes taught me a few things."

"Remind me to buy Fes an expensive bottle of wine."

"Are you kissing me yet?"

"I'll get there."

He did.

~

Adam's Journal

"How will we know if it worked?" Kiarra paced inside the kitchen at EastStar.

"We have to wait—the same as we were doing before. I'm cautiously hopeful," I said.

"I never want his hands on me again," she shuddered.

"I'll kill him again," I growled.

"Mom, stop fretting," Franklin walked in, closely followed by Shane and Trace. "This isn't good for you or anybody else."

"I know, honey. Where's your father?"

"He's talking with Pheligar, Graegar and Garegar. They said they'd be here shortly."

"Did anything else happen while I was asleep?" she asked.

"Not that I know of, and we've been checking the vids regularly. No new information, just rehashes of the old."

"At least nobody else is dead."

"Sweetheart, slow down," I said. She was back to pacing.

"I want my hands around his throat," she muttered. "Or a sword in my hand that will kill him."

"I assume you're talking about the General now?" I asked.

"Yes. Saxom I leave to you. I want the other bastard. The one responsible for bringing Saxom back."

"My darling, are you discussing someone's demise again?" Merrill appeared, accompanied by four generations of Larentii—Pheligar, Renegar, Graegar and Garegar.

"You know it," Kiarra huffed.

"My love, stop with this incessant pacing." Pheligar lifted Kiarra and soothed her gently.

"Honey, I really love you, but you ought to put me down. I have a snit going and I don't want to be interrupted."

"A snit? My love, a snit only agitates you, and then passes like a virus to the rest of us. I prefer snit-free mornings. They go much better with my sunlight consumption."

"Mom, let's have breakfast and table this for now, pun intended," Franklin suggested. "Then you can snit again if you want. Shane and I will cook."

"No snits," Shane declared. "I don't like it when somebody snits where they eat, more pun intended."

"What in the name of the Dark Realm is going on?" Kevis arrived, pulling Breanne after him. I wanted to laugh—she didn't look very willing to interrupt our morning.

"Snits and breakfast," Pheligar offered a long-suffering sigh and set Kiarra down.

~

Breanne's Journal

It looked as if we'd interrupted a family discussion. I wasn't comfortable with that.

"Hello, Love," Graegar stepped toward me and gathered me up. "How are you feeling?"

"I'm fine." I leaned in to kiss him. He offered me a dazzling smile afterward. "I've missed you."

"And I you. Conner wishes to see you soon."

"Then I'll visit."

"I'll take you."

"Okay."

"Breakfast first," Franklin announced, pulling pans from a cabinet and setting to work.

We had breakfast. Franklin cooked a vegetarian version of an egg and biscuit casserole. The dish was outstanding, so I gave him a hug for it. Lissa came in while we were eating, herded by Karzac. She sat beside me and had ham with her biscuit and egg casserole.

"What are your plans for today?" she asked.

"Seems I'm expected at Conner's," I said. "Graegar is taking me."

"Can I go?" Lissa turned to blink at Graegar, who sat on my other side, watching me eat.

"Of course. Kiarra may come as well, if she wants."

"I do." Kiarra nodded.

"Barrigar?" Graegar spoke to empty air. His protector appeared quickly.

"Hello, my love," Barrigar leaned in to kiss me.

"Have you had breakfast?" I asked him. Honestly, Barrigar was amazing. I thought that about him and Graegar, actually. Kal still had a way to go, in my opinion.

"I have collected a sufficient amount of sunlight," he smiled and kissed me again.

"You smell like sunlight," I said. "That's wonderful."

"We will take you to Conner, when you are finished eating," he said.

"That's great, hon. I'll be done in a minute."

"We just ate," I waved off an offer of tea or coffee from Conner when we arrived in England later. This was England present and not past, although Conner's manor had been placed in stasis and looked exactly as it had centuries earlier.

"Hello, ladies." Lynx wandered in dressed only in pants, a cup of tea in his hands.

"You just wanted to show off, didn't you?" Conner pointed a finger at him.

"Caught in the act," he laughed and pointed his cup to her. "I wanted to get more tea." He rummaged in a cabinet while all of us watched shamelessly.

"Now, down to business," Conner said when Lynx walked out of the kitchen. "I have this."

"What?" Kiarra asked. Conner didn't seem to have anything.

"Me." Someone I didn't know walked in. Yes, I read her—and almost recoiled. She was Sirenali. Not only was she Sirenali, she was V'ili's sister. His older sister—V'era. She was supposed to be dead— V'ili killed her long ago, so he'd be first in line for the Sirenali throne.

"The Ear, the Eye and I went after her," Conner said with a shrug as V'era sat at the island across from me. "Pulled her out minutes before her death, Cleo fixed her and here we are."

"How did you know to do that?" Lissa asked.

"Nefrigar," Conner said. "He showed me the history of the Sirenali he keeps in the archives. It shows that V'era died—just not how she died. One of the High Council members suspected treachery, but he was shouted down and V'ili was named crown prince. We three went backward in time to do some sleuthing, and brought V'era back with us."

"V'era, how do you feel about all this?" Kiarra asked. She couldn't read everything from V'era, as I could.

"I despise my brother. Many did. Sirena wasn't always as it turned out to be."

"I'm not surprised," Lissa said. "Put a few bad ones in charge and things go south in a hurry."

"I think I grasp the concept of your words," V'era nodded to Lissa. "Yes, things began to go badly when V'ili gained control over several highly-placed members of the King's Council. Together, they drove a wedge in the Council and then began working to drive a wedge in the people. Dissatisfaction came quickly, and neighbor turned against neighbor. You can imagine the results—many weaker ones died at the hands of those stronger and more capable of placing terrible obsessions."

"Let me guess—a few well-placed economic disasters also arrived?" Kiarra asked.

"Exactly. The level of dissatisfaction grew, my father the King, who was an even-tempered Sirenali, was termed weak and ineffective. V'ili was often hailed as a hero when he made suggestions to repair an economy that he'd manipulated to fail beforehand."

"And then came the suggestion to invade the Larentii homeworld."

Graegar and Barrigar had stood by quietly, listening to the conversation, but Graegar spoke now.

"V'ili believed that all our troubles would be remedied if we had at our command even a small portion of the Larentii—they could form anything with the power they had and command atoms. V'ili's greed would know no bounds, if he could only enslave a handful of the blue giants."

"Likely, Acrimus was whispering in V'ili's ear," I sighed. "Although he seemed to be an apt pupil."

"He was always grasping for what he shouldn't have, even as a child," V'era said. "Our mother had to watch him closely or he'd harm himself, attempting to get whatever caught his attention."

"It seems he wants his homeworld back," Barrigar interjected. "That is what his goal has been ever since he and others were rescued by Acrimus and the General, to achieve their domination."

"I know now that the Larentii were forced to destroy my world," V'era nodded to Barrigar. "But it was already beyond saving—most of it, anyway, when V'ili lured me into a trap and killed me. I have Conner and Cleo to thank for restoring my life."

"Thank Nefrigar," Conner said. "The Larentii Archivist. He holds the records and made the suggestion."

"Then I will thank him, should I get the chance."

"What we're faced with now is exploding Sirenali," I said. "I heard from Hank earlier that their cells have been manipulated and packed with tiny explosives—enough to take down a building—if the Sirenali is killed."

"So it is dangerous to kill these enemies," V'era considered the problem. "Is it any death, or only certain types of death?"

"No idea," Kiarra said. She'd gotten the same report I had—only from Pheligar instead of Hank.

"Are there any others we should go back for?" I asked. "Of your kind? Allies, perhaps, or the like-minded? We could use your help—if you're willing."

"I am certainly willing. It angers me that my brother has brought our race to this—and to their destruction. Yes, there are two I trust. I would appreciate their assistance, and I believe they would be willing to help."

"Who?" Conner asked.

"My two younger sisters. V'ili killed both of them."

"We will bring them," Graegar offered. He and Barrigar disappeared.

Bree, make sure all three are on the up-and-up, Lissa sent.

Already there, sister, I replied.

Tory's Journal

"Stop worrying," Sali punched my arm. He led my squad of High Demons—I'd been surprised when he selected me as his Second-in-Command. We were scheduled as third responders—Caylon's Group was first, Crane's group was second. There were four groups altogether, and Drake and Drew had taken the fourth squad. Caylon charged them with clean-up, in case the first three squads were in danger. I knew Dragon Taylor functioned as Caylon's Second, while Crane Trevor worked with his father in the second group.

Dragon was in charge of the entire operation, and would remain in contact with Li'Neruh Rath and Kifirin when the squads were dispatched. They'd come in last of all, if they were needed.

"They're worried about those arena rentals on old Earth, aren't they?" I asked.

"Yeah." Sali shook his head, as if he knew something I didn't. After considering it, my assumption was likely correct.

I'd gotten word from Ry and Erland, too, telling me to call for them if things got out of hand. I hoped that wouldn't be necessary, and had no idea what they might do anyway, against rogue gods.

We're ranked among them, now, Ry pointed out when I sent a half question in his direction. *No offense, bro, but we might be able to hold our own, depending on what's thrown at us.*

Do they know—that this is what you are, now? I asked.

Not yet. I worry that they're attempting to draw us out, just to see who the enemy is.

Then hold back unless there's no other option, I returned.

Did you get the blades from Nissa, Toff and Trik?

We did. Tried them out yesterday. It's amazing how well they work.

I talked to her several times while they were designing them. She asked a couple of questions, too, and Dad and I made suggestions. I hope they work like I think they will.

I hope so too, bro. Look, Sali's asking for help to go over the roster. Gotta go.

∾

Breanne's Journal

I read V'ala and V'orla the moment they arrived. They were more than angry that their brother commanded their deaths, and like their sister, felt he'd led their race and their world in the wrong direction. That direction has resulted in their destruction.

"I just want to make sure you don't mind going with some of ours—to keep them safe and hidden from enemy eyes," Conner said. "In exchange, we'll offer your world back to you, to rebuild."

"I find that completely acceptable," V'era agreed.

"Good. I'd like to send one of you with Kiarra," Conner said. "And the other two to Dragon and his command of High Demons."

"Again, acceptable," V'era nodded.

"You'll be kept as safe as we can keep you," Kiarra said. "You have my promise, as long as our agreement stands."

"I have one request," V'era said.

"What's that?"

"That you remove our ability to create obsessions, if we regain our world. That talent led to this. I'd prefer not to have it."

"I think we can manage that," I said. "If we survive this war, you may certainly have your wish granted."

"Calhoun may still attempt to take you," Conner informed Kiarra later, after the three Sirenali women were given rooms in Conner's home for the night. Their help would be required the following morning. "Since he likely isn't aware of how we've altered Moxas and Saxom."

"The longer he doesn't realize that, the better off we'll be," I said.

"What about the Tanners and Wildrif?" Lissa asked.

"I'm hoping they stay out of this," I said. "Since they have important roles in the future. Like Calhoun."

"You know that's not likely," Conner pointed out. "Those rogue werewolves are in this up to their necks, unless I'm very, very wrong."

"This sucks," Lissa muttered. "We have to do our best to keep some of these assholes alive while trying our damnedest to wipe out the rest. I have a headache."

"I think I can fix that, at least," I offered.

"Yeah. Thanks." I reached out to touch her forehead, eliminating the tension and sending a bit of *Love* to make her feel better.

"I wish I knew how you did that," she said when I pulled my hands away.

"If I knew, I'd let you know," I said. "Can we go home, now? I'm really tired."

"I think we can," Lissa agreed. "We missed lunch a couple of hours ago."

"How's my baby?" Hank was waiting when Graegar and Barrigar ferried Lissa and me back to EastStar.

"Tired," I said. "Maybe a little hungry, too."

"I'll take you out to eat and see you get some sleep," he offered.

"Yeah. That sounds great," I sighed.

"Fes, I'm sorry about Desh's," I said when Hank landed me inside the kitchen at my San Rafael home.

"We needed to remodel, and nobody died except the bad ones. Win-win," he grinned at me. "I can get my brothers on the rebuilding, while I concentrate on what we need to do."

"Did you quit your job?"

"Yes, and I shut off my phone. I had dozens of calls, with job offers. Some of them for obscene amounts of money."

"What are you cooking now?" I asked. He had a towel over a shoulder while stirring something in a pan.

"Fresh tomato soup, to go with the cheese bread in the oven."

"You really do know me, don't you?"

"I've done some homework. Mostly, I bothered Hank until he told me what you liked."

"You did that? For me?" I turned to Hank.

"I don't mind, if it makes you happy," he smiled.

"You make me happy anyway. Food is just a bonus."

"It's ready," Fes said, dipping soup into a bowl and placing two slices of cheese bread on a plate.

"Thanks, honey," I said.

"How about a kiss?" Fes grinned.

"I think you can have several."

I ate, sitting between Hank and Fes. They had cheese bread while I ate soup, since they'd had lunch two hours earlier.

"I hear we have Sirenali to help," Hank said as I leaned back after finishing my soup.

"We have three. I read them—they're trustworthy. They're also very, very pissed at their brother V'ili, who is likely in charge of all the Sirenali the General brought back."

"These aren't booby-trapped, then," Hank nodded in satisfaction. "I heard from Dragon—he's prepared to send a Sirenali with the first wave of High Demons, when the nexus net gets a hit."

"I hope that works," I said, leaning my forehead against Hank's shoulder.

"Baby, I know you're worried about more worlds getting destroyed. I am, too." Hank stroked my hair. "Things have to happen as they will. It'll hurt in the meantime, I know. We just have to get through it."

"I don't know if I can handle too much of that," I whispered.

"I'll get you through it. Fes, Bill, Trajan and the others will help, too."

"We help," Chazi, Bekzi and Perzi walked in with Jayson. I could see that they'd been at the shooting range; all of them carried pistols. Jayson and Chazi also had a rifle with them.

"Blowing stuff up?" I asked Jayson.

"Paper targets," Jayson grinned and leaned in for a kiss. "We're not dangerous to you, baby, trust me. Unless it's in bed."

"Jayson," I whined.

"Hey, everybody here knows exactly what I'm talking about. Why are you embarrassed?"

"You'd walk around naked, wouldn't you, if your ass didn't get goose pimples in cold weather."

"Hey, I look good in goose pimples."

"Unbelievable."

"He trying to distract you," Chazi shouldered his way in and put his arms around me. "We be naked if you want naked. We be dressed if you want dressed. Simple. What Bree wants, she gets."

"Honey, I love you," I said and wrapped my arms around him.

"Are we ready to go in Chicago?" Zeke Tanner asked.

"Everything's in place," Obediah nodded. "We'll have a baptism like nobody's seen before."

"Welcome to the world of the werewolf overlords," Zeke grinned. "Piss us off, you die. I like it."

CHAPTER 14

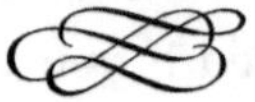

race's Journal

"Look, I don't know how to handle this. I was hoping you would." I gave Frank and Shane a pleading glance. "Jayson brought her in and asked me to take care of her. Now what?"

"Maybe Willem knows," Shane shook his head. We watched Belinda from the house—she lounged by the pool wearing a thong and nothing else while drinking a rum drink.

"You called?" Willem appeared at my side and lifted his head for a kiss.

"That." I jerked my head toward Belinda, after a second kiss. Willem knows how to kiss, that's for sure. He knows how to fuck, too, but that had to be tabled until later.

"What are those marks on her back—wait. She likes kink, doesn't she?" Willem stared at Belinda. Hell, we may be gay, but we know bodacious ta-tas when we see them. Belinda had no trouble showing them off, either.

"My worry is," I began, when Kathleen walked up and said, "What in the name of California is that?"

"My dear, those are rather large breasts," Casimir pulled Kathleen against his chest and wrapped arms about her.

"Jayson's playmate," Shane shook his head. "For his ah, kinkier tendencies."

"Does he care about her?" Kathleen asked.

"If he didn't, I don't imagine he'd bother bringing her here," Franklin replied dryly.

"If he cares about her, then I don't care that she's here. I think she ought to cover up, though. It makes the rest of us feel inadequate."

"There's your excuse," Willem said. "Ask her to cover up because it makes the other women feel inferior. Surely she'll respond to that plea."

"I'll speak with her," Casimir offered. "And if that doesn't work, there's always compulsion."

"Thank you," Kathleen breathed. "They're mesmerizing, aren't they?" None of us could take our eyes off Belinda's largesse.

"I believe your son responds to that," Casimir chuckled. "Perhaps we ought to find a distraction for her while she's here. Can she cook or perform some other function?"

"I'll find something," I said. "I tried frying bacon while I was naked once. That requires clothing," I added.

Breanne's Journal

"Belinda's at SouthStar," Jayson said.

"Good for her," I nodded.

"She's running around half naked. Or was. Mom and Trace had to convince her to get covered up. And they put her to work in the kitchen. I didn't know she could cook."

"Because you were too busy with other things," I pointed out. "You weren't thinking about food."

"I can't tell you how nice it is that you don't mind," Jayson said.

"I like her. Why would I mind?" I asked. "I don't have anything to compete with her chest, but she doesn't have what I have, either."

"Definitely agree with that, baby." Jayson nuzzled my neck.

"Hey, now, there are others in line ahead of you," I said.

"We in line," Chazi agreed. He and his brothers took up the sofa opposite the one Jayson and I occupied.

"Then I'll wait. It'll be sweeter when I get it," Jayson grinned and stood.

"How's Terry?" I asked.

"I'll check on him." Jayson disappeared, leaving me alone with my reptanoids.

"We alone. Finally," Chazi grinned. Before I knew it, I had all three around me. Two of them were lion snakes. Their tongues tickled my chin and neck while Chazi leaned in for a kiss.

Hank's Journal

"Everybody is feeding her energy. While having sex," I said. "That way, she won't notice so much. I told them how to do it—so she won't get too much before she's ready for it," I added. "She feels better every time she wakes afterward."

"Good idea," Trajan said. "I'll take care of her when it's my turn."

"You and I need to be last in line this time. We can give her the most, and she'll be better able to accept it by that time."

"What I'm concerned about in the interim is the arena rentals, the Tanners, Wildrif and Calhoun," Trajan growled.

"We're all concerned about that," I agreed. "Kifirin is working with the High Demons under Dragon's command, and everybody is ready to go, we're just waiting for the hammer to drop."

"Let's hope what we have will be sufficient to withstand the attack when it comes."

"I worry about that, too."

"Have any preparations been made in Chicago?"

"Nothing yet, but with Calhoun and other rogues available, that's a moot point. They can have something ready in seconds. I asked Jayson to take Terry with him to Chicago, to watch for anything suspicious. So far, there's nothing."

"With the Tanners involved, you know it won't be good," Trajan said.

"I dislike the fact that we have to leave them alive, to maintain the integrity of the timeline," I muttered.

"I may have to experiment with the smoke thing," Trajan nodded at the curl of smoke drifting from my nostrils. "It's an effective way of telling everybody how pissed you are."

"In the High Demon language, it's called *kiffel*—the manifestation of displeasure," I explained. "*Kiffelan* is past tense."

"Is there a connection between the word and Kifirin's name?" Trajan asked.

"A referential nod," I agreed. "He was the first to employ the gesture, and it grew from *Kifirin-fel*, or Kifirin's anger, to *kiffel*—the expression of displeasure—as the language evolved."

"It's appropriate," Trajan grinned. "I like it."

"You may be seeing a lot of it before this is over," I warned.

"Yeah. There's that," he agreed.

Lissa's Journal

"I just finished adjusting the orbit of the other planets around Yalles' sun," Charles said as he took a seat next to me. I'd gone to the arboretum to think. Charles found me.

"What a nightmare," I mumbled. I was still upset over the deaths of innocents—those through Song and Serenade, in addition to Yalles.

"Lissa, you have to trust," Charles said cryptically. "If you don't trust me, trust your sister."

"I do trust my sister. She'll do the right thing, even if it kills her."

"I know that, too."

"Where is Griffin? Kee says he disappeared from Fresno, and Thurlow isn't in San Rafael."

"I know. I sent out a call. They're working together on a project for me."

"That sounds like trouble in the making."

"I told them they had to get along and play nice."

"How long will that last?"

"As long as I tell them to."

"You can be a hard-ass when you want, you know that?" I said.

"I've been a lot harder, trust me," he said. He wasn't looking at me—instead, he gazed through the tall windows at the city below us.

"What did you think of being Wlodek's right hand?" I asked, changing the subject. His words troubled me in some way, but I didn't want him to know. "Was it a chore, being at his beck and call?"

"Most of it I enjoyed. I had my fingers on the pulse of the vampire and werewolf races, which became more important as time passed. We needed the treaty. We needed it kept. Too many things needed to happen, and they couldn't be tampered with. I hope you understand that."

"I sort of do, but a bit less suffering would have been good."

"I know. For Bree, too. I couldn't see or feel her, so I was operating blindly where she was concerned. You have no idea how badly I feel about that."

"What about Ashe?"

"I knew the minute Wlodek informed me that there was a talented child in the experimental group in Oklahoma. There was too much coincidence there, so I knew Ashe was one of us. I didn't know which one at first, but it became clear quickly."

"You helped him, didn't you?" I asked.

"As much as possible, without being obvious about it."

"But Breanne—no information came on her, did it."

"No. I was beginning to worry, too, back then. I did know, through Thurlow, that you had a sister—he owned up to it. After she was brought to Le-Ath Veronis by Jarnis, I did research. Everything started to add up. Belen didn't realize that several mind clouds had been laid when Bree was brought in—he merely saw her as a replacement for you while you were on assignment."

"She did such a good job, and got persecuted for it," I shook my head.

"I know. I sent mindspeech to her once during a Council meeting

—I couldn't help myself. She didn't know who it was. She probably does, now."

"Did you remove the mind clouds from Gavin and Cheedas?"

"Yes. Once I discovered their existence. It was a delicate matter, though—I had to search for the one who placed them. Once I found that information, I was able to destroy them undetected."

"Acrimus."

"Quislus."

"Fuck," I sighed, rubbing my forehead. "So much of this is beyond comprehension."

"I concur."

"Cheedas still slinks around like a misbehaving child," I said. "I wish he'd stop. I know it wasn't him when he," I didn't finish.

"I know that, too. I believe he needs what Breanne can do, and she may not feel charitable toward him."

"She did it for Gavin."

"Then I'll ask. For you," Charles nodded. I realized then that his mind was elsewhere—probably several elsewheres—while he and I spoke.

"I'd appreciate it," I said. "I didn't want to upset her by asking."

"I don't believe she'll be horribly upset."

"Is she strong enough?"

"I believe she is now." Charles smiled—I watched as a corner of his mouth curled nicely. "I'll pay her a visit." He disappeared.

Breanne's Journal

I stretched lazily. Somehow, I felt amazing instead of tired. Going to bed with three lion snake shapeshifters ought to tire anyone. I wasn't tired. Thirsty, yes. Tired? No.

"You liked." Bekzi, Chazi and Perzi grinned at me.

"I liked," I agreed. "We do again."

"Now?"

"Not now, I need Breanne for a mission," Charles appeared inside my bedroom, startling all of us.

"You certainly pick your moments," I said, offering Charles a pointed look.

"I could have shown up sooner."

"Thanks for not doing that," I replied.

"Get dressed. Your lion snakes may come if they want."

"We want," Bekzi nodded enthusiastically.

"Then get dressed. We're going to Le-Ath Veronis."

"Oh, no," I moaned. Charles had taken me to the wide doorway that led into Lissa's kitchen. Cheedas, looking harried, worn and depressed, herded kitchen staff about while dinner was prepared.

"Yes," Charles insisted. "Bree, you gave of yourself to Gavin, and saved Gavril's ass several times. Do this. If not for me, for your sister. She loves Cheedas. He has been a comfort to her through too many troubles to count."

"She could have asked," I pouted.

"Love, you're adorable when you pout, but we need to get this done."

"Fine. What do you want me to do? Just walk up to him?"

"Let's go." Charles pulled me into the kitchen, while every comesula there stopped what they were doing to stare at me. Yes, they'd all mistreated me in the past. They had no idea why I was in their kitchen, now. Most of them wore expressions of shame or guilt.

"We're here for Cheedas," Charles announced. Cheedas, startled, looked ready to bolt—or cry. Perhaps both. Was I supposed to feel sorry for him? A part of me did. He'd been manipulated, but his actions, although atypical, still stung. Nevertheless, I reached out and infused him with *Love*.

Lissa's Journal

Come and see, Charles sent. I folded into the kitchen. There, I found Cheedas on his knees, holding onto Breanne as if his life depended on it. She'd given him *Love.* Probably forgiveness as well. He'd received a gift that defied all logic.

Is that what Love—my sister—is? Something that defies logic? I asked Charles.

I have known it to defy logic too many times to disagree, Charles confirmed. *Your sister has something that I have never seen in any other. I don't care if it defies logic. It is a very great gift.*

"Cheedas?" I stepped forward and placed a hand on his shoulder.

"Why didn't someone tell me?" He turned dark eyes toward me. I saw the tearstains on his face—but these were tears of joy.

"Stand up, honey," Breanne said, taking Cheedas' elbow and lifting him to his feet.

"I will do anything for you," he breathed. "Anything."

"Even cook vegetarian and let me in the laundry room?" She smiled to temper her words.

"All you have to do is ask."

"Honey, don't worry. We'll get along fine," she said, patting his cheek as he smiled down at her.

"What is going on—ah." Gavin entered the kitchen and took in the scene before him.

"I would like for you to visit often. I want to introduce you to my sire. Please, let me know if there is anything I might do for you," Cheedas pleaded. He wasn't ready to let Breanne go.

"I'll let you know, I promise," Breanne said, attempting to move away.

"Ah, forgive me. I forgot that I was preparing a meal." Cheedas stepped back before barking at the staring comesuli all around us.

"He's fine, now. Back to normal," Charles said. "Your Papa Cheedas is back."

"Thank goodness."

"Thank Breanne."

"I owe her too much already."

"As do I."

~

Breanne's Journal

I rested in the crook of Charles's arm while sipping a glass of wine. My lion snakes were draped over both of us. Yes, I was already half asleep after eating with Lissa and her crew. Cheedas sat near Lissa for the first time in a long time and ate with the rest of us. Lissa was overjoyed. Roff and Cheedas seemed to have plenty to talk about, and the rest joined in from time to time.

I was content to watch the others, and Charles was content to watch me. We lounged in a sitting area of Lissa's library, in comfortable seats. Drake, Drew and Gavin clustered about Lissa, while Charles, my snakes and I sat opposite them, drinking companionably.

"Here, honey," I held my glass out for Chazi to sip. It was funny to watch the lion snakes dip their tongues in my wine.

"I think Cheedas will sleep soundly tonight for the first time in a long time," Lissa said. "Bree, I don't know what to do to thank you. For so many things."

"Don't worry about it," I said. "Just the thought is enough."

I love you. More than anything, Charles sent. *Don't ever forget that.*

I won't, I promised.

~

"How?" I asked when I woke the following morning. Yes, I was in my own bed—Charles had seen to that. I just didn't remember being in bed with anyone else when I went to sleep.

"What's wrong?" Salidar DeLuca blinked dark eyes at me.

"Did you ninja your way into my bed?" I asked.

Sali muffled his snicker against my shoulder. "No," he chuckled moments later. "I didn't ninja my way into your bed. Although it's a good idea. I'll try that next time."

"Uh-huh," I said. "You're full of surprises."

"I could take that so many ways," he grinned. "But I won't. What's the best way to get you so hot you're all over me?"

"I'm not the idea woman. Hank is the idea man. He always comes up with something."

"Did you say up?" He scooted closer and slid his "up" against my leg as he nuzzled my neck before placing a kiss or two.

"You're taking everything with a grain of sexual salt, aren't you?" I said.

"Sexual salt?" He moved closer.

"What happened to our clothes?"

"We were naked all night. I just waited—like a gentleman, I might add—for you to wake up."

"Are you serious? Where is Charles?" I demanded.

"Come on, let's do this, then you can be mad at Charles."

"Honey, what's," I moved. "Oh, lord. Is that you?" I'd put my hand on a very rigid, very strategic spot.

"That's me. Is this you?" He thumbed my right nipple. "Oh yeah. That's nice. Really nice. I want some of that."

"Looks like you're getting it," I mumbled.

"Mmm-hmmm." He didn't say anything else—he was polite enough not to talk with his mouth full.

I took the opportunity to run my fingers through his dark hair—it was like thick, black silk. Sali wasn't hard to look at, by any stretch. I had another werewolf, looked like, and wondered briefly if he'd howl like Trajan did afterward.

There was one way to find out. I shifted so my body was beneath his. He took full advantage of my invitation. The truth was, after it was over, I wanted to howl, too. That's how good it was.

Ashe's Journal

"Good morning, sweetheart." I reached out to pull Kay to me for a kiss when she shuffled into the kitchen at SouthStar. I'd taken her there the night before and we'd fallen into bed and slept soundly. I'd left her asleep earlier while I went to the kitchen for coffee and to check in with Trace.

"Want more coffee?" Belinda asked.

"No, thanks." She was dressed, thank goodness. I'd already gotten a mental earful from Trace, who sat across from me, going over reports.

"I'd like coffee," Kay said.

"You got it," Belinda smiled and went to find a cup.

Lissa's Journal

"One more day. I hate waiting like this."

"We know."

I'd spent the night with my Falchani. Drake stood behind me, his arms wrapped around my waist and his head on my shoulder while I considered what to wear for my return trip to Fresno's past. I'd already gotten a mental message from Merrill, Kiarra and Adam—we'd go back together after we had breakfast.

"The Larentii say the nexus net is in place."

"Good. Is everybody prepared on your end?" I turned in Drake's embrace and touched his face gently. He smiled and kissed my fingers.

"We're ready," he agreed.

"Then be careful. Tell the others to do the same."

"We will. Dad wants Travis and Trent to work at the command center on Falchan. He wanted us to ask if that's all right with you."

"Not in harm's way?" I frowned at Drake.

"As far out of it as we can keep them. Dad says it's good experience —for them to see things from that angle."

"I suppose it's all right," I sighed. "As long as you and Drew are okay with it."

"Dad put us in every position before we were ready for battle," Drake said. "We acted as assistants, runners and messengers before we were ever stuck in the back of a unit. We worked our way up honestly, and we know what it's like to see a battle from all stations."

"Then it's fine. Just make sure they stay out of trouble."

"We will." Drew walked in, freshly showered and wearing a grin. I should have known they were connected while Drake and I spoke. They usually were.

~

"I have received no new visions," Moxas said.

"So we proceed as planned?" Calhoun asked.

"Of course."

"Excellent."

~

Breanne's Journal

Bree, can you come? Mindspeech came from Lissa, along with information that she'd just arrived in Fresno with Merrill and the others. Sali was already gone, after having breakfast with Fes and me.

On my way, I replied. Opal, Jayson, Bill, Trajan and my reptanoids insisted on going with me, so we arrived in a group.

"What's the problem?" Bill asked the moment we landed in the compound's kitchen.

"Spawn attacks. On sixteen worlds. Too many spawn to count, actually, and they're biting everything humanoid they can reach."

"Oh, no," I muttered.

"Too many for Kay to deal with—if she can even change them back after they've been bitten by spawn," Kiarra said. "Part of their plan, no doubt. If they add this to whatever they're plotting, things are definitely not looking good."

"Too many for me to deal with, too, right now," I sighed. If I were at full strength, I might make a difference as far as *Changing What Was* for those bitten by spawn, but I had to conserve what I had in case it was needed for a larger encounter.

Regardless, I wanted to weep for lives lost—spawn virus took over in a matter of seconds, and the human soul fled, leaving the body at the command of its attacker. There were only a handful of instances where that didn't hold true, and those exceptions were extremely rare.

"The strange thing is this—most of those worlds we'd term not worth saving, because they're already headed in a dangerous direction," Pheligar said. He lounged comfortably in the kitchen, using the island as a stool to accommodate his height.

"That is a little weird, but that's beside the point," Kiarra said. "People are dying, no matter how you look at this."

"And with our High Demon army held back for what looks to be a battle, we don't have anyone to send. Even ours are scattered about, working on other problems. All we can do is sit back and watch the destruction," Merrill said.

"Let's worry about that later—that's all we can do at this point," Hank appeared, breathing smoke. "Now isn't the time to be distracted. We need focus."

"You think that's the ploy—to distract or scatter us?"

"It's possible."

"Fuck." Kiarra shook her head. "Sixteen worlds destroyed—as a distraction."

"Prepare yourselves—this may only be the beginning," Pheligar warned.

I was the one to say *fuck* this time.

"Where are we going?" I asked Hank.

"Down the coast. We never got our day, remember?"

"I remember you pissed me off," I said.

"I know. I didn't mean to."

"Is this to take my mind off things?"

"Mine, too."

"Where are we going?"

"For a walk on the beach."

"This isn't Earth." Hank had folded space, landing us on a beach. Tiny shells littered the sand, and none were the familiar ones from the

California coast. The sand was a pale pink, as if coral had been ground into the mix. There were no trees near us—only the strip of sand we walked between pools of blue water and white surf.

"I know. I wanted it to be just us."

"I think you achieved your goal. Unless you count birds, fish, mollusks and gastropods."

"Leave it to you to toss gastropods into this. They're quite gossipy, you know."

"Gossipy gastropods?"

"Galloping gossipy gastropods."

"You know, if I live over this," I stopped walking and tapped his chest, "I may make Pluto bigger. It'll be a regular planet again."

"Are you sure you want to add fuel to that hotbed of controversy?"

"I didn't realize it was such a contentious hotbed. Wow."

"You didn't realize that scientists are arguing the topic in every coffee shop on Earth?"

"I had no idea."

"Because they're not." Hank grinned. "Look behind you."

I turned. Yes, any woman's breath might catch. It was a dream. A big, canopy bed stood on the sand, with lengths of white, gauzy fabric blowing about it in the ocean breeze. "What?" I began.

"I'm gonna fuck you, baby. Right here and now. I'll make sure you like it. A lot."

"You get away with those presumptions because you know you're sex on a stick, don't you?" I pointed a finger at him.

"I do. But I'm *your* sex on a stick."

"Even better."

"Lord Kifirin?" Zendeval Riin rose from his seat and dipped his head respectfully to Kifirin. "Welcome to my study. What may I do for you?"

"Your army is still well-trained and battle ready?" Kifirin took a seat before Zendeval's desk and nodded for Zen to do the same.

"Of course."

"Good. I wish to borrow your troops. You may come, if you are so minded."

"I'll come. Might I see Reah? I haven't seen her since before the baby's birth."

"If you wish. I have one other request."

"What is that?"

"Arm the dwarf and bring him with you."

"What in the name of Baetrah?" Jaydevik Rath stared as Greater Demon troops began to appear in his courtyard.

"You realized I have been reborn?" Kifirin appeared beside Jayd. "Call your brother. I wish to speak with both of you."

"I did not know," Jayd bowed to Kifirin. "Will you bring Baetrah back?"

"I will consider it, if we are victorious."

"Victorious?"

"If the General finds himself under attack by High Demons, he may turn his attention in this direction. I have brought Greater Demons to defend you in the absence of much of your army."

"We need Greater Demons to defend us?"

"They have been battle ready for centuries. Zendeval Riin has seen to that. He had foresight, even when I did not."

"I'd like to argue with you, but that has never gotten me anywhere," Jayd conceded. "I will make preparations for their stay."

"Good."

"Zen, I have no idea why I'm here," Perdil muttered.

"You're not staying here," Kifirin appeared.

"Where am I going?" Perdil studied Kifirin suspiciously.

"To Le-Ath Veronis. You'll be placed in the palace guard."

"You cannot be serious."

"I am most certainly serious. Come. I hope you know how to use that sword you carry."

"Zen forced me to improve," Perdil grumbled. "I had some knowledge, but he drove me to be better."

"Good. I hope you know not to anger vampires," Kifrin smiled. "Because you'll be working with many of them."

"I've learned manners. Zen drove those into my head, too."

"Then Zendeval should be commended. Come, you will be guarding the Queen's suite." Perdil gasped when Kifirin folded him away.

~

"Have you commanded them?" The General demanded.

"Yes. They do not respond." Quislus worked to keep the agitation he felt from showing. It wouldn't do to display weakness to the General.

"How many?"

"Nearly one hundred, General."

"Find them, then. Bring them to me. They will learn how disobedience displeases me."

"Yes, General."

~

Charles's Journal

"This is quite a collection," Nefrigar said.

"I've been busy."

I had been busy. More than a hundred bodies of rogue gods, all drained of their power, lay in an underground section of the Larentii archives. Kaldill had supplied excellent information; all I'd had to do was travel to the locations given and take down unsuspecting rogues.

"Are they looking for these yet?" Nefrigar asked.

"If not, they should be. It would be negligent not to do so."

"Will they find the reason behind the disappearances?"

"If they do, they're welcome to have a chat about it."

"Do you suppose they will?"

"No," I chuckled. "They won't talk. They'll be out for revenge."

"That concerns me," Nefrigar said.

"Don't let it concern you," I replied. "Just be concerned for the rest of us."

"As if that had not already occurred."

"I'll bring more," I said.

"I have sufficient space," Nefrigar said. "Bring all of them, if you wish. I do not mind gazing upon the nonfunctioning bodies of rogues."

CHAPTER 15

*B*reanne's Journal

"How do you feel?" Trajan rubbed his nose gently against mine. Hank had gotten the previous afternoon, but the night belonged to Trajan.

"I feel good. And worried. I guess good and worried ought to describe how I feel."

Morning light filtered across my bed as Trajan and I lay comfortably together. "You're almost too tall for the bed," I said. Trajan was nearly seven feet tall, and his feet nearly reached the bottom of the mattress.

"I always get questions from people, asking if I played basketball," he grinned. "I started saying yeah, I played basketball. Did you play miniature golf?"

"Honey, you didn't," I snickered.

"I did. I thought Winkler was going to fall on the ground laughing the first time I said it to a waiter."

"Maybe you ought to hang around the Larentii, just so you know how the rest of us live," I grinned.

"They're tall, but I don't mention basketball to those guys."

"Barrigar is almost as tall as the goal," I said.

"Dunking from the charity stripe for them? No problem," Trajan laughed.

"Honey, what do you think is about to happen?"

"Baby, I don't know," Trajan sighed. "We're in a place where we can only react to what they throw at us. We can't plan against what we can't see coming."

"That's for sure." I snuggled against his warmth and tried to shut off the worries crowding my mind. I'd had dreams the night before—of people being bitten by spawn and losing their lives in seconds as the virus took over, turning them into what had bitten them.

"Do you think Acrimus designed the Ra'Ak and their spawn, or did he and Quislus plant the idea in Kifirin?"

"I don't know," Trajan mumbled. "Let it be, sweetheart. Let's be comfortable and happy for this moment. We've gotten very little time together, and I like waking up with you. Let's enjoy the morning. We'll have to get up soon enough and face the day."

"Yeah." I scooted as close as I could, laid my cheek against his shoulder and closed my eyes with a sigh.

"That's my girl," Trajan mumbled against my hair.

Lissa's Journal

"What?" I stared at what I found. I'd folded to Le-Ath Veronis for a Council meeting and discovered a dwarf standing guard outside my suite.

"Lord Kifirin assigned me to guard your door."

"I know you," I said, eyeing him suspiciously. "You're Perdil. Probably the only Liffelithi Dwarf still alive."

"I beg you not to point out the flaws or take pleasure in the destruction of my race," he said, lowering his eyes. "I am here to guard you. It is a very great pleasure for me to do so."

"Kifirin sent you?"

"Yes. I could not be here, otherwise."

"He must have had a reason."

"I trust that he does."

"Have you had breakfast?"

"Lady Queen, I have not—I have stood guard for hours, and my shift is about to end."

"Then come with me. You can sit and tell me how the Greater Demons are getting along while we eat."

"I thank you," he bowed. "I will be happy to tell you anything you wish to know."

"I love that in a man," I said, and motioning for him to follow, we made our way toward the dining hall.

The top of Perdil's head is just higher than my shoulder. He and I had a private breakfast while I scrolled through the agenda for the meeting and asked about Zendeval Riin and his Greater Demons.

"The army is stationed on Kifrin," Perdil informed me. "Kifirin thought it prudent to guard the Royal family and the surrounding city."

"Because we're borrowing the best of Jayd's army, right?"

"I believe that is correct."

"Not a bad idea," I conceded. "How many troops?"

"Three thousand."

"Not bad."

"Your kitchen staff is competent. These eggs are almost as good as Reah can make."

"She gave them the recipe," I said. "I'd forgotten that she cooked with you before."

"I should have known better, before."

"Have you had any dealings with Sirenali?" I asked.

"Only peripherally, through Cayetes and his horde. I hear he's dead. I'm glad. He was filth."

"Agreed," I nodded.

"Dantel Schuul only used him to hide assets; even he found him repulsive," Perdil grumbled. "And if Schuul found someone repulsive," he shrugged.

"Then they're the worst of the worst," I said.

"I hear through gossip that something may happen soon."

"You heard correctly. We just don't have any idea what it might be."

"I'd expect attacks on multiple fronts. Those brief forays employing flesh-eating monsters? Just an appetizer."

"You've been keeping up with the news?"

"Always. I understand how the criminal mind works. I hope that doesn't offend you."

"It doesn't, as long as you're not involved in the crime."

"I won't be."

"Hello," Breanne appeared with Trajan and both took seats at the table. Comesuli rushed to get the new arrivals something to eat. I'd sent out a mental message for Breanne, because I was curious about Perdil and wanted her to read him. I wasn't really prepared for her answers.

He loves you, Breanne sent as tea and plates of food were placed in front of her and Trajan. *Has, for thousands of years.*

Are you kidding? I sent back.

Not kidding. He'd do anything for you. He thinks Kifirin gave him the universe on a plate when he set him to guarding your door.

Unbelievable, I replied. *How is he otherwise?*

I think he's learned some hard lessons, and knows not to repeat past mistakes. He's changed over the years.

Good to know, I said. *I won't kick Kifirin's ass, then, for springing this on me.*

He left a rose on your pillow. Kifirin did. Perdil knows that, she added.

I wanted to sniffle at Breanne's message. Kifirin left me a rose.

"How about coming to the Council meeting with me?" I pleaded aloud.

"I can come," Bree shrugged. "Maybe it'll distract me."

"Good. Perdil, thanks for guarding my door. It was nice having breakfast with you," I nodded to him.

"You are welcome." He stood and bowed before walking away softly.

❧

Breanne's Journal

"Breanne," Gavin kissed my cheek when I walked into Lissa's suite —I had to borrow something to wear from her to attend a Council meeting. I couldn't go dressed in jeans and a sweater.

"Hey, Gavin," I said. Yes, I still tensed whenever he was that close, but things had certainly improved between us. I didn't bother to read him—I didn't want to.

"Will you advise the Queen today?" He offered a wry smile.

"If that's what she wants," I shrugged.

"I want," Lissa walked out of her closet, carrying two outfits. "Which do you want?" she asked. "The blue one or the yellow one?"

"Give her the yellow, it will look very nice with her dark hair," Gavin said.

"Good. I look better in blue," Lissa grinned.

"You planned this," I accused, shaking a finger at her.

"I had a few things made for you, yes. Gavin paid for them."

"Then thank you," I nodded to both. "I like yellow silk."

I borrowed Lissa's bathroom to dress. The yellow, raw silk tunic and loose pants were made by a popular designer and fit perfectly. "Shoes," Lissa opened the door slightly and handed in a pair of pale-brown slippers.

"Nice," I said, slipping them on my feet.

"We'll make a grand entrance," Lissa said as we left her suite together, with Gavin walking beside her. Other guards fell in with us as we passed from the residence wing into the grand hall, heading toward the Council chamber.

Aryn said, "All rise for the Queen," as we walked in, and the Council members rose as Lissa walked toward her waiting throne. Gavin escorted me to a chair near the door, and I waited for the command to be seated.

"At least we have plenty of help," Amara shook her head. "And enough space."

"You may have anything you want, where these are concerned." Andeleda, formerly high in the rankings of the Nameless Ones, was now among the Al'Riyu and in charge of a large nursery. She smiled and rocked an infant in her arms as she spoke.

"Did you wonder what had happened to us—to the faithful ones?"

"I did, but I was afraid to ask."

"We received our assignment several of your months ago. As you see, we have plenty of work. Children are being brought to us by the hundreds."

"I do see. I'm glad Edan and I can help. Might I ask—who is bringing them in?"

"The children are being gathered by Griffin and Thurlow," Andelida nodded. "At the command of Wisdom."

"That is a good errand for both of them," Amara agreed. "A very good errand."

≈

Breanne's Journal

Breanne? Corent's voice floated into my mind.

Hi, honey. How are you?

Acting as peacemaker between vampires and werewolves, Corent replied, a mental smile in his sending.

I'll bet they're eating out of your hand, I teased.

Not in the physical sense, although Flossie Thompson and I are having difficulty cooking enough for werewolves. They certainly have an appetite.

I've seen them eat, I agreed. *You have your work cut out for you.*

I miss you, he said. *Very much.*

Me, too, I said. *I have to go, the Council is about to begin a trial.*

I will contact you later, he said. *I love you.*

I love you too, I sent and turned back to the meeting.

≈

Bree? Lissa sent. Evidence had been presented against a business owner from Casino City. He'd been accused of defrauding business partners and not paying sufficient taxes.

Guilty. Not just of those charges, but he's had a hand in several murders, I responded.

Do you have names?

Of course. Taddus Rox, Evard Gindly and Parl Nevu, I sent.

Those are on the lists of missing persons, Gavin broke in.

This guy killed them. With help from an assistant. The bodies are buried in a field on the light half.

Where most vampires can't go, Lissa muttered. *Trevor?* She sent.

"Come with me," Trevor grinned at Kooper. "If this goes right, we'll get to see Breanne."

"I'm with you, brother," Kooper stood immediately. They'd spent most of the day marking worlds off lists—worlds being taken over by Ra'Ak spawn and populations destroyed. The count was up to thirty, and looked to be growing. "Where are we going?"

"To the light side on Le-Ath Veronis," Trevor said. "To dig up bodies."

Breanne's Journal

They'd bent time to arrive before the trial ended, but they'd managed to do a lot. Trevor and Kooper held a guilty assistant between them, while vampire guards hauled in skeletal remains of those killed. If I'd wanted a distraction from what was about to go down, this was a good one.

"I suppose you wouldn't want to confess to these murders, now?" Lissa stood and glared at the prisoner. "Your assistant has already confessed, and he named you as the one who murdered these three." She swept out a hand, indicating the remains.

"I'll kill you," the prisoner lunged at his assistant. His chains held him back. Aryn calmly ordered him back to his seat, placing compulsion to answer questions honestly about the murders. The Council had a full confession in a matter of minutes.

❧

"I could smell it on him, but couldn't pinpoint who or how many," Lissa said, removing the gold circlet from her head. "You don't need a nose—you can see it in them."

"I'm glad I can block it when I don't need it now," I said. "I'm glad to help, but the visions of those murders were pretty grisly."

"Yeah. Sorry about that."

"Don't worry. He'll get proper justice now."

"Bree, what do you think will happen today?"

"Something we won't like, no doubt," I said. I couldn't stop the shiver that accompanied my words.

❧

Trajan's Journal

Still nothing, Jayson reported. *Terry and I have been waiting in a coffee shop nearby, and there's absolutely no activity.*

It's nearly sundown in Chicago. This bothers me, I said.

Me, too. I feel itchy, but there's nothing to indicate a cause.

We have to consider that they may be more devious than we think. They have plenty of power, after all, and who knows what the Tanners, the Sirenali, and Moxas and Saxom have brought to the table. Granted, Moxas has been taken out of the game—at least that is our hope, but there are others in the General's arsenal.

Did Breanne read Moxas and Saxom, or could she see through their disguise without reading them? Jayson asked.

Good question. I'll ask her. She hates reading people unless there's no other way.

Let me know what you find out.

Will do.

~

Breanne's Journal

Bree, did you read Moxas, Saxom and the others at Fes' restaurant? Trajan sent.

No. I can see through any disguise. I knew it was them and frankly, I really didn't want to see their plans for Kiarra.

What about the Sirenali?

She didn't know anything. I shut down her reading fast. I didn't try reading the rogue god. I could see in the Sirenali that he was a rogue.

Bree, I hate to ask this, but I think you ought to go back and try reading them. Can you be in the same place at the same time?

I can.

I think this is important, Trajan said. *Would you mind going back?*

I'll go back.

~

I chose an appropriate moment to bend time and mist into the restaurant. Saxom, Moxas and the others had just been seated and were giving their drink orders to the waiter.

Lowering my mental shields, I read them. And then I began to scream a warning to anyone listening.

~

Tory's Journal

The nexus echo net alarm sounded, but Dragon sent all of us at once. Twenty arenas on old Earth—at different times, were being hit. My blades were in my Thifilathi's hands the moment we hit the floor, and I barely had time to notice that the arena was filled past capacity with humans. What concerned me—and the High Demons around me—were the creatures pouring out of the gate at the center.

Were the humans hoping for a reenactment of those vids they'd seen on their archaic Internet? If they were, they were more than surprised to find they were the targets this time.

All the exits are blocked, Sali shouted into my mind before turning into the largest werewolf I'd ever seen and snapping heads off rogue Ra'Ak.

"Get to work," I shouted at those around me. With blades flashing, thirty Thifilathi stalked forward, intent on destroying monsters. That's when the explosion came.

Ry, we need you, I sent. *The roof is about to cave in.*

~

Stellan, Astralan, bring your brothers, Ry sent a desperate message. *We need your help for Crane, Caylon, Drake and Drew. Dad and I have our hands full, helping Tory and Salidar. It'll take your power to hold up large roofs while they kill monsters spewing from temporary gates.*

On our way, Stellan replied.

~

Lissa's Journal

"We were overwhelmed, but we did take many down." Dragon dropped his blades on the edge of my desk with a weary sigh. "We only lost twenty-six. That in itself can be counted a victory for us, although the enemy won the battle."

"Attacking twenty at once was something we weren't prepared for." I dropped my head into my hands. "We managed to save four cities out of twenty on Earth. Former Saa Thalarr attempted to help those attacked in both Alliances, but fifty venues were hit there at once. We were overwhelmed. There's no other way to describe it." I didn't mention that my son might have died had he not called for Ry and the Starr brothers—Ry and Erland held the huge arena together while Sali and Tory's High Demons killed monsters. The Starr brothers helped Crane, Caylon and my Falchani.

Ry also managed to get the doors open, too, allowing some of the humans to escape. I held little hope for their continued survival, however. They'd been marked by the enemy, and he likely didn't appreciate his targets slipping through his hands.

"Chicago, New York, Atlanta and Los Angeles survived—for now," Dragon agreed with a nod. "Phoenix has been taken over by spawn. Kansas City, Miami and thirteen others are overrun by spawn and monsters. Those cities are also on fire, thanks to the General's chimeras. We were thinking in a linear fashion. We won't make that mistake again."

"We got a little bit of warning from Breanne as to what was coming, we just didn't have enough ready to go," I said. "We need wizards and warlocks, too, looks like."

"They'll need the power of gods to get around the High Demon ability to nullify their power," Dragon pointed out.

"Take a look at this," Grant walked in with a comp-vid in his hand. "These are the feeds I'm getting through Trajan, who is still on Earth in the past with Bill, Jayson, Opal and several others."

Dragon and I watched as Ezekiel Tanner announced that he and his brother, Obediah, were leading the new world order of werewolves and other unsavory characters.

Then, as if that weren't enough, a video was shown of the U.S. President's office exploding, followed by the bombing of the White House. Then the Houses of Parliament and every other powerful government was taken down across the globe.

Grant's face paled as he watched with us, and I held a shaking hand at my mouth as I considered what this meant. People screamed while rogue werewolves led an army through the streets of major cities, gunning down any in their path.

"Pull all of ours away from old Earth," Charles arrived and sat heavily on a guest chair. "It's a lost cause."

Breanne's Journal

"Somehow, they chose the ones who kept watching those internet videos," I said. "If the same person watched it more than five times, they were targeted for an arena."

"There were plenty of those, then. The arenas were packed full."

"Zeke and Obediah are gloating. They think the planet is theirs," Bill muttered. "If you don't count Calhoun and the General, that's pretty much correct."

"Charles just pulled all of ours away from Earth. He declared it a lost cause," Ashe sat heavily beside me. We'd gathered at SouthStar to discuss what had happened—and our loss—to the General's forces.

"Fuck," I muttered, dropping my head onto the island with a small bump. "We may as well have walked away from it in the beginning. We lost twenty-six High Demons in those battles."

"Spawn have taken over sixty worlds, by the latest count," Trevor took a seat on my other side. "Love, I'd like to tell you not to fret, but I can't stop myself from doing it."

"Trevor," I sat up and held out my arms to him.

"Hush now, no tears," Trevor brushed moisture away from my face. "We'll figure something out. These things take time."

"Time just ran out for too many," Ashe mumbled. He rose and stalked angrily away. Trevor pulled me tighter against him as we watched Ashe leave.

Lissa's Journal

"The nexus echo net operated perfectly. Our preparations were flawed," Dragon admitted. "While we were prepared for four attacks, the enemy had prepared more than seventy."

"You're not counting the worlds taken by spawn," Kooper pointed out. "More than a hundred of those, now."

"I'm not ready to raise a white flag," I snapped.

"I'll die fighting before I bow to the General," Dragon huffed.

"That's probably what he's hoping for," Aurelius said. "To engage us in combat and destroy us. He's confident that he has sufficient power."

"It's done—all those who were currently alive and important to the future have been pulled away from old Earth, but the rest," Weldon announced. He, Wlodek and Winkler had arrived at SouthStar. "We put them with the others that Corent, Flossie and Amos are watching. Obviously, we didn't bring any of the bad ones forward. They will remain with the General."

"Do we need to bring the ones you saved to Avendor?" I asked.

"Charles says no. He says they're fine where they are, but they are getting a bit testy. I suggested separate quarters. I think they enjoy arguing with each other, so we left things alone."

"It's mostly vampires," Winkler pointed out. "A few wolves. Shapeshifters. A handful of humans."

"Are they well-supplied?"

"Yes. Conner is seeing to that, with Larentii assistance."

"Good."

"Corent seems to be an effective peacemaker," Wlodek said. "If the arguments get too heated, he places a sound shield around the verbal combatants. Nobody hears them until they cool down again. If it looks as if it might come to blows, Amos Thompson builds a power shield around them. Nobody sees or hears them until they calm down. It appears to be quite effective."

"Too bad we can't do that for a lot of folks," I sighed. "We need another meeting. I just don't want to have it right away. Ask everybody to bring their best ideas in two days. Maybe I'll be better prepared by then. Right now, I have nothing."

"This has been tampered with." Calhoun shoved the Sirenali to her knees before the General. "I asked her to place obsession. She attempted it. It failed to work. Somehow, that ability has been removed."

"When did this happen?" the General demanded. Calhoun wanted to back away from the immediate anger. He couldn't.

"I do not know. I never felt an increase of foreign power while she was with me, and she has been with me continuously."

"Give me all your locations—when you have been among others," the General snapped. Calhoun opened his mind and prepared himself for the mental rape.

~

"Brother, I have been rendered blind," Moxas whispered.

"What?" Saxom's concern was immediate. "You cannot see?"

"I see in the physical sense, but my visions do not come. I can no longer command even the simplest thing to appear in my mind."

"How?"

"I never felt it," Moxas wailed. "I do not know."

"We are in danger," Saxom muttered. "Come. I will employ what I have to keep us safe."

"What?"

"I still have my vampire abilities, although Calhoun made it so I might walk in daylight and eat normally. Those filthy Saa Thalarr think only they might do that. Calhoun can accomplish it as well."

"Calhoun will kill us if he discovers I am no longer of use to him."

"I'm attempting to prevent that, brother. Let's leave before we are discovered."

~

Charles's Journal

"Just stack them. Have you never seen the catacombs in Paris?"

"I will stack them, although I bemoan the fact that we cannot properly catalog them first," Nefrigar sighed. "How many are there?"

"I brought two thousand, this time. As you see, I've been busy."

"I see you have been quite busy. Has the General not noticed their absence?"

"He hasn't missed these—yet. That may be about to change."

"I shudder at what he may do when he learns of their demise."

"As do I. Things will go as they will, Archivist. Keep your faith and remain strong."

"That may become difficult in the coming days."

"I know."

∾

"Quislus, I am incensed. Call the Hidden. It is time they obey my commands. One of mine has been altered by the enemy. I wish to make retribution."

"As you command, General," Quislus bowed and sent out a message.

∾

Breanne's Journal

"Ildevar?" He'd surprised me by knocking on my bedroom door. He stood in my doorway, smiling.

"I can kiss you now," he said. "Without worry that I might damage you."

"How about eating real food—at least something cooked," I said.

"I can also do that. I've developed a taste for rare steaks. I can still change to my other form, and continue to consume ah, criminals," he added.

"Not a problem."

"I hoped you wouldn't mind. Might you join me for a walk through the groves?"

"I might."

He offered his arm.

I took it.

∾

Ashe's Journal

"I've never seen you drink," I said.

Charles sat beside me, tossing back expensive bourbon.

"Stop worrying about me," he said. "I just want to be inebriated for a short while."

"I have no problem with that," I said. "In fact, I'll join you."

Charles slid the bottle toward me with power. *Pulling* a highball glass to me, I lifted the bottle and poured out four fingers' worth.

"Trying to catch up?"

"As quickly as possible." I downed the whiskey in two swallows and poured more. "Kay's asleep, thank goodness. We had to tell her about the children. She was understandably upset."

"At least those two women are dead."

"She took small comfort in that."

"We were never going to get out of this with no losses," Charles sighed.

"I know. I just wasn't prepared for the losses we've had already, with more expected."

"Agreed. There really isn't a way around it, you know."

"That's what worries me."

"I know."

"What do you think the General's next move might be?"

"You don't want to know."

"Yes I do."

"No you don't."

"You don't want to tell me, do you?"

"No. And I won't."

"Fine. Keep it to yourself, then." I drank my second glass of bourbon and poured a third.

"Thank you. I will. Hand the bottle back, please." I pushed the bottle toward him, with a tiny bit of power. It slid into his hand, like a bottle sliding on the bar in an old western.

"This universe ain't big enough for the both of us, General," I quipped and lifted my glass.

"Exactly," Charles agreed and drank straight from the bottle.

~

"Where are Moxas and Saxom?" Calhoun snapped. "I ordered you to guard them." He glared at Reedy.

"I was asked to run an errand by Saxom. He ordered dinner. I went to get it," Reedy mumbled.

"Faugh, you have compulsion in your eyes," Calhoun growled. "I should have known to rid him of that talent. They have escaped, probably because they were tampered with, just as the Sirenali was. This will not please the General."

"What do you want me to do?" Reedy whined.

"You? Come with me. I can set you on the population," Calhoun shrugged. "That's all you're good for now. If you find Saxom and Moxas, kill them."

"Saxom and Moxas have also been altered, although they managed to escape before we discovered it," Calhoun groveled before the General.

"Then the enemy will pay," the General replied. "Where is Quislus? I ordered him to bring the Hidden to me."

"I will search for him, General."

"Look no further. The Hidden have been taken by the enemy," Quislus dropped to his knees before the General. "Just as Jarnis and Hydel were taken."

"We will prepare a message," the General hissed.

Lissa's Journal

We were all wakened. There was no need for anyone to tell us—we knew immediately. All of us gathered in the kitchen at SouthStar. Most of us wept. Le-Ath Veronis, Campiaa, Wyyld, Falchan, Refizan, Tulgalan and Earth had all been destroyed—blasted to atoms by the General's wrath.

CHAPTER 16

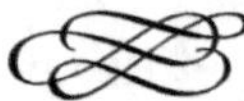

*A*she's Journal

"All news outlets have received the same message," Kooper handed a comp-vid to me. He and Trevor had managed to get away from Le-Ath Veronis, but everyone else, including Aryn, Perdil and Cheedas, had perished.

"It's from the General," Charles appeared and read the message with me.

Choose your battlefield, the message read. The journalists reported the message, but they had little information regarding what it meant. The destruction of seven worlds terrified them, too. They had no idea what to do against an invisible foe. Ildevar and Tybus had already done several interviews, calling for calm, but there was little of that precious item anywhere.

"We need a meeting," Charles said.

"How do we get a message to the General?" Kooper growled.

"That's the easy part," Charles replied cryptically.

"I will let you live—for now."

Saxom cowered with his brother. If he hadn't provided information as to which worlds would most harm the enemy if they were destroyed, he and his brother would be dead already. They hadn't gotten far after their escape—Calhoun had found them easily.

"I will do anything you ask." Saxom worked to keep the quiver from his voice.

~

Breanne's Journal

"This is for messing with Saxom, Moxas and one Sirenali?" Kay asked. She shivered in Ashe's embrace.

"Sweetheart, it would have come anyway. He was likely looking for any excuse to hurt us like this."

"It would have happened, no matter what," Charles soothed.

"Did you hear? Seven hundred worlds destroyed by spawn," Trevor walked in and sat beside me. We'd chosen Ashe's solarium for the meeting. Sunlight, uncaring that so many had died, shone brightly on rows of gishi trees below the house.

"The gates of hell are opening everywhere," Macy wiped tears away after Kooper folded her, Elizabeth, Luanne, Philip and Keith in. "Dragon is holding the High Demons back—he says they'd be ineffective against such a widespread attack."

"Ineffective doesn't describe it properly." Dragon walked in, followed by Crane, Crane Trevor, Caylon, Sali and Dragon's sons. Tory followed Sali. Both looked exhausted. "We just moved our High Demon troops into the southern reaches of SouthStar, and I've asked Jayd and Glinda to move the rest of theirs, plus the Greater Demons in as well. They'll have to occupy jungles for a short time, but it's better than being obliterated."

"You think Kifirin will be next?" I asked.

"I think Kifirin will be next," Kifirin appeared, blowing angry smoke. Hank was with him.

"Quislus will likely name it a target," Hank agreed. "We just sent a message his way—he's been calling for the Hidden among us, and he recently discovered that they're all dead. Kifirin heard the call. I told him to answer and let his former parent know his rogue underlings are dead and that we are searching for him, now."

"So he knows Kifirin is alive, then?"

"Yes."

"Good. At least he knows we have some power against him," I said.

"How will we answer the General?" Lissa asked. Her voice was thick with tears as she walked in, followed by Gavin, Tony, Rigo and several others.

"We do what he says," Charles replied. "We choose our battlefield. Not just where, but when."

Kal? I sent.

What, Love?

I need that meeting with the Larentii Council. Now. And we don't have a lot of time.

I understand. Come now. We will be ready.

"I'm going to run an errand," I announced and stood to stretch.

"Where?" Hank turned dark eyes toward me.

"The Larentii homeworld. You sort out the battlefield. I'll be back in a few."

Lissa's Journal

All my people, wiped away in an instant of the General's anger. Aryn, Cheedas and so many others that I loved—all gone. I felt helpless against what the General could do. He had no care for anything, except his own bloated power.

He recognized the need for underlings, but that's all they were to him—underlings—to do what he had no desire to do for himself. He could reject them at a moment's notice if they displeased him in any way. Likely, he might destroy them, too—but I didn't know that for certain. Again, I wondered what he was and how he'd been created.

Acrimus had a hand in it, if my suspicions were correct, but how had the General grown so strong? Other godlings that had been created were all less than their parent—none of them could create an equal or something greater than themselves.

"I believe we should choose a battlefield—and a battle—that has already been fought," Charles said, breaking into my thoughts.

"What do you mean by that?" Dragon asked.

"What was the last real battle we fought?" Charles asked.

"The battle against the rogue elves and all the creatures they'd summoned from the Dark Realm of the past," Edward replied as he walked in with Reah. She'd been grieving too—for Tulgalan and all the other worlds destroyed.

"Exactly. I say we choose that place and time," Charles said. "Most of you are already there. The powerful can be in the same place at the same time. This will serve to double our forces, will it not? As long as you are alive now, you can go back. The General's forces who are dead cannot be brought back to stand beside themselves and fight again."

"Will that be enough?" I asked.

"It is my hope that we will stand against them until they are all gone," Charles shrugged.

"Then we'll pull up that battle in a three dimensional hologram and begin to study it," Dragon said. "We need every advantage, and if our enemies join those who are there already, we will have our hands full."

"Remember, many of you were not as strong then as you are now," Charles pointed out as Dragon formed an image of the battlefield in the middle of Ashe's solarium.

"The shield is here, separating armies," Dragon began, pointing a finger at the proper spot.

"I wasn't able to be there before, Gavin. I was pregnant with Travis and Trent, remember?" He and I walked through rows of gishi trees to discuss the meeting—and the subsequent decisions. We had three days. Charles and Ashe had left afterward, to deliver the message. At least that's what they said they were doing. Hank and Kifirin went with them.

"Reah came in at the end, with Edward. They bent time to do so," Gavin nodded. "The battle would have been lost, had they not done that."

"I know. But it's as Charles said; most of us are stronger now than we were before. I just don't know how," I wiped tears away. I couldn't finish.

"Because Gavril was there before. I know this," Gavin nodded, his face paling. "I may find it extremely difficult as well."

"And Norian," I mumbled.

"Tybus will go back with us instead, giving us two—at least for a while."

"I still don't like the odds," I wiped away more tears. Gavin pulled me to a stop and I melted into his embrace.

"Cara, remember that I love you, no matter what the outcome might be," he murmured against my hair.

"Gavin, I love you so much," I sobbed.

Adam's Journal

"I suspect that Saxom and Moxas still have cards to play," Merrill said. "We managed to get Kiarra out of their sight, but they repaid that debt by giving the General a list of which worlds to destroy to harm us most."

"I agree," Pheligar said. "That is my conclusion as well. Who knew the fangless serpent would have one last bit of poison to fling in our direction?"

"And he may have more. I curse the day he was formed," Merrill growled. "Breanne and Kay saved lives in that restaurant, only to see them destroyed when the General discovered their subterfuge."

"Meanwhile, worlds are overrun and destroyed by spawn, which no doubt count in the trillions," I said, shaking my head at the complexity of the General's attacks. "We don't have enough to do battle against the army at his command."

"Which of the Mighty is responsible for the deaths of the Hidden? I don't believe it is Breanne," Pheligar said.

"Wisdom, most likely," Merrill observed. "Remember, we saw two killed before Breanne and Ashe were strong enough corporeally to return."

"Very true. Wisdom has had to employ stealth, no doubt, to take those he has without the General's knowledge."

"At least until now," I said. "The General certainly knows now."

"The worlds taken by spawn are mostly those that do not belong to either Alliance, and are generally warring amongst themselves," Pheligar said. "I will not miss many of those, they were so destructive."

"That doesn't make complete sense to me," I said. "I'd assume those to be the ones the General might want to keep."

"Regardless, he has taken seven worlds we hold dear, and Saxom may supply more names in the coming hours. He offered no promise to hold destruction at bay before we meet on the battlefield."

"That is not comforting in the least," I jerked my head at Merrill.

"I understand, but that doesn't alter the possibility."

Charles's Journal

"After you get this taken care of," I told Griffin, "I want you and Thurlow to show up on the battlefield and speak with Breanne."

"You want me to grovel before my daughter?"

"I know it makes you uncomfortable, but yes. Offer apologies or whatever you think might persuade her to talk to you."

"I'll do it, but only because you command it."

"Good. Go now, we don't have much time left."

I watched while Griffin and Thurlow disappeared. I'd thrown the dice, now it was a waiting game—to see if the numbers I wanted came up.

Reah's Journal

"Promise to keep her safe," I begged. "If we don't come back."

Aedan Evans looked over Adele's shoulder as she cradled Lexsi in her arms. "Do you think we might survive, if you do not?" Aedan studied me with concern in his dark-gray eyes.

"I hope so. I have to believe that you will." I wanted to weep. I forced back tears instead. "I hope Ashe's shield will hold," I added. "It has held so far."

"I will have faith in his strength, if nothing else," Adele murmured as she rocked my youngest to soothe her.

"Ashe has always done his best to protect us, even when we didn't deserve it," Aedan agreed.

"Then I hope he is able to protect us in the future," I said. "For my children and their children."

"Hope," Adele crooned at Lexsi. "Hope is exactly what we need."

Breanne's Journal

"Will it come to this?" Kal asked.

"I hope not, but that's all it is at this point—hope."

"Then I hope it works, should it come to this."

"Me, too."

"Will we be together, for more than a few moments at a time, if we are successful?" Kal watched me carefully.

"Honey, I can't make any guarantees. You ought to know that. Will Nefrigar keep my secret?"

"Nefrigar is the most reliable and secretive Larentii, should it prove necessary."

"Good. I'm gambling, here, Kal. I hope you understand that."

"There's that word again—hope. I will hold hope in my heart as long as you survive, my love."

"Hold that thought," I sighed. "I need some time to think."

"You may do that here, on the Larentii homeworld."

"I'll consider it," I said and folded away.

~

I didn't stay on the Larentii homeworld. Instead, I went to find Kay. "We have something to do," I said after waking her from a healing sleep.

"What's that?" she asked, yawning.

"Come with me; I'll show you," I helped her sit up. "We need a few other folks to back us up, but that shouldn't be difficult."

It wouldn't be difficult—if we bent time to appear at the proper place and time.

~

"This is SouthStar in the past, isn't it?" Kay looked around us.

"It most certainly is in the past," Renegar nodded congenially at me when he appeared. Several who'd lived in Cloud Chief in the past gathered about us as well. I recognized Marco and Cori, Ace, Wynn, Amos and Flossie Thompson—those who'd be waiting when the teens walked through the gate that a young Ashe would form on the other side. This required my talent of butting two timelines together, and this act would be crucial to the future.

"Is everyone ready?" I asked.

"Ready," Amos Thompson nodded. "Bring 'em."

Nodding to Kay, I stepped away from her—she'd be the first one Ashe would notice when he opened the gate. Light formed before us and the gate opened. I held the gate open from my side while a thirteen-year-old Ashe held it open in an Oklahoma field in the past.

Teen versions of Macy, Edward, Keith, Luanne and Bryce came through with their parents. I shone brightly as I held the gate open. Then, I saw the older version of Bill, staggering toward the gate.

"Wait. Wait," he said. I wanted to weep—the side of Bill's face was covered in blood as he stumbled toward me. Somehow, he knew I stood there waiting for him to cross over. The young Ashe thought the former Director wanted to stop the families from getting to safety, but that wasn't the case. Bill wanted to get to me. I wanted him to get to me, too. I sent a bit of power through the gate, to help.

The moment Bill reached the gate, I stepped forward and held out my hand. Bill took it gratefully and moved to embrace me. I held him while I fed him power and healing. Last of all, the ghosts of Philip and Elizabeth ran through, just before Ashe closed the gate behind us.

"Welcome home, honey," I dimmed my light and kissed Bill, leaving him stunned in a grove of gishi trees as Kay and I disappeared.

~

"I probably shouldn't have, but Ashe looked so sweet, I told him I loved him," Kay slumped on her bed with a sigh.

"Kay, you did just fine," I sat beside her and gave her a hug. "In fact, you did exactly what you were supposed to do." I sent her *Love*, and she smiled and leaned her head on my shoulder.

Later, when she was asleep again, I sneaked away to visit one more place. Three reptanoids needed their lives back after the first battle, and I intended to take care of that.

~

"Get things taken care of?" Charles waited for me when I appeared in Ashe's kitchen late that evening.

"I got plenty taken care of," I said.

"Congratulations," he said. "Are you hungry?"

"A little."

"How about I take you to dinner?"

"Where?"

"I believe we have a reservation at Dee's in the past."

"Then let me rescue Dee from Campiaa from before it was blown to bits, and he can come with us."

"Sounds fine."

"Good."

~

"I don't know why I knew you'd come for me, I just did," Dormas sighed as we were seated at a table at the restaurant he and Teeg purchased for Reah years earlier.

"You should trust Bree before anyone else," Charles smiled and nodded at the waiter, who offered a bottle of wine.

"I saved you once; I wasn't willing to let you go a second time," I said, watching as the waiter poured a glass of wine for me.

"You saved me before. Yes, it makes sense," he nodded. "I was dead, wasn't I?"

"Yes, but not very long," I said. "Tybus will be glad to see you. The Starr brothers, too."

"Speaking of the Starr brothers," Charles said as Stellan pulled out the fourth chair at our table.

"Hey," I touched his hand and smiled. "What have you been up to?"

"We helped Dragon and his High Demons," Stellan said. "We held arenas together while they battled monsters. Before that, we held off raiders from Karathia for Ry and Erland. Charles here had all sorts of assignments," Stellan grinned. "But I'm here now."

"I'm glad. Want this glass of wine? I can wait for another."

"Let's share, until they bring another glass," he said.

"Sounds good."

Another glass of wine was poured quickly and the specials were given. Our orders were taken and the waiter walked away discreetly. "How are the preparations coming along? I received information secondhand through Ry," Stellan said.

"I have everything in place on my end," Charles said. "I just hope things go as I think they will."

"I worry about what they have to throw at us," Stellan muttered before sipping his wine. "And what they may do in the next two days."

"Whatever they do in the next two days can't be helped," Charles said. "We have to concentrate on the battle."

"I know how it went the first time," Dee said. "We lost some there."

"And we may lose some again," Charles agreed. "Things will

happen as they will. I suggest keeping your worry in check. It can prevent us from operating at our best when the time comes."

I watched Charles carefully throughout the meal. The food was excellent, as was the wine, but something concerned me. I couldn't put a finger on it, but it niggled my brain, like an itch I couldn't scratch.

He paid for the meal and transferred all of us back to SouthStar, before kissing me goodnight and going to bed. Dormas, too, went to find Tybus, leaving Stellan and me alone in the solarium.

With no sunlight and little moonlight, the groves were dark under the stars. "Let's go outside and sit by the pool," Stellan suggested.

"Let's get in the hot tub," I countered.

"I'm all for that. With or without suits?"

"Oh, without," I shrugged. I knew we'd both be naked before the night was over anyway.

"Sounds good," Stellan grinned.

~

Tybus' Journal

"Breanne saved me—for the second time, as I understand it," Dee said.

"I am grateful," I said. "For both times. The memories I have from Gavril tell me when it happened the first time. He should have listened carefully to Breanne, yet he did not. I understand that his spirit was being siphoned away, but the mind cloud obviously destroyed what little reason he had left."

"He was a good child when he was young. Curious and capable. It was a joy to teach him."

"When did things begin to change?" I asked.

"Shortly before he took Campiaa to begin forming the Alliance. I was shocked by his treatment of Reah. I cannot say that taking the reptanoids with him wasn't a good idea—they were important, just as the Starr brothers were important in building the Campiaan Alliance. He could have reassured Reah, yet he did not."

"He wanted her love, yet he blamed her for so much," Kevis appeared and sat at the small table in Ashe's library, where Dee and I had settled to talk. "He and Kifirin—so much was the same with them."

"Then we ought to blame Quislus—and Acrimus—for much of that. Kifirin interfered with Gavril, but Acrimus and Quislus interfered with Kifirin." Karzac nodded to his son and took the last chair at our table.

"Healer," I nodded respectfully to him.

"I hope we can sort all this out, if we survive the battle," Kevis said, *Pulling* a bottle of bourbon in, with four glasses. "Care to join me?"

"Yes," Karzac nodded. "We all need a drink."

Hank's Journal

Kifirin and I stood upon the edge of Baetrah, where Quislus had killed him before. Below, the caldera was cold and dead. Kifirin had created it in the beginning, and allowed it to erupt at times to express his anger.

"It feels empty. The planet. It has not been empty since I first created it," Kifirin breathed smoke as he looked about him.

"Are you prepared to call Quislus?" I asked.

"I am ready," Kifirin agreed. "He knows I live. Will the General appear a second time?"

"I doubt it. Quislus killed you with little effort before. He assumes you are the same and he might do it just as easily a second time."

"How does he suppose I live again?" Kifirin asked.

"I suspected that one of the powerful remade you," Quislus appeared, nodding in my direction. "You know what happened the last time we met, don't you?" Quislus crossed arms over his corporeal chest and glared at both of us.

"Last time, I was dead before Li'Neruh arrived," Kifirin snarled.

"I intend to make you dead again."

Kifirin didn't bother with a reply. He merely sent a mental flick of power, holding Quislus immobile while I held the shield around the rogue.

"Kill him. Once his body is dead, pull the power into yourself," Charles arrived and instructed Kifirin. Kifirin's eyes widened as Quislus died quickly and he absorbed his former parent's power into himself.

"Time to go, before the General becomes suspicious," Charles grinned. We folded to SouthStar without a backward glance.

Lissa's Journal

"Where have you been?" I asked as Hank, Charles and Kifirin appeared in the kitchen and pulled out an expensive bottle of whiskey.

"On an errand. If my calculations are correct," Charles began. "Yes, as I expected—the General has just destroyed Kifirin's planet."

I felt it—as if something in me was lost. I nodded at Charles. I had no idea what he, Hank and Kifirin had done, but it was clearly satisfying to them in some way.

"Pour me a glass too," I said. Kifirin delivered the glass of whiskey to me personally, then leaned in and kissed me gently after I sipped it.

CHAPTER 17

Ashe's Journal

"I'm not sure I can fight back," Kay murmured. I'd joined her in bed early the following morning.

"I know. Sweetheart, just stay toward the back. Protect yourself. Don't worry about the rest of us, all right?"

"When will we go to Xordth?" Kay asked.

"Charles and I discussed that this morning. We'll go tonight and join the others who fought in the past. While Charles, Breanne, Hank and I weren't there before—at least for the battle, most of the others were, so they'll have to have a short talk with their former selves—about what is going down and why they're there, squared."

"So we can form battle plans, right?"

"Yes. Dragon will discuss this with Dragon, as they'll be the field commanders. Crane and Crane will back them up and dissect the first battle with all of them, so they'll know what to expect."

"What about the ones who died—the first time? Won't they know something isn't right when their second self doesn't appear?"

"We're trying to avoid that. Remember, not everybody there was given extra power, so they can't be at the same place at the same time. I'm hoping we can skirt that issue."

"Let's hope it doesn't come up, then," Kay shivered in my embrace.

"Sweetheart, it'll be okay," I held her tighter.

"Ashe, we don't know that," she whimpered. "I lost you once. I can't face that again."

"I hope you never have to deal with that again," I said and leaned in to kiss her.

~

Breanne's Journal

"We're going tonight, baby," Hank crooned against my collarbone before kissing it. Yes, I'd spent the night with Stellan, but he'd been called away early to meet with his brothers, and Hank found me in the shower afterward. We'd ended up back in bed.

"So you have time to plot and plan?" I asked, running my fingers through thick, black hair as his head moved down to my left breast.

"Exactly. And to get the others there used to the fact that they'll be backed up by a second, more powerful versions of themselves." His teeth locked on my nipple and bit gently before sucking and kissing.

"Oh, honey, that feels good," I mumbled. How does Hank do it? I always feel wanton in his arms—as if I can't get enough of him.

"Want more?" he teased, pulling away and grinning at me.

"Oh, yeah." I arched my body toward him.

"Then come and take it." Hank rolled over on his back, still smiling.

"What?" I stared—he wasn't moving. Naked and erect, yes, but not moving.

"Come on, your turn." He stroked himself, just to taunt me.

"Uh, okay," I mumbled uncertainly.

"Come on, I like my nipples played with, too."

"Okay." Well, they'd always fascinated me, but I'd never had an open invitation from him before, so I'd held back. Mostly, he liked to be in the driver's seat, with me not moving so I wouldn't distract him.

I reached out and pinched his right nipple gently. He seemed to like that. I moved closer, pulled a leg over one of his and proceeded to rub myself against him. I think that was good—for both of us.

"I think I like this," I said, moving to straddle him and leaning down to give him a kiss. "I think I like it a lot." I moved to cover him and went to work to make him moan for a change.

~

Lissa's Journal Past

"Cara Mia, you cannot go. You are pregnant," Gavin pointed out.

"Tell me something I don't know," I muttered. I'd wakened that morning feeling queasy and Connegar and Reemagar had both shown up before I could make it to the bathroom. They cleaned up the resulting mess, too.

"But you, Winkler and Drake and Drew are going," I grumped, rubbing my belly. Drake and Drew were with me more often than not, and while they normally were the most easygoing of my mates, fatherhood had turned them into almost-tyrants.

"As are several others," Gavin agreed. "All the vampires who can stand in daylight are going. Our son holds most of the talents you had before you became a Nameless One. He will act in your stead."

"It just isn't fair," I huffed. "Reah and I can't go, for the same damn reason."

"Lissa, are you belittling your unborn children?"

"No. Hell, no," I turned away, rubbing my forehead. "But the timing sucks. Even you have to admit that."

"I will not deny it," he sighed. "Although a part of me is glad you won't be placed in danger."

"Gavin, everybody on that field will be in danger. Admit it. We both know the god wars are coming—what if this is the beginning?"

~

Lissa's Journal Present

Before the original battle, I'd mentioned the god wars to Gavin, and asked him whether that battle might be the beginning. As it turns out, it was the ending instead. For good or bad, one side would walk away victorious. I worried that it wouldn't be my side.

So far, the General had hurt us every time we'd stood against him. He'd taken Bree down, too, and only the combined power of the Larentii had pulled her back to us. The difference then had been that he hadn't destroyed her body. She'd had that to return to.

Somehow, when the Three had joined together to destroy Acrimus after Ferrigar fell, they'd moved their bodies to a safe place. We'd all thought those in the Larentii Archives were the real ones, but that hadn't held true.

"Does the General know the Three have returned?" I asked.

Kifirin blew a warm breath against my neck. "I do not believe he does, although I cannot say for certain. He will not expect the One to interfere—that has been the belief—according to the books and prophecies. Acrimus believed that to be true, as did I and all the others."

"Do you think they allowed that misconception to be carried forward?"

"It would be logical, don't you think? To allow those who work against them to believe themselves safe from the One?"

"Unless they kill a Larentii," I pointed out.

"True. Acrimus acted before he considered the situation, and that led to his death. I am not sorry he is gone."

"I don't think anybody is sorry he's gone," I agreed.

"I feel nothing for Quislus' death. Should I?" I turned to gaze into Kifirin's dark eyes. Stars—brighter than I'd ever seen there—fell through their depths.

"Honey, that's not your parent. Not this time. Why would you feel anything for the death of an enemy who betrayed you?"

"Breanne did this for me. I cannot repay her for this gift, or for the gift of your life, Avilepha."

"I don't think she expects repayment, and she just gets embarrassed if somebody grovels and thanks her profusely. I think she takes joy in our joy, and appreciates our love for her."

"I have that," Kifirin agreed, kissing me. "I certainly have that."

~

Breanne's Journal

"How are we supposed to dress for this?" I asked, sorting through the collection of clothing in my closet at SouthStar.

"I don't think it matters, sweetheart," Bill said. He stood behind me while I flipped hangers across the rod. Nothing looked good—or appropriate—for a battle.

"Honey, I'm really glad you're here," I said, turning to kiss him. "I don't ever want to see you hurt again."

"I don't want to live without you," Bill sighed, hugging me tightly.

"Then we'll hope it doesn't come to that. Won't we?"

"Yeah. I think hope is about all we have left, now."

"You could be right. But you know, hope may see us through."

"Then we'll have hope. Until we don't have it," Bill murmured against my mouth.

~

Lissa's Journal

"Look at this." Drake and Drew folded me to a portion of SouthStar I'd never seen. Ashe had built this for the people of Star Cove, who'd come from Cloud Chief in Oklahoma before that. The town was small and beautiful, fitting architecturally with the groves surrounding it.

All of those living there worked in the groves or had something to do with the business end of things, and through the years, some of them had traded duties just to learn how to do as much as they could.

They'd prepared a feast for us, with food covering long tables, which were surrounded by fruit trees in a park at the center of their town. "Smells good, too," Drake grinned. "This is a good idea—I didn't feel much like eating, but this is too good to pass up."

"We made vegetarian dishes, for Breanne," Fes walked up to us. Reah wasn't far behind him, and I realized that this was how two master cooks chose to use their free time before going to war.

Tybus, grinning broadly, followed Reah closely. He was happy; she was his, completely, for the first time. I hoped their love would continue instead of being destroyed by the General, who only seemed to understand hate and destruction.

"Wow," Breanne breathed. She and Bill folded in next to my Falchani. Then, to make things even better, Travis and Trent appeared with Dragon and Crane.

"Hey," I held my arms out. They came to hug me. I kissed both their cheeks. Their fathers, accompanied by their grandfather and great-uncle, had traveled into the past and pulled them away from Falchan before it was destroyed. So many others weren't so fortunate, however. I still wanted to weep for them. I didn't. I presented a brave face to my youngest, so they wouldn't break down, too. They'd lost too many friends to count and already grieved their loss.

"Grammy," Bel Erland arrived with his father and grandfather.

"Erland," I offered a trembling smile to my Karathian warlock mate before he kissed me. I hugged Bel Erland after that, and then his father, Ry.

"Looks like an appropriate feast," Erland nodded as Bel took off with Travis and Trent.

"Gram?" Wyatt stood next to Edward, who'd gone to fetch him earlier. Edward grinned while I hugged Wyatt and then sent him off to find the other three.

He still doesn't suspect about Tybus, Edward shook his head as he sent mindspeech.

"Don't worry," Breanne said, patting Edward's shoulder. "If we survive, I think I might help with that."

"Reah and I would appreciate it," Edward nodded. "Thank you."

In half an hour, we were seated together and sharing food with the powerful and non-powerful—vampires, shapeshifters, werewolves, humanoids—all sorts.

"We need to do this again, if we have the opportunity," Ashe declared. Kay sat quietly beside him, nibbling at this or that and listening to the rest of us talk. I knew she was worried, as did Breanne. Kay thought she might be a hindrance instead of a help, and that was a shame. Her past had made her weak and frightened. I hoped that somehow, Bree might change that in the future. She'd done so much for Kay already, however, that I didn't want to bring it up now.

"Dude, you gonna eat that?" Sali grinned at the extra roll sitting on Ashe's plate.

"It's yours." Ashe laughed and tossed the roll to Sali, who buttered it carefully, then consumed it in two bites.

All too soon, the meal was finished and people rose to clear plates and scraps away. I sighed when Bree put an arm around my shoulders and sent me a bit of *Love*. "Three more hours," I said.

"Three more hours," she agreed.

~

Hank's Journal

We gathered at the designated time in Ashe's courtyard. Our army. All the Saa Thalarr, including healers. Lissa and all her mates. Reah and her mates. The High Demon army, which included Jayd, Garde and Glinda. For the first time, Jayd had bowed to Glinda's wishes, allowing her to wage war.

So many others appeared that I hadn't suspected might be among the powerful, now. Jett Riffler arrived, leading a contingent of others gathered from this world or that. Many of them were werewolves, from Harifa Edus. Some of them, including Casimir, were vampires from Le-Ath Veronis. I'd never met Montrose, Susila or Oluwa; nevertheless, there they were, as Nameless Ones. Charles had likely been busy, replacing the Hidden with allies.

Ildevar Wyyld appeared, with the twenty former Ra'Ak who'd formed the Grand Alliance Council so many centuries ago. With them were Youon, King of the Black Ra'Ak, Maldak, Prince of the Copper Ra'Ak and many of their people. All of them had been added to our army of the powerful. They were closely followed by Kaldill and Lendill Schaff, with an army of elves behind them.

Last of all came Zendeval Riin, with his army of Greater Demons.

Most of those hadn't been given power, but a few had. Regardless, they all wanted to fight on our side. I silently applauded their resolve. All of them preferred to die rather than serve the enemy. I felt the same.

"Are you ready?" Dragon bellowed.

"Ready," we shouted.

"We go to war," he cried and folded us to Xordthe in the past.

Breanne's Journal

"Holy shit." Kiarra stared at her future self. If things weren't so serious, it would be comical. I hid my smile anyway.

"Things are about to go down," Merrill nodded to his mirror image. "The god wars," he added.

"This is the time and the battlefield chosen. We need as much of an edge as we can get," Charles said. Adam from the past stared at him.

"Meet the Mighty Mind," Adam from the future made introductions.

It looked to be a standoff between Gavin of the past and Gavin of the future, with Lissa standing between them to prevent blows. Drake and Drew couldn't get over their doppelgangers; they'd already had a discussion with Lissa, who was pregnant in their timeline. She reassured them several times that Travis and Trent were fine.

"Stuff it, Gavin," I snapped, causing the old Gavin to swivel in my direction. Lissa began to laugh, and that caused the future Gavin to smile.

"I'd never have believed that, if I hadn't seen it for myself," Gavril stepped to my side.

"Hello," I said, holding out my hand. "How are you?"

"Good," he shrugged and took my hand. "I'd just like this to be over with."

"Ain't that the truth," I muttered.

"If you need help, let me know," he nodded toward his parents—

Lissa and both his fathers, past and present. "Dad can be a bit testy, even in the best of times."

"I'm glad you said that and not me," I said. "I'm your Aunt Bree."

"I never knew I had an Aunt Bree."

"Your mother didn't know she had a living sister," I said. "It was a surprise for everybody."

"Have you met Tory and Ry?"

"Yeah. Earlier," I hedged.

"What the hell is Nissa doing here?" he asked. "And Toff and Trik, too? Man, I have to talk to them." Gavril stalked off, heading for the contingent from Grey House. I shook my head as he walked away—this was the Gavril I should have met in the beginning. The one Lissa loved. My shoulders sagged as I considered the damage that Acrimus, the General and all their followers had caused.

"If Dragon and Crane can get this bunch together, then they're miracle workers," Bill muttered beside me.

"Hi, honey," I put an arm around his waist. "Who knew it would be such a chore to get on the same page with yourself?"

"At least we weren't here before," he said with a nod. "We don't have to argue with Bill and Bree."

"I'm glad about that."

"I hear that more Larentii are coming, but there will only be one of each. Somehow, Kal has instructed only the ones from the future to appear, since they are stronger and more knowledgeable."

"That makes sense," I agreed.

~

Charles's Journal

"I know you're about to tell me that things will go as they will," Ashe sat beside me. I'd chosen a seat in the grass atop a small rise, watching those below with interest. We had a short time to convince everyone to work together. The rogue elf army would be engaged first, but the General wouldn't be far behind.

"Do you think the General has approached Naldill and Reldill already?" Ashe asked.

"Possibly."

"Will Naldill cooperate with him?"

"It matters not if Naldill doesn't want to—he can't deny the General."

"This is so messed up," Ashe muttered.

"An appropriate term. The Larentii shield," I nodded in the proper direction. "They're just on the other side of it."

"Yeah. I can see right through it," Ashe replied. "I don't see the General, but I don't know what he looks like anyway. Not really."

"You'll know him when he uses power," I said. "It vibrates the opposite of ours. If nothing else, it'll just feel wrong."

"Great."

"I'll be watching for him from the side," I offered. "Be prepared when the time comes." I stood and surveyed the field, making sure it was large enough to accommodate everyone and give them sufficient fighting room.

"What time?"

"You'll know," I said and folded away.

Lissa's Journal

Old Gavin was skeptical. New Gavin was confounded. I never thought I'd see Gavin second guessing himself, but that's exactly what was happening. New Gavin couldn't understand why Old Gavin was so grumpy and uncooperative. I wanted to say, "Welcome to my world," but I didn't.

"Just keep in mind that you'll both do your best," I said. "No matter what. You've always done that," I soothed New Gavin. Actually, I preferred New Gavin to Old Gavin—by a very wide margin. I didn't say that, either. Breanne had worked wonders with him, and I didn't want to jinx any of it.

"How much longer?" Old Gavin whined.

The shields are coming down, Pheligar's voice sounded in our minds.

"Farzi! Take your brothers through there," Gavril shouted. There was a path between roaring Ra'Ak, leading past the vanguard to the creatures standing behind them. Some of those might be vulnerable to lion snake poison, and the lion snakes might be difficult to see crawling through the grass. Farzi nodded and Norian, standing with him, joined Farzi and his brothers.

Kiarra's unicorns, both of them, led the charge of the Saa Thalarr, with dragons and giant birds flying overhead. The unicorns ran at the forefront with two giant snow leopards and two enormous black gryphons on either side.

Werewolves, many of them huge, raced closely behind. The enemy rushed forward, eager to join in the battle. Ry and Erland, with their former selves, led the contingent of warlocks and wizards, destroying the ground beneath the feet of minotaurs, kobolds, satyrs and cyclops.

Eight dragons landed upon the enemy in the center of the rogue army, coming to ground with a thump and a mighty roar. Dragon breathed fire, scorching any who dared approach him. He and his sons formed a ring that none dared breach as their circle widened to fight retreating enemies.

The great cats crashed into a line of enemy Copper Ra'Ak, and behind them came Maldak and Youon's armies. There was growling, hissing and screaming as the enemy died.

Lissa's Journal

We're beating them back, Old Gavin shouted in my mind.

Shut up and keep fighting, New Gavin snapped. *This is far from over.* He was right. I heard Faldill's mental scream as he fell. I knew he'd died in the first battle, but nobody prepared me for the hopelessness of it as others began to fall, filling our minds with their agony as they died.

Dragon, both of him, became infuriated. He and his sons, including Drake and Drew, went into a higher gear, crushing and burning anything they could reach. Power blew out around us—Ashe had joined the fight.

Still, the sounds of the dying could be heard in our heads. Wizards from Grey House screamed as they were burned alive by rogue High Demons. The battle was changing; the General made sure of it. When Li'Neruh Rath led Jayd and his High Demon army into the fray, he even stood above Kifirin, who fought at his side.

Another blast of power came from Ashe as I misted through the battlefield, relieving any enemy I encountered of their heads. There were so many, even at the blistering pace I set for myself there seemed to be no end to them.

❧

Breanne's Journal

I followed Lissa's example and became mist, to relieve the enemy of their heads. It kept me busy while I contemplated where the General might be and whether he was merely toying with us, waiting for us to feel a bit more confident before employing power. That's when I heard it—Griffin—sending mindspeech. Calling my name.

"What?" I landed before him and Thurlow—they stood well back from the last of our army, and I still heard screams of the dying—on both sides in the battle behind me.

"I just wanted to explain," Griffin began. He looked guilty about something, and I didn't have time to hear him out. Too many needed my help. Lowering my shield, I read him.

Yes, it made sense. That didn't mean it didn't upset me. It did. And it confirmed some of my suspicions, but there wasn't time to dwell on any of it.

❧

Ashe's Journal

A power opposed mine—whenever I sent out a power blast, it should have cleared the field before me. It didn't. Yes, many fell, but most of those rose again and began to fight anew. The General was certainly making his presence known. I suspected he might be toying with us, to make our suffering greater in the end, but I had plenty of power left. I loosed another power blast.

This time, it was answered. I didn't recognize the scream from my throat as I was hit and tossed backward, and didn't realize that my body might plow up earth as I slid backward from the force of the blow.

Somehow, Kay heard me. I wanted to shout at her to stop, but my voice wouldn't work. Kay, my precious girl, appeared in front of me as the General removed the shield about him. I blinked. He looked very much like someone I'd seen before. I attempted to shout again at Kay —to get out of his way. He'd come for me, not her.

Gathering her strength, she stood her ground and threw everything she had as one of the Bar'Mirha at the General.

He laughed. And then he raised a hand, sending a careless bolt against her. In slow motion, I watched her fall, tears coursing down my face as I wept soundlessly. Where were the others, who should have come to her aid? They fought their own battles, I realized. All of them fought for their lives, as Armageddon descended.

Now you, the General's voice sounded in my head. He raised a hand the second time. I gasped, but it wasn't because he'd sent a killing blow against me.

No.

Time slowed. Something tugged at me. Just as my body was blasted to bits behind me, my essence was jerked away—pulled toward a destination I couldn't refuse. Yes, I might have screamed mentally in anger and anguish, but I made the unwelcome journey anyway.

Hank's Journal

What have you done? escaped my mind as my spirit was jerked from my Thifilathi, leaving it behind to be destroyed by a horde of rogue Copper Ra'Ak. They had no care that they'd been dying by the hundreds as I battled them; they seized the opportunity now to destroy the body I'd left behind. How was this possible? I shouted again, but there was nobody to come to my aid.

~

Charles's Journal

I suspected it might happen, but there was no way to predict the time or the method. I only knew something would come. The General had achieved the unthinkable, and I marveled at the preparation to make this possible.

Kay—Kalia, had died at the General's hand, and I, along with others, were being pulled away, leaving our bodies behind to be destroyed. Still I marveled at the idea, as my spirit raced toward a destination I couldn't slow or prevent.

~

Lissa's Journal

Lissa, it's time, filtered into my mind. And then my energy was pulled away from my body. I recall hurtling toward a destination so fast, everything was a blur around me. Could I stop it?

No.

I wanted to weep. I had no eyes to cry as my body was destroyed behind me. Gavril and Gavin's voices sounded in my mind, screaming. Others took up the sound. Some died. I couldn't really say who.

~

Griffin's Journal

Screaming would do no good. This had been decreed long ago. I just had no idea how it might be manipulated to achieve the desired outcome. Yes, my daughter, the Mighty Heart, had read in me what Wisdom knew she'd find. That Thurlow and I had been sent out to worlds uncounted, not just to collect children, but to set spawn loose to devour populations.

We'd seen nearly a thousand worlds destroyed. Yes, these were worlds not worth saving or nearly so, but it was a wrench anyway. There was a purpose, he'd said. I knew there was. That didn't mean it wouldn't hurt, or bring everlasting grief to me. And to Thurlow.

I'd seen him weep. Had finally come to have sympathy for my old enemy. Discovered how he'd changed from the one I'd known.

We suffered together, now. And only the other of us might understand how and why.

Through tears, I watched as Charles, Ashe and Hank, who called himself Li'Neruh Rath, were pulled away from their physical bodies. I watched in sorrow and disbelief as their bodies were destroyed behind them.

The General grew at the center of the battlefield, and he laughed. He had no worries—he could destroy the powerful. He'd proved it by destroying Kay. She lay lifeless in the grass, until a kobold approached and ripped her torso in half.

Two of my daughters were still on the field. Where were they? I began to search frantically for them. They'd be destroyed, just as the others had been.

I watched Lissa fall. Wept harder when her body was crushed into a bloody mess beneath a giant's foot.

I found Breanne. She stood alone, watching as the General raised his fist in victory.

<h1 style="text-align:center">CHAPTER 18</h1>

she's Journal
I only recalled this once before, and found that somewhat curious as my energy joined with that of Charles and Hank.

What the hell?

I heard Hank's mental message clearly, before we became one with Charles. Yes, he was the Mind. He would make the decisions. My consciousness fled.

Lissa's Journal
Now I knew. I couldn't fathom the how of it, but it had been carefully planned. If not recently, then in a past I couldn't recall. Yes, it amazed me. No, I couldn't keep it from happening.

My energy slammed into Breanne. She became filled with what I had. I saw through her eyes. Could she see them?

Yes. She saw them clearly.

"So," the General turned. "The One appears. I have done nothing to provoke you." He turned his empty visage toward the combined energy of Charles, Ashe and Hank.

"You killed a Larentii," the One announced. I took a moment to marvel that Breanne hadn't been forced to join Ashe and Charles. Instead, Hank had been pulled in.

"I killed no Larentii."

"It may interest you to know," Breanne stepped forward, growing as she walked through trampled and bloody grass, "that the Larentii have named many as members of their race. They are Larentii, according to the laws of the Larentii."

"You think that matters to me? I can destroy all of you, should I choose. You don't have the power to defeat me."

To illustrate his statement, he killed thousands, ally and enemy alike, with barely a flick of a hand. They didn't even have time to scream before they died.

"I could do the same," Breanne shrugged. The deaths troubled her, though. I could feel it. "But that would be wrong," she added.

"You think I care about right or wrong?"

"No. You only care about yourself. Tell me, who are you? How did you come here? Where do you get the power you're so proud of?" she asked.

"Acrimus woke me, but I have always existed."

"Acrimus woke you, all right. But you didn't always exist."

"Then please, before I destroy you, tell me what I am." He waved a hand magnanimously, as if I—or any of us—didn't matter.

Breanne's Journal

Unfortunately, I recalled this same conversation from once before. I hoped this one would have a different ending.

"I'll be happy to tell you what you are. You're a construct. Acrimus fed the myth of you to the people. They began to believe. Their belief made you strong, and as more believed, you grew in power. Instead of giving them the idea of a benign god, however, Acrimus led them to believe in a vengeful one instead. All the ideas of a god who loved have been destroyed. You took over, fed by the fear, hate, cruelty, prejudice and above all, the belief that if they served you, you'd save them. Only that last part isn't true, is it?"

"I grow weary of your lies," the General snapped.

Lissa's Journal

"And I grow weary of you." Breanne lifted our hand. Yes, for now, it was our hand. Breanne could connect one timeline to another. That was now common knowledge among the powerful.

What I didn't realize until now, was that she could also connect one bubble of the multiverse with another.

Now, she said. At first, I didn't know what would happen.

I felt the tunnel open over us, however.

With a roar, the One, comprised of Hank, Charles and Ashe, pushed all their power at the General, who'd been weakened by the destruction of nearly a thousand worlds filled with believers.

With a scream, the General leveled the field around us, killing everyone there before he was shoved through the portal. He screamed again before the opening snapped shut behind him.

Lissa's Journal

"I hoped you would come. I hoped your sister would come as well." Nefrigar helped me sit up. I recognized the Larentii Archives immediately. Nearby, Nefrigar's sons helped Hank, Ashe and Charles to sit up.

Breanne had found a use for the decoy bodies in the Archives. She'd also formed two others, if my guess was correct—one for me and one for Hank. Hers was missing.

"How long?" I asked.

"Only an hour, as Earth measured time," Nefrigar soothed. "You appeared here quickly. Your sister did not."

"We were right behind you," Ashe said. "I don't feel as weak as I did the last time," he added.

"You won't. Bree saw to that," Charles sighed and rubbed his forehead.

"I can't believe she did that," Hank said. I watched as a thin curl of smoke escaped his nostrils.

"She had a plan, independent of ours," Charles muttered. "I don't know if she'll come back to us after, well, after she found out what I've been doing."

"I think she may have outgrown us," Ashe said.

Charles snorted, as if that were a given.

"Many are gone," Nefrigar reported.

He was right. Many were gone, including Kay and all my mates. All destroyed by hate, jealousy, lies and power gone wrong. I was too numb to cry.

"Archivist, come and see," Kalenegar appeared in the room with us.

"See? Kalenegar, you almost sound excited," Nefrigar blinked at him.

"I am. The worlds, they are reappearing."

Ashe's Journal

From SouthStar we watched it. The recreation of so many things. Le-Ath Veronis appeared on a holographic image that Hank set up.

"People are there," Lissa breathed, vibrating with excitement.

"Look, Tulgalan," Charles said.

One by one, they returned. Refizan. Falchan. Wyyld. Campiaa. Kifirin. And then Earth. Many of those destroyed by spawn were left empty, however. Worlds not worth saving.

"The populations aren't what they were," Charles pointed out as he studied many that had returned.

Love

So many of the General's believers trusted that he'd take them to their version of the afterlife one day—that they'd just be pulled away from the planet and relocated to a better place.

I decided to fulfill their desires. I removed them from their planets, once I recreated them. And then, I sent them to live in the universe the General now occupied. It had been empty before; there were none for him to destroy. I sent his followers to live with him.

As long as they could.

I also made sure there would be no young, once they arrived on virgin planets circling this sun or that.

They were sterile. No children would be born to perpetuate their beliefs. Once they died, the General would also die. I wouldn't miss him.

The only thing they had going for them, was that they'd be reborn. They'd have a chance to do things right another time.

The General couldn't be resurrected. He also couldn't create. Acrimus had only designed him to destroy. He had no knowledge of how to make something. He only knew how to bend to his will what had already been created.

Nobody would miss him. His myth would die when he did.

Reaching out with power, I recreated another world. It gave me joy to do it.

Hank's Journal

The Three were now the Four. Charles made the announcement, but Lissa and I already knew. When Breanne left us behind, she'd seen to that. Lissa and I had received a promotion, but there was little joy to be taken in it. We were now Wisdom, Strength, Hope and Wrath. Yes, I was named Wrath. Lissa laughed and said it was a pun. I knew Earth English well enough to recognize that. It gave me no joy.

Because I missed Breanne.

It hadn't taken long for the others who'd been taken away from us to reappear. I almost wept when Ashe was reunited with Kay. She held no memory of dying, and for that we were all grateful.

I marvel at the power it had taken to bring back worlds that had been obliterated. Charles had told me that I would be included when the One reformed, but Breanne was supposed to be with us, instead of Lissa.

Breanne had seen what Charles planned, and then formed her own plan, leaving the rest of us out of it. I couldn't argue with the results of her plan, I only grieved for her disappearance from the rest of us. I believe Charles might know the reason, but I didn't want to press him about it. He seemed to be grieving in private for Breanne's loss to us.

We'd all attempted mindspeech, but there had been no replies. We knew she was out there—things were being set right at a steady pace.

Lissa almost fainted when all her mates reappeared at once. That was a joyful reunion. Yes, some of her vampires and many other residents of Le-Ath Veronis weren't recreated with the planet, but I knew Breanne had a reason for that.

Ashe called it the reverse rapture. I'd had to *Look* to study the concept. And then I laughed at Breanne's logic. She'd given the recreated worlds to those who might deserve them, taking those who didn't away or leaving them dead. It didn't matter which, after all.

I just wanted her back.

Everybody else was reunited with those they loved. Except those who'd loved Breanne. Bill disappeared on most days. Nobody knew where he went. I didn't ask.

I forced myself to help Kifirin with the Dark Realm—oddly enough, many of the worlds were recreated and repopulated there, and it was our duty to see that the new residents understood that someone would be watching.

Jayd, Glinda and Garde were properly grateful that they had a world to return to. They thanked me. I told them to send their thanks to Love.

Love.

The reason we now exist.

It is fitting.

~

Ashe's Journal

A year has passed. Kay and I are together, and as happy as possible without Breanne. We both avoid that subject.

Sali and the rest of Breanne's mates still mourn her loss. No, she isn't dead. She just didn't come back to us. We miss her. Sali has almost become mute, only speaking when it is absolutely necessary. On the eve of the anniversary of the battle, I went looking for him.

"Sal?" I tapped him on the shoulder, making him jump. I'd folded in, so he hadn't heard me approach. He'd been sitting on the perimeter of the shield around the '57 Cadillac, staring wistfully at the classic vehicle.

"Ashe?" He stood gracefully, as only those trained by the Falchani might and blinked dark eyes at me.

"Sal, you said something to me once—mentioned something you'd like to do. We're about to do it."

"What's that?"

"Come on, man," I slapped him on the back.

Moments later, we were driving over the speed limit on South Padre Island Drive in Corpus Christi, the top down on the car and Sali's werewolf sitting in the passenger seat, his tongue lolling and the fur blowing back from his face. If a wolf can grin, he had the biggest grin on his face at that moment—we were doing something that neither of us might have thought possible—living a wish—or a dream. We'd had to travel to the past to do it, but it was more than worth it.

Forming a pair of Wayfarers in my hand with power, I slipped them on and pressed the accelerator, smiling as the waters of Corpus Christi Bay flew past us on our journey.

~

Reah's Journal

"Sweetheart?" He walked into the room. I'd been combing my hair at the mirror, and I watched him as he stepped behind me, lifting my comp-vid off the bedside table and examining it for a moment.

"Chash?" I turned to smile at him.

This was my gift from Breanne. Gavril had come back to me. He and Tybus now coexisted at the same time. Love had made that miracle for me. This wasn't Teeg; Teeg was gone. Gavril remembered all our exploits when we were young. He constantly worried about my comfort. Made sure I had anything I wanted.

He and Tybus. So different. And now, equally loved. I felt like weeping, I was so happy. "Want to sleep in my bed?" He smiled and slipped an arm around my shoulders as he sat beside me on my dressing bench.

"Is it as comfortable as mine?"

"I think so. Farzi and Nenzi are already there, waiting for us."

"Then we'll sleep in your bed." He leaned in to kiss me and folded us to his bedroom at the same time.

Lissa's Journal

"Drake, we can't celebrate. Not without—you know." I shook my head at him.

"But we'd like to have another feast—like the one we had at SouthStar before the battle," he said. "Call it the Feast of Rebirth, or whatever you want to call it. To mark the General's destruction and the recreation of Le-Ath Veronis, Falchan and all those other worlds."

"Where?" I sighed.

"Here, Falchan, it doesn't matter," Perdil walked in and handed a comp-vid to me. I wanted to shake my head at what my sister had done—she'd given me a dwarf who loved me.

There was something else I wanted to thank her for, too.

Gavril had come back with the others. He and Tybus looked like twins, and I found it amusing that they often switched off as the ruler of the Campiaan Alliance. Mostly it was so the other could spend time with Reah, but I wasn't about to argue that point.

Somehow, they'd received permission from Breanne to occupy the same place and time. She'd given my son back to me, and this was the Gavril I'd known when he was young, before Kifirin stole him from me. And from Gavin.

He laughed often, teased his siblings and sent gifts to us. Usually it was gishi fruit from Avendor, when it wasn't in season on Kifirin. He had few memories of his previous years, when his spirit was sapped away. For that, I was grateful.

The one who hadn't returned, however, was Norian. I think Breanne knew that he needed to be reborn and learn new lessons. Perhaps he would come back to me in the future.

Perhaps not. I chose to let her decide.

"Fine. Let's have a feast. At SouthStar," I nodded to Drake, who grinned.

"Thanks." He turned to go.

"Wait. That was already in the works, wasn't it?"

"Yeah. We just had to figure out how to convince you to go."

"I ought to throw things at you."

"We can have a food fight—tomorrow."

"And waste good food? No way."

Wisdom's Journal

At times, I want to laugh at my title. At other times, I feel compelled to agree with it. Wisdom means learning from your mistakes. I've made plenty. I learn from all of them.

You see—I am the fraud. The pretender in all this.

Why?

I was the first version of the General. I could remove power from any legitimate god or godling, by sucking it away from them. I'd been created by multitudes of people, searching for something to believe in. I was weak in the beginning, but I gained strength as time passed and populations grew on many worlds. All of them believed in me—and taught their offspring to believe in me. I grew so powerful none could stand against me.

That's when I began my bid to take everything.

Not realizing that I was destroying it in the process.

I grew fat on the power I drained from those I killed. Until I found the last two. Strength and Love. I chose Love as my next target, believing her the weaker of the two. Exultantly, I took her and began stripping the power from her.

Little did I know, then.

I know better now.

The last thing I stripped away was Love.

Pure Love.

I'd never felt anything like that, and I thought I knew everything. I'd never known Love.

It changed me.

Forever.

I wanted more of it, and realized that if I killed what I held, I'd never have it again.

Love changed me. I felt for the first time. Felt so many things.

Sorrow.

Regret.

Pain.

I felt lonely, too. I had billions who believed in me, but they were afraid. Afraid that if they failed to obey my every whim, I'd destroy them. I realized that I had none as companions. I realized that I was destroying everything.

I changed.

Fed energy back to Love. Held her. Nurtured her. Restored her.

Then, I allied with Strength. Together, we rebuilt what I'd destroyed. To do that, however, I had to accomplish one thing.

I had to make Love and Strength forget what I was in the beginning.

I've always had a talent for that. They thought we'd always been together, and that we'd defeated what I was.

I hate that part of myself. That I was a bloated, power-hungry construct, just as the General was. Breanne finally remembered.

That's why she isn't with us now. She knows what I was.

I kept telling her that I loved her and always would. She has seen fit to let me live now, instead of shoving me into another multiverse bubble with the General.

I couldn't blame her if she did.

I want to beg her to come back to us. I'm afraid to tell the others that it's my fault she left us alone. Afraid that they'll leave me, too.

I've discovered that I can't live without them, either.

Now, I don't know what to do, and that is both humorous and sad at the same time. Wisdom doesn't know what to do.

Laughable.

"Charles?" Lissa appeared next to me.

"Hey." I slipped an arm around her—she'd found me sitting on the cliff beside a massive waterfall on SouthStar's southern edge.

"Looks like we're having a feast tomorrow, to celebrate the anniversary of the battle."

"A celebration without the guest of honor?" I pulled her closer and kissed her cheek.

"Yeah."

"Why did Breanne join with you instead of letting you join with the rest of us?" I asked.

"I really don't know," Lissa shook her head. "I know through Bree that you instructed Griffin and Thurlow to set spawn loose on worlds not worth saving. I understand that it was to weaken the General. I know you had them remove children from those worlds before they were taken over. That's what the faithful were doing—taking care of children. I think she wanted me to know those things."

I considered that for a moment. Lissa had no idea—Breanne held that back from her. Kept my secret. I breathed a sigh. "Your sister is perhaps the most generous soul I've ever met," I said.

"When she gave Gavin and Gavril back to me, I knew it too."

"Because of her, we have love in the universes. I don't know what we would do without it."

"I know. Are you coming to the feast tomorrow?"

"I'll be there."

"Good." Lissa kissed my cheek this time. "Thank you."

"For what?"

"For saving me from the Council. For keeping me from dying when I tried to give myself to the sun. For being a friend."

"You are welcome," I smiled at her.

"I like this version of you. Not just the way you look, but the way you are. Powerful and gentle at the same time. It looks good on you, Charles."

"Thank you for that."

"You're welcome."

~

Lissa's Journal

"Do you think we need to give this feast a name?"

"Like what?" I turned to Karzac, who offered me a smile.

"I have no idea," he said. "But feasts generally have names."

"Sounds like something a Council might submit to a committee, who would then choose subcommittees to set up meetings and throw out ideas that everybody hates and it takes months to whittle it down to ten choices."

"Just listening to your description wearies me. And makes me hungry."

"Then let's table the naming of it and just go eat. I'm starved."

~

Trajan's Journal

"When?" I studied Ashe's upper arms. The crowns were missing. He still held eight medallions, but those were his to give away.

"A week ago." Ashe took a seat at the kitchen island, a cup of coffee in his hand. "A single crown, forged from the two, appeared at the foot of my bed this morning. It's time to bring the

Elemaiyan race back. This time, it won't be interfered with by rogue gods."

"Who's gonna watch over them?" I asked.

"Lissa and I will have joint custody, relatively speaking."

"Good idea. Who will wear the crown?"

"You'll see." Ashe grinned and shook his head, as if he held the punch line to the best joke ever. I didn't press him for it.

Ashe's Journal

White tablecloths lined long tables as the feast was laid out. Everyone was coming. Except one. I felt her absence. Regretted so many things. Kay smiled at me as she carried a tray of rolls to set on the table. And just like that, everybody folded in.

"Thank you for joining us," I announced as everybody gazed at me expectantly. "Before we celebrate our Feast of Love, I'd like to make an announcement."

Several in the crowd gasped as I *Pulled* the new crown into my hand. "This has been remade," I said, turning toward Kifirin. He offered a slight nod—he recognized it, as he'd made it in the beginning.

There was no taint on it, now.

"This," I said, "belongs to Luanne. She is the peacemaker among the Elemaiya. I can't think of anyone else who deserves this more than she."

Luanne stood, blinking at me in surprise. I approached and placed the crown on her head.

It's heavy, she sent.

It's a reminder, I returned. *The rule of any race is always a burden to the mindful.*

I'll remember that, she replied.

"Let's eat," I said aloud. The celebration began immediately.

Hank's Journal

I don't know why I hoped she'd show up for the feast. Perhaps we all hoped the same, we just couldn't voice that hope aloud. Other than feeling empty, even after stuffing myself with exceptional food, the feast was a success.

Are you ever coming back to me? I sent.

There was no reply.

Lissa's Journal

I was supposed to be in bed. I'd misted away from Karzac after he fell asleep and now I sat atop the high dome of my palace, staring out at the city that bore my name. A few of the houses that had lights the last time I was here were now dark. For whatever reason, they hadn't been brought back. I didn't question Breanne's decisions. If anyone knew better than I about these matters, she was the one.

"This timeline was the easy thing. The hard thing was putting old Earth back together. I had to maintain the integrity of that timeline so everything would turn out the same."

I gaped—I know I did. So many things wanted to come out of my mouth. "What the fuck?" was the first thing. Unfortunately.

"Nice to see you, too," my sister said.

Charles's Journal

I was the first one she visited, before she went to see Lissa. Yes, she's a little angry with me. I'll settle for that. She let me know that if I ever fucked with her mind again (her words, not mine), she'd kick my ass.

She can do it, too.

"How?" I asked. She knew what I was asking.

"I ripped a page from your book," she snapped, her cobalt-blue eyes flashing a warning at me. "I bent time and sucked up power from about half a million rogue gods, before they flew through the tunnel I'd created, linking one timeline with another. And then, because the former me was really weak and about to wander too far into the tunnel, I shoved myself back."

"Only you had so much power by that time, you ended up slapping yourself into a wall in your sister's palace," I nodded.

"Yeah. I was really pissed at whoever did that. Turns out I was pissed at myself."

"How mad are you? Really? Do you hate me now?"

"I don't hate you."

"Good."

"I love you."

I could have said something stupid, then, like *even better*, but there are times when it's wiser just to say *thank you*. "Thank you," I said, dipping my head. "I love you more than anything. You are the first thing I ever loved, and you'll be the one I love forever."

"And that's why I'm not kicking your ass right now," she informed me.

"Thank you," I repeated. "When?" I didn't finish the question.

"Someday. But you got moved to the back of the line."

"I can live with that."

"Good. I'm going to visit Lissa, now." She disappeared without another word. I sighed then, before smiling broadly. She loved me. That's all I'd ever need.

Breanne's Journal

"Old Earth, huh?" Lissa asked after she got her senses—and her profanity—under control.

"Real bitch," I agreed. "But everything should be fine now. It pisses me off that I had to leave that fool Calhoun running loose for a while, but that's all right. I caught up with him a few years later."

"So you took out the Sirenali too?" she asked.

"Most of them. I'm still hunting V'ili and a handful of others. I may need help with that."

"Any idea who?"

"Right now, I have V'ili's sisters on his tail. If they can't take him down, well, I have my eye on someone else," I replied cryptically.

"So, what's next on your agenda?" Lissa asked.

"I need a drink," I said.

"There's plenty of stuff in my liquor cabinet."

"Nah. I want to go out."

"There's a really good bar in the Chessman," Lissa suggested.

"Sounds good. Let's go." I let her fold us there.

Sounds of slot machines, gamblers, talking, laughing and a few happy shrieks greeted us as we headed toward the bar in Adam's casino. Lissa paused for a moment before we went through the doors of the upscale bar she'd chosen.

I watched as she took a breath and squared her shoulders before reaching for the door handle.

"Two vampires walk into a bar," she said. Without a word, I followed her inside.

Bill's Journal

We'd gathered there after the feast, and decided to stay—unless we were needed elsewhere—all of Breanne's mates except Charles, Ashe and Hank.

"So Charles built this for her," Jayson stared at the ceiling over our heads. It was high, that ceiling, with a rectangular skylight over the kitchen island, where we sat.

"He asked her what she wanted. She told him she wanted a house big enough for all of us."

"So she was thinking about us, too." Jayson nodded his thanks as Belinda set a fresh cup of coffee in front of him.

"You sound so surprised." Breanne appeared at the end of the island and blinked at both of us. I folded space to hug her first.

EPILOGUE

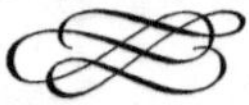

HANK'S JOURNAL

"So you finally get to me," I muttered. I even breathed a bit of smoke.

"Are you planning to waste time being mad?" My back was to Breanne, so she walked around to look at me. Her arms were tightly crossed and I knew—she was still afraid of my anger.

I had no idea if she'd ever get rid of what that bitch in Texas did to her. "Breanne," I breathed. "When will you know me well enough to realize I will never harm you?" Untucking her hands, I pulled them into my own, then drew her into my arms.

"I love you more than anything," I whispered. She trembled against me. I leaned down to kiss her. Was it perfect?

You bet your ass it was.

The End